THE LAND

OF GRACE

Mike Burrell

Livingston Press
The University of West Alabama

Hardcover binding by: HF Group
Typesetting and page layout: Sarah Coffey, Joe Taylor,
Proofreading: Daniel Butler, Erin Watt, Nick Noland,
Tricia Taylor, Daniel Butler, Debra Burrell, Sarah Coffey

Cover Design: Amanda Nolin and Joe Taylor

Cover photos are of various Elvis impersonators:

Paul Hyu, Juha Laitila, Dwight Icenhower, doullen

Marco la voz del rock and roll, Elvislomenea, Elvisimpersonator,LasVegas

This is a work of fiction. Any resemblance
to persons living or dead is coincidental.
Livingston Press is part of The University of West Alabama,
and thereby has non-profit status.
Donations are tax-deductible.

First edition

6 5 4 3 3 2 1

THE LAND OF GRACE

For Debra

PART ONE

PROMISED LAND

1
LIGHTNING IN A BOTTLE

From where he stood, backstage at the Willow Ruth AMVETS, the murmur of female voices and the clamorous shuffling sounded like a pretty lively crowd swarming into the club. And after a few minutes all the clapping and the foot-stomping, accompanying the furious chant of "WE WANT ELVIS! WE WANT ELVIS!" had him imagining a standing-room-only throng of rabid Elvis fans. It even ignited an old, familiar spark down in his gut that he thought he'd lost somewhere on that long road he'd been traveling.

"This is why I do this," he told himself under his breath. "By God, this is what gets me up in the morning."

As if he'd recited some magical incantation, the memory of the latest string of skimpy, unresponsive audiences across the plains of Kansas and Nebraska faded into a mist. But when he drew back the musty stage curtain and peeked down on all the white hair and wrinkled faces scattered over a dozen rows of metal folding chairs, his sudden euphoria dissolved into the trickle of bile he felt rising up in his throat. He washed down the bitter taste with a hard slug of his Pepsi and wondered if this was what seven years of lugging his *King of Kings Elvis Tribute* through every little Walmart-raped town to-hell-and-gone had finally come down to: senior night at the AMVETS.

"Well, what the hell," he said, shrugging. "It's show time, and they got out of their rocking chairs to see Elvis." He crushed his Pepsi can, dropped it at his feet, and cued his backing tracks with his remote. The club lights dimmed, the overture to *2001: A Space Odyssey* swelled through the room, and the unruly knot of old ladies fell as silent as pallbearers. But as the overture segued into the "That's All Right, Mama" vamp they sounded like a cage of hungry animals about to be fed. When the curtain opened and he walked onstage through a swirl of lights in the white Aloha jump suit with the E-L-V-I-S sign flashing red behind him, turning while spreading out his cape to let the spangled eagle on the back glitter like the Las Vegas Strip, he felt as if he were in the middle of a prison break.

Except for one old lady in a wheelchair, they all bounced out of their seats and jammed in around the foot of the stage. A couple of the club's employees tried to get them to sit down but gave up when it looked as if they were going to have a riot on their hands.

All the excitement and the beat of "See, See Rider" kindled a firestorm inside of him. Next, he kicked straight into "I Got a Woman," already soaring on a hot wave of senior hysteria.

Right in the middle of his hunka, hunka move in "Burning Love" he experienced that rare moment all the great entertainers speak of in whispered reverence; that moment, often compared to lightning being captured in a bottle, when singer and audience magically become one. And the magic stayed with him all the way to the end, though one granny had thrown off his timing a little between "Teddy Bear" and "Don't be Cruel" by pulling up her dress and flashing her black panties.

If anyone could tell his vocals had stumbled for half a minute, they didn't show it. All through his performance they stood, squealing at every wiggle of his leg, every curl of his lip, sounding as feral as any mob of hormone-charged teenage girls he'd ever heard.

As the final notes of "Can't Help Falling in Love" faded and he handed out the last of his scarves, it dawned on him that the youngest one out there had to be somebody's great-grandmother. So getting laid was way out of the question. But he figured that loss was more than compensated by knowing that these ladies were the King's contemporaries, the only audience that could appreciate a truly artistic interpretation of Elvis' persona.

While taking his final bow to raucous screams and applause, he felt as if they had given him the power to rise up from that drab little club and take his place among all the stars in the galaxy. Before he could make his exit, one old woman was flailing away to swing her leg over the stage apron. Afraid she might fall, he bent over to help her to her feet.

A squad of AMVETS employees jogged over to intercept the invader, but he waved them off. She looked harmless enough, and from the way she tilted her head back, he figured she was just excited from the concert and wanted a kiss. But when he dipped down to give her a little thrill, she said in his ear, "You were purty good out there, son. But you wouldn't make a pimple on the King's ass."

Now, he knew he wasn't Elvis. Not really Elvis. Nobody had to tell him that. But as he tossed back another cold Pepsi and rested his haunches on a ragged lawn chair in what passed for a dressing room, he had to admit that the old woman had kind of hurt his feelings. And it wasn't so much what she said, although that was bad enough, it was the trouble she went through to deliver her message. He felt a sinking sensation accompanied by a wave of nausea as if he were on an elevator that dropped a little faster than he expected. It was a feeling he often had anytime he suspected he'd never be anybody but ol' Doyle Brisendine from San Angelo, Texas.

The only thing left was for Mr. Parker, the club manager, to deliver the rest of his fee. Dressed in jeans and a red and blue plaid sport shirt, with the Aloha airing out on a rack behind him, Doyle waited. "What does that old bitch know, anyway?" he snarled. "The rest of them liked me. Hell, they loved me."

The room was powdered in dust and carried the faint scent of a wet dog. The spotted mirror in front of a cluttered table told him it had tried to be an actual dressing room at one time. But all the broke-leg chairs and cracked table tops piled in the corners made it look more like a storm-littered beach on Galveston Bay.

He'd gone over the graffiti on the walls a couple of times and didn't find any of it very interesting—just a few numbers to call for "a good time" and the names of a some people who were "here" on various dates. The art work, mostly crudely drawn genitalia, did have one sketch of a vagina that, to the best of Doyle's memory, looked like a pretty convincing representation of the real thing.

Something written over the mirror caught his eye, but the lettering was too small to make out from the chair. When he got close enough, he saw that the words were drawn in such a fine calligraphy that he figured it must have taken its author a long time to write. It declared simply, "If you're reading this, you are standing in the heart of my broken dream." And it was that inscription along with the old woman's harsh assessment of his act when he exited the stage that made him wonder if it was too late to go back home and take his uncle up on that grocery clerk job at Albertsons.

After a while, he consoled himself by thinking the money he had coming would go a long way toward getting him back to San Angelo. He could stay in a couple of nice motels, even eat a few decent meals along the way. But he couldn't get away from the thought that whatever amount the wild flock of old ladies had spent out there would have covered only a fraction of the fee he'd been promised. The more time that went by, the more he was convinced that the five-hundred they'd paid up-front would be the only money he'd ever see from this down-at-the-heels, geriatric gig.

While cramming the Aloha into his garment bag, he cursed himself for being so stupid. He wondered what could have made him believe an AMVETS in an Alabama town barely on the map could pay him over six times his usual fee. Of course, he did suspect it was bullshit till they actually wired him the advance to the Check-and-Go in Bellevue, Nebraska. With his bookings calendar blank for the next three months, it was either the Willow Ruth AMVETS or nothing. So he had packed up his van and headed toward Alabama, stopping only for gas and nature while living on Pepsi and two bags of beef jerky.

A hard rap at the door startled him. And Parker poked his head in the room. "Hey, boy," Parker said, "'fraid you might've give up on me."

"Oh, no," Doyle said, pointing to his garment bag. "I was just packing."

Parker, a bald man with smiling eyes and puffy cheeks, ambled into the room. A fairly imposing belly poked out of his olive plaid sport coat. As Doyle shook hands with him, he noticed Parker wore more rings than he had fingers. Doyle figured he wanted to make everybody think he was some kind of a big-shot impresario.

"Great show, boy. Grrreaaat show," he said, chuckling as he pumped Doyle's hand. "It was so good, I thought we'd have to call the sheriff to clear those biddies outta here. Boy, I'm telling you, that bunch really wanted a big chunk of your ass. 'Specially one of em."

"The one in the short pink dress who climbed up the stage?"

"The very one," Parker said, a big grin stretching his cheeks as he reached into his coat pocket and extracted an envelope. He handed the envelope to Doyle and said, "You earned ever' goddamn dime of this."

"Thanks," Doyle said, hefting the envelope that was a good bit thicker than he expected. He thought it was probably half the cover charges in ones.

"Go ahead," Parker said. "You need to count it."

Doyle ripped open the envelope and began stacking hundred dollar bills on the dressing table. He felt confused when they added up to six thousand, and he thought he must be too tired for this level of serious ciphering. "This is..." he said. "Hell, this is way too much."

"Well, no, see," Parker said, "Your act tonight? Well, it was kind of subsidized. And you put on such a good show and all, our sponsor decided to pony up a little bonus."

"Subsidized?" Doyle said, his fingers caressing the hundreds. "Who...?"

"Hey, somebody out there wants to talk to you if you

got time."

"Well, it's getting kind of late, and I don't usually..."

"'Course you don't have to, but she said she'd really appreciate it."

"It's not one of those old...?"

"Oh, hell, no," Parker said, chuckling. "I wouldn't do that to you after what you did out there. I'll swear, son, you are a true professional if I've ever seen one. You took to our little humble stage like you was performing at the International. And you sang to that hand-full of biddies like they was two thousand débutantes, sipping champagne out of crystal. And I'll be damned if you didn't look and sound like the real thing, too. And, believe me, I know. I'm an Elvis fan from way back. Might even call me a Elvis scholar."

"Well, thank you, sir," Doyle said. Disarmed by the compliment and his newfound riches, he couldn't come up with a reason to refuse. So he shrugged and added, "Sure, I'll talk to her. Why not."

The club had looked seedy enough in the dark, but with its harsh overhead lights glaring down and Ernest Tubb rendering "Walking the Floor" from the house speakers, Doyle thought the joint had taken on the ambiance of the underside of a rock. That is, with the exception of the woman sitting at the table near the wall. She stood and smiled as Doyle and Parker approached.

"Mr. Brisendine, this is Ms. Rhonda Price," Parker said.

"You were just wonderful out there tonight," she said, holding out her hand.

"Well, th...thank you, ma'am," Doyle stuttered while holding her soft hand as if he didn't quite know what to do with it.

Doyle liked her large brown eyes, her throaty voice, and he liked the hue of her skin that told him she spent just the right amount of time under a good tanning lamp. He liked the way her black hair, bound tight behind her head, shimmered in the light. He especially liked the fragrance now wafting in front of his nose. He couldn't decide if it was flowers, exotic spices or something good to eat, but he was sure he was looking at the personification of that scent, and it scared him. He had no doubt that she was way out of his league, and that he had no chance in hell of getting in those high-class panties.

"That's great," she said, as she retrieved her hand and eased back into her chair. "That yes ma'am, no ma'am stuff. You're still in character, aren't you?"

"Well, I'm, uh...Yes ma'am. I guess so," he said as he pulled up the chair across from her and sat down.

"Well, hey, I'm gonna let you two get acquainted," Parker said.

Doyle couldn't think of anything to say, but she looked perfectly content to just sit there and smile at him from across the table. That was okay with him too. He just wished whoever had put together the playlist they were listening to had picked out something a little more romantic than Eddie Arnold wailing "Cattle Call."

Doyle finally pulled the envelope from his pocket and thumped it on the table. "You uh... are you the one I should thank for this?"

"Well, the people I work for," she said.

"Who is that, by the way?"

"It's a faith-based organization you've probably never heard of called Our Lady of TCB."

"You mean like, taking care of business?"

"Taking care of business," she said. "Very good."

"How would they, I mean how did they ever find out about me?"

"I couldn't really say other than the fact that I know they stay plugged into the entertainment trade. Especially the Elvis acts. Well, the really good ones anyway."

"Tell them I really appreciate it."

"I will. They tell me you changed your act a few years back."

"Man, those cats really do keep up with this stuff," Doyle said, nodding, feeling a little more comfortable with the conversation now that it had turned to something dear to his heart. "Yeah, actually, I used to do Elvis, 1956. You know how he dressed with the pegged pants, the loud shirts and sport coats."

"I get it," She said. "With the simple trio backing him—Scotty, Bill and DJ."

"Exactly. During the first set, all my backing tracks were just rock-a-billy stuff. The second set was the '68 comeback, and I came out in a tight leather jumpsuit."

"You know," she said, giving him that smile again. "I can see it. If you had on that leather jumpsuit right now, you'd be the '68 Comeback Elvis right down to the ground."

"Oh," he chuckled, feeling himself blush. "I don't know about all that. I did it like that for a few years. But it got to where all people wanted was the Las Vegas Elvis. You know, like I did tonight, with all the capes and the spangles and the karate kicks."

She shook her head and said, "People can be so stupid."

"Yeah, tell me about it," he said. "What really gets me is all those overweight clowns out there doing Elvis, and comedians still doing fat Elvis jokes." He shook his head. "Its got to where people forgot that for most of the twenty years that we saw Elvis, he was as streamlined as a race horse. Then he hit his forties and sickness got the best of him that last year. Damn vultures," Doyle snarled. "They just lay around and wait for somebody who's on top to stumble a little. Oh, hell. Look, I'm sorry, I kinda get on my soapbox sometimes about Elvis."

"Oh, don't apologize," she said. "We feel exactly the same way."

It was late, and he knew she would get up and leave at any moment. But he wasn't quite ready to lose her yet, so he blurted, "Hey, I know he's trying to close, but I bet we could get Parker to hustle us up a couple of drinks."

"Wouldn't you rather go get some dinner?"

"Dinner? You mean, go somewhere? Like together?"

"That's sort of what I had in mind," she said.

"Well, I guess I could eat," he said, his stomach growling at the memory of gobbling down the last of the jerky coming out of Little Rock. "You know a place open this time of night?"

"Oh, I know the best place of all," she said as she stood. "Come on. We'll take my car."

He glanced over at his computer, his amp, his mic, his speakers, his neon sign and the light show. Then he still had all his makeup, not to mention the Aloha he had worn during the show and the Fringe he'd broken out for back-up. Damn near twenty thousand dollars worth of gear and wardrobe not counting his van. That was a lot of money, but it made him a little sick every time he thought about what all that stuff had really cost him. "I got all my..." he said while pointing to the stage.

"Don't worry about your stuff," she said. "The Col-onel'll take care of it for you. Won't you, Colonel?" she called.

"Safe as if it was in a bank," Parker answered from somewhere in the shadows beyond the bar.

Doyle followed her to the door through the wonderful scent she left in her wake. "Hey," he said. "Colonel Parker. Man, that's a hell of a coincidence, isn't it?"

She didn't answer as she walked ahead of him, clutch-ing a black leather purse in her arm like a running back carrying a football. He couldn't help but notice that she had a couple of very playful-looking legs working under a tight knee-length skirt. She and those legs led him across the parking lot to something that made him think of a hulking mass of pink candy perched on four monstrous marshmal-lows. The headlights of a passing truck shimmered over its glossy pink finish. "*This* is your car?" he said, easing around the vintage automobile as though it were a ticking bomb sitting on gangster sidewalls.

"My mama's. Beautiful, isn't it?"

"It's something," he said.

"It's a '55 Fleetwood Special. You won't see many of these around."

"I know. I know. It's just like the one Elvis bought his mother."

"Yes," she said. "Now that you mention it, I think it is."

"Can I drive?"

"Nah, better not. Mama'd kill me if I let someone she didn't know behind the wheel of her baby. Hop in."

He opened the passenger door and settled into a pillow of plush white leather. "No seat belts?" he said.

"You won't need one," she said, sliding behind the wheel. "I'm a real good driver." She started the car and pulled out onto the road.

After a few miles, he leaned his head into the soft leather, the cushy suspension making him feel as if he were sitting on a big pink cloud floating through the night.

2

WHAT WOULD ELVIS DO?

They were quiet for a while, and as the pleasure of the ride waned, the anticipation of what would happen at the end of it flooded into Doyle's mind. He fantasized that she might actually be hot for him. And he figured that they would probably just grab a quick sandwich at a Waffle House somewhere and find a motel. Or maybe they would just do it in the car since the damn thing had enough room for an orgy.

The longer she drove, the more he worried that he would be a big disappointment to this beautiful woman. The women who usually waited for him after his Elvis act were somewhere south of beautiful—many of them even south of cute and most of them north of forty. He didn't have to be a psychologist to figure out that many of them were damaged by their lack of self-worth, willing to lie with him in the back of his messy van or a cheap motel room while imagining themselves getting screwed by a big star.

And what was her name, anyway? When he saw her, sitting there in that dingy club, he had been so stunned that Parker's introduction shot through his ear like a bullet. Did he say something like Donna or Roxanne? He thought about a dozen female names and nothing seemed to stick.

As she drove through the shadows of the dark pines he asked himself the question he always asked in moments of doubt—what would Elvis do? Elvis wouldn't care what her name was. The King knew the power he had over women and would now be imagining how that confident expression of hers would soon be melting into one of surrender under his kisses. Doyle stretched out his hands, thinking how they'd fit nicely across her firm ass while she locked her legs around him. She cleared her throat as she drove the big car, and he thought how it wouldn't be long before he would be hearing her sweet sighs. And her scent. He didn't know what that was, but he was pretty sure that from now on he'd get a hard-on every time he passed a Cinnabon in the mall.

He knew Waffle Houses were more common than poor kinfolks, but he was sure there weren't any this deep in the woods. "Where the hell you taking me, anyway?" he asked, chuckling behind his words to hide the concern creeping into his mind.

"I thought we'd go to my place."

"Your place?"

"What's the matter? You're not scared are you?"

"Scared?" he said through a nervous chuckle. "You kidding?"

She stopped at a crossroads, the stop sign an octagonal shadow towering over a dark tangle of sumac and honeysuckle. "You know, you might be more comfortable if you moved over here a little," she said, patting the seat beside her. And when he slid over, she rested her hand on his thigh, quashing the creeping anxiety caused by all that dark, rural space.

"Where the hell are we?" he said as the woods opened into a field where a lighted brick wall stretched out like a shining dam against the surrounding woods.

"It's kind of a gated community," she said. Her warm hand moved higher, giving him all the reassurance he needed as he watched the headlights gleam from a wrought iron gate shaped like an open hymnal with musical notes filigreed across its open pages. One of those weird, déjà vu feelings he had sometimes was interrupted when she stopped. The gate cracked open, and a dark figure stepped toward them, a flashlight beam jiggling from his hand.

"Don't worry," she said. "It's just Uncle Vester."

The passenger side window rolled down with a hum, and a wiry little man with narrow smiling eyes and a full head of white wavy hair leaned against the car. "I see you came back," the old man said.

"Well, I live here," she said.

"Yeah. For now. Who you got here?" he said, poking his head in.

"Uncle Vester, this is Doyle."

"How you this evening, Doyle?" he said, nodding.

"Fine, sir," Doyle said, thinking the old man's bulbous nose looked a lot like a gnarly potato.

He stared at Doyle for a moment as though he were trying to remember where he had seen him before. "Damned if you don't look like you belong in there, son." Vester said. Then he backed away, patting the side of the car as though it were some living thing. He strutted toward the gate, waving his hand in the air without looking back as he called out, "Y'all have a nice evening." In a moment the gate swung all the way open and the woman drove the big car through.

"Am I imagining things or did the old guy sound like he didn't like you very much?"

"He's just being Uncle Vester," she said as she drove on.

He thought it was some kind of trick when he saw the house projected by the broad spray of floodlights on the dark lawn. In front of four towering columns two benches looked as if they were designed for some purpose other than sitting, and the two white stone lions guarding the steps made the place look more like a library than a house where people actually lived.

While she fumbled with the keys at the door, he looked around in wonder at the stone walls and the reflection of the floodlights gleaming from the door-length arched windows. "Graceland," he said. "This place looks like Graceland."

"You think?" she giggled. "Come on in."

He followed her into the foyer, feeling the need to tip-toe over the white carpet at his feet while the woman stepped across it as though stomping through grass. Though overwhelmed by the house, he remembered what he had actually come for and had his attention appropriately riveted on her butt working against her skirt until he saw an eerie light dancing to his right.

It was dark in the Living Room, and beyond the room, the light flickered blue, red and gold from two stained glass peacocks across snow banks of white chairs and a long white couch perched on a tundra of white carpet.

He walked across the Living Room and stepped between the peacocks into the Music Room where the light shimmered across gold colored drapes covering the back wall and a mirror on one of the side walls. Beside a white baby grand piano stood a life-sized figure of Elvis Presley in his Sundial jumpsuit. His legs were splayed apart as if they might shake furiously at any moment, and his lips curled in that sneering smile of his as he looked down upon an audience of at least a hundred votive candles melting into puddles below him. A guitar with a blond soundboard dangled down the Elvis figure's chest on a thick strap that looked like a blue suede stole around the neck of a priest.

He thought the thing was damn sure life-like, and he stepped in, slowly, feeling that the figure might bolt and run if he made any sudden moves. With his mind lost in this weird effect, he was startled when the woman walked up behind him. "There you are," she said. "I just looked around and you'd disappeared on me." She emitted a deep sigh, shook her head and said, "Mama left those candles burning again. I'll swear, that woman's going to burn this place slap to the ground one of these days."

For a moment his curiosity about the Elvis figure shriveled into sickening disappointment as "You mean, your mother's here?" rose from his throat like a bad taste.

"No, silly. I wouldn't invite you all they way over here and spring Mama on you without warning you. She was here earlier, but she said she had some work to do at the Tupelo House."

He'd driven by Tupelo on his way and remembered it had to be at least a hundred-fifty miles from there. He figured that ought to be far enough to keep her from spoiling his fun.

"Come on, let's eat," she said.

"Yeah, you did say something about dinner."

In the Dining Room he eased around the long table perched on an island of shining black marble and surrounded by a border of the seemingly unending white carpet. A centerpiece of exotic flowers he didn't recognize sat in the middle of the table, and the crystal spears of the sprawling chandelier hanging overhead looked like ice melting from the pale blue ceiling.

"Sit right there." She pointed to a chair at the head of the table in front of one of the two place settings. "In the place of honor."

"Honor?" he said as he sat down. "Hey, this place?"

"Yes?" she said, smiling as she sat beside him.

"What's up with this place?"

"You do a tribute to the King with your act, right?"

"Ummhum," Doyle said, nodding.

"Well, Our Lady does the same tribute with this house."

"Man, this is a..."

"A what?" she said, removing the dome from a serving tray.

But the aroma of the fried chicken in front of him made him forget what he was going to say.

With the food settling warm in his stomach, he realized that he had become relaxed in his chair and that his eyes had grown accustomed to the opulence of the house. He could see the glint of the chandelier and his own face and hands moving in the china cabinet against the wall. And he tossed a little conspiratorial wink at his Elvis-like reflection as he thought he could get used to some of this in a hurry.

"I was just thinking," Doyle said. "With all this hot food and everything waiting on us, it sure looks like you were expecting me to come home with you all along."

"I wasn't really sure, but I was hoping," she said, blinking her eyes and returning his smile.

"Hoping, huh?" Doyle said. She had been thinking about him and he liked the sound of that. She reached out and caressed his forearm. Then they sat without talking for a while. Before long, his curiosity about the flickering candles and the huge Elvis icon seeped back into his mind. "Hey, about this house. Y'all must really be Elvis fans."

"We all love Elvis," she said. "If you're finished eating, I'll show you some more."

"More's what I want to see," he said. "You got a Jungle Room and everything?"

"Right back here," she said. "Come on, I'll show you."

Walking with her out of the dining room, he chuckled to himself. She stopped and turned to him. "What?" she said.

"Oh, I was just thinking how I was expecting to walk out of the dressing room and have one of those old ladies from the audience waiting for me."

"Oh, so you like em young, huh?"

"I like em like you," he said.

Thinking the words of an Elvis song, "It's Now or Never," he pulled her to him and he could feel her surrender in his arms and see that the closer she came the more her eyes closed as her lips parted. Her purse fell to the floor with a clunk, and her arms slid up around his neck as their lips melted together. When their lips parted, he caught his breath and tried to kiss her again, but she pushed away and picked up her purse from the floor. Then she grabbed his hand. "Come on," she said in a whisper and led him past the Jungle Room, through a narrow hallway down one of the wings to a bedroom.

Compared to the rest of the house, the bedroom would have looked kind of ordinary if every bare space on its walls hadn't been splattered with frame photos of Elvis—Elvis as a kid in a cowboy hat, Elvis on a motorcycle, Elvis onstage in Vegas. It had a bathroom and a closet just big enough to stand in. One full-length mirror hung on the door, another over the dresser and a bronze bust of Elvis surveyed the room from a chest of drawers. The brass headboard on the bed looked as if it had been polished recently, and the mattress didn't fight back when he gave it a couple of punches.

The woman had excused herself to the bathroom when they walked in. And after he lost interest comparing his own image in the mirror to the ones on the Elvis-strewn walls, Doyle sat on the bed and listened to her shuffling around.

The toilet flushed. Water splashed. Then she swung the bathroom door open and stood there so naked she was like a flash of bright light that caused his vision to blur for a moment. He thought the thing that made her look even more naked was her long, black hair, loose from whatever binding she'd had it done up in, now lying free on her back.

His eyes lingered on her breasts, the size of a couple of small cantaloupes, whose only imperfection he could see were the brown nipples pointing in different directions that made him think of twin sisters who didn't like each other very much. He didn't want her to think he was a complete pervert, so as his gaze drifted on down her tight waist to the swell of her hips, he was careful not to stare too long at the neatly trimmed V between her smoothly muscled legs. And he was thinking that this is the kind of stuff that happened to Elvis not Doyle Brisendine when she said, "Well!"

"What?" He gasped, realizing that he hadn't been breathing.

"You going to get out of those clothes?"

"Yes," he said. "Yes I am."

3

ONE NIGHT WITH YOU

*I*t looked as if he'd hit the Elvis trifecta. He was practically sleeping in Graceland, he had a pocket full of cash, and he was about to make love to the most beautiful woman he'd ever been with. She looked good, smelled good, and from the way she sighed as her tongue danced against his, she really wanted him. "You look just like Elvis," she gasped, coming up for air. "God, you feel just like him."

A few hours earlier, he'd represented the King on stage. Now he had the chance to represent him in another way. And he had the want-to. Oh, he definitely had the want-to. But the problem was, the want-to was all in his head and not where it counted. He'd eaten way too much of that chicken. But the worst part was, he'd been running on adrenaline for better than twenty-eight hours, and when the rush of adrenaline dwindled to a trickle, he could feel every mile of the non-stop drive from Nebraska, every move from the vigorous performance at the AMVETS. It didn't matter how beautiful the woman in his arms was, the pillow beside her looked a hell of a lot better than she did.

He rolled over on his back and let his head sink into that pillow, his brain drifting into a haze with her attached to him like a hungry predator and her hot breath and quick, wet tongue working its way down his chest. She almost scared him into a heart attack when her head popped up from under the covers like a prairie dog springing out of its hole. "It's just lying there," she said as she pushed the hair from her face. "Doesn't it stand up?"

"Well, usually," he groaned.

"I mean, I've been, you know...for the longest time. And...and it's still just lying there."

"I'm sorry, baby. I'm just wasted."

"You think it'd help if I kissed it some more?"

"You're welcome to try, but, the way I feel right now? I don't think it's gonna stand up if you blow 'The Star Spangled Banner' on it."

She scooted up in the bed and dropped her head down on the pillow beside him so hard the bed bounced as if she'd dropped from the ceiling. "Shit!" she said.

"Look," he said. "I said I was sorry. What can I say? It's never done this before. Honest. I guess I've never been this tired before."

"You're sure it's not about me?"

"About you? Oh, Baby, how could it be about you? You're the sexiest thing I've ever seen."

"Really?" she said. "You're sure?"

"I've never been more sure of anything in my life. It's just that my, uh, equipment..."

"Your little Elvis?"

"Hey, you don't think it's too little, do you?"

"No, that's just what Elvis calls his."

"Oh, yeah? Okay. My little Elvis has just run out of gas along with the rest of me."

"You won't say anything about this will you?" she said.

"Who the hell would I tell?"

"Well just don't tell anybody."

"All right. I gotcha, but I want a rain check, okay?"

"A what?"

"A...you know. Another chance. I'm sure it's going to rise again."

"Like Elvis."

"Yeah, like... What?"

"Elvis. You know how when Satan tried to destroy him by having him drafted in the Army, and he rose to become a movie star. And after he got lost and tempted in the Wilderness of Hollywood, he rose again in his '68 Comeback. And when everybody thought he'd died, he rose again. And again. Just like he said he would."

He never thought he'd get tired of hearing about Elvis, but she got dangerously close to his threshold. He tried to sleep while she rattled on about the King—how wonderful Elvis sang, how beautiful Elvis was, and how Elvis had been sent by God to bring the lost children to the Land of Grace or some shit he couldn't quite figure out.

From the looks of this place, this outfit had some deep pockets. They had already paid him six grand for his performance at the AMVETS. If they went to the trouble of researching him, they probably had an intention of paying him some more. He figured he'd hang around and see what they had in mind. Right now though, he just wished she'd shut up so he could get some sleep.

4

EVERYBODY'S A CRITIC

The woman sat up as if she'd heard a gunshot and shouted, "Shit!" While he rubbed sleep from his eyes, she kicked back the covers, sprang to her feet, and walked over to the window. After pulling back the drapes and releasing a flood of blinding sunlight into the dark room, she said, "You've got to get up."

He buried his face in the pillow and moaned, "I'm not sure I can."

"I've got to get ready for church," she said as she scampered into the bathroom.

"Church?" he called after her. "Did you say, church?"

He dozed and awakened again when she stepped out of the bathroom, skirt and blouse wrinkled, hair a little more together but still looking like it had gone twelve rounds with the pillow. "You want to go to church with me?" she said in the same tone she might use if she were asking if he wanted a blow job.

"I'm not really the church-going kind," he said behind a yawn. "I haven't been to church in..." he shook his head, "I don't even remember."

Her lower lip poked out and her eyes clouded up as if she were going to break into tears. "Last night. You know. We...we didn't. I mean you couldn't..."

"Hey," he said. "I was tired."

"If you'd go to church, I would be willing to give Little Elvis another chance."

He did want to prove to her that last night was a fluke. But going to church? "You know, I don't have anything to wear."

"I'll get you something to wear."

"I just remembered I left my van and all my gear back

at the AMVETS."

"Give me the keys, and I'll ask one of the apostles to get your van and all your stuff for you."

"Apostles?" he said.

"That's what we call our Board of Directors or elders," she said. "They really wanted to talk to you about your future and stuff."

He was right. There was some more money in this deal.

"Well, if you can find me some clothes to wear, I guess it'll be all right."

She picked his jeans off the floor. "Your keys in here?"

"Yeah," he said. He sat up and shook his head as she turned her back and rifled through his pocket.

"Well," he said. "I guess it'll be okay. Hey, you know something?"

"What?"

He stood, inched over to her and pulled her close to him. "I think you may have woke up Little Elvis."

She pushed him away. "We don't have time for Little Elvis," she said. "Come on, let's get you some breakfast."

The dining room smelled of burnt bacon and dark French roast coffee left on the warmer a couple of hours too long. The two men sitting at the table were dressed in garish blue suits, white lacy shirts with blue bowties. Both looked as if they could be professional wrestlers with broad, rugged faces, one with black hair styled neatly over his ears, while the other sported short-cropped red hair and a devilish goatee. The red-haired man, crunching a mouthful of bacon, sounded as if he had chomped into one of the water glasses. The other sat rubbing his jaw and staring down at the table.

"When you gonna let Doctor Nick take a look at that tooth?" the redhead said around a mouthful of bacon.

"That creepy sumbitch ain't looking in my mouth. Besides, I think it's getting better."

"Bullshit! I heard you whining last night when I got up to piss."

The red haired man shook his head and pinned an egg to the edge of his plate with his fork as he sliced a knife into it with all the concentration of a brain surgeon removing a small tumor. "Keep on hurting," he said. "It gets bad enough, you'll come around."

"Doyle, this is Red and Sonny," the woman said.

The two men looked up and gave Doyle and the woman a nod.

"You're kidding," Doyle said. "Hey, that's like Red and Sonny West."

"That's who they are," she said.

"Oh," Doyle said. "I get it. This place is like Disney World where everybody has to stay in character."

"Well," she said, shrugging, tossing her head from side to side. "For want of a better reference."

"Uh," Red said. "Mama wants to see you."

The woman winced as if she'd been stabbed, and she slumped over the back of a chair. "What does...? Do you know what she wants?"

"Hey," Red said. "I'm just relaying information. Said she'd be in the Music Room till nine. I'd get on over there, I was you."

"I've got to run," the woman said. When she got to the door, she turned and said, "Can you boys fix Doyle up with a suit for church?"

Red chewed thoughtfully as he looked Doyle over. Then he nodded. "Think I can handle that," he said. Doyle damn sure hoped it wasn't going to be a replica of the clown outfits this pair of faux West brothers had on.

"Sit down and help yourself," Sonny said. He wiped his mouth with a cloth napkin and pointed to a chair.

When Doyle dropped into the chair, Red said, "Coffee?"

"Please," Doyle said.

"Glad to meet you," the redhead said. "I'd shake hands with you, but I've got grease all over my fingers. Heard you put on a pretty good show last night."

"I don't know about that," Doyle said. "I think the audience had a good time."

After a couple of hard slugs of coffee strong enough to prop open the eyes of a corpse, Doyle reached for the only thing on the table he knew he could choke down—one of the flaky biscuits. He cut it in half, slathered it in butter and thick sorghum syrup, then ate it with a fork as if it were a pancake.

"Now, let me get this straight," he said. "Everybody here's supposed to be like a Graceland resident."

"Everybody *is* a Graceland resident," Red said.

"Who is she supposed to be?" Doyle said, thinking he would catch her name.

"She lives in the Big House on a temporary basis," Red said.

"Oh," Doyle said. "But how about Uncle Fester. That's from the Addam's Family, isn't it?"

"You misunderstood," Sonny said. "That's Vester with a V. He's Elvis' uncle who guarded the front gate at Graceland."

"*Guards* the gate," Red corrected.

"Yeah, that's right," Sonny said. "Guards the gate."

A wiry old woman tromped in, wiping her hands on her apron as she took in the room through the narrow slits of her eyes. Doyle could tell from the straps and the stitching along the edges that the apron had once been white before it became soaked in grease and splattered in vintage tomato paste. And her tattered jeans were in bad need of a washing or maybe just an oil change. A cluster of hair pins over her forehead held on to dingy gray hair that drooped on her head as if it had grown tired of being there.

"Look who honored us with his presence," the old lady said, spitting out the words with bitter sarcasm. "The big star. Keep your seat, your majesty," she said worshipfully bowing a couple of times when Doyle started to stand. "Can't have a big star like you standing for a peasant like me."

"Oh," Doyle said. "Ma'am, I'm not a star."

"You goddamn right you ain't," she snapped.

"Now, Granny," Red said. "Take it easy. Doyle here's our guest."

"Oh, I'm gonna take it easy," she said. "You want some notes on your performance last night, big star? Some honest criticism from a real fan?"

"Well," Doyle said. "Yes, ma'am. I'm always open to honest criticism."

"See, you think you've got the look down, don't you?" Granny said. "Well, you have if a real fan don't look too close. When somebody does look close, they can see the hair don't tumble down just right over your eyes. And that smile. That smile's got to smolder like you was a young bull that just pranced out in the pasture, sniffing a herd of heifers to pick out the ones in heat."

"Granny," Red said. "I heard he was pretty good."

"Purty good's a good description," she said behind a sneer. "But purty good's not good enough. If you want to really be Elvis, you got to live it. When you're doing a fast number you got to be nothing but rhythm and sex. On a ballad, your voice has got to be fucking velvet. And the expression on your face? Well, shit, the expression on your face has got to make every woman in the audience think you're over her getting ready to come."

"Don't you think you're a little hard on the boy," Red said from across the table.

"He needs somebody to get hard on him," Granny said. "Y'all need some more eggs?"

"No," Red said, "I think we done all the damage we got time to do."

The old lady looked down at Doyle as if he were something she'd scraped off the heel of her shoe, then she walked into the Kitchen.

"Guess she told me," Doyle said.

"Ah, don't pay her no 'tention," Sonny said. "Heard she fell off a Harley somewhere around Trussville few years ago. Kinda fucked up her head. Gang of bikers she was with wouldn't even go back for her."

"She's such a bitch, I don't blame 'em," Red said.

"When you get back to the room you slept in last night, just go ahead and shower or whatever you need to do. I'll send you a toothbrush, a razor and some clothes down there in a minute."

"Hey," Doyle said. "What time do all the tourists get here?"

"The what?" Red said.

"The tourists. You know, to look the place over."

Red and Sonny looked at each other and shrugged. "Why the hell would we want tourists in here?" Red said.

5

MAMA

From the foyer, Rhonda could see Mama kneeling in front of the shrine in the Music Room. After slipping the compact mirror from her purse, she raised it to her face, slowly, as if she were trying to sneak up on her reflection. She looked worse than she thought. Her lipstick looked as if she'd slapped it on in the dark with a paint brush, her mascara clumped in her lashes like blue mud, and though she had fought with her hair for ten minutes in the bathroom, it was all warped on one side. On top of everything else, the skirt had spent the night on the bathroom floor and now looked as if she'd pulled it from the bottom of a laundry bag. She sighed as she wondered what Mama would say when she saw her.

Anytime she thought about Mama lately, she couldn't help thinking of former Joe Esposito who had smuggled a letter out of the compound for one of the women in the Village. Like everyone else who had broken the law, poor old Joe had vanished. "The Lord must have called him up," Sonny said. "So he can get his mind straightened out. You know, like he did those other guys."

As far as she knew, this was the first time it happened to an apostle. Rhonda knew if it happened to an apostle, it could happen to her. But it wasn't long before another guy started walking around the Big House, saying he was Joe. "Mama said the spirit of Joe entered him," Sonny said. So she thought the apostles kind of reincarnated sometimes like Elvis did.

With her breath catching in her throat, she trudged across the Living Room floor toward the Music Room as if the carpet were a bog of white gumbo mud. Ahead, Mama still knelt in front of the Elvis shrine. The scent of candle smoke drifted out into the Living Room, and from the speakers under the drapes came the high, lonesome sound of the Louvin Brothers singing "Satisfied Mind."

After stepping through the doorway, she glanced at her watch. She hated to interrupt Mama's prayers, but she was late. If she were in her room right now, she'd still have to scramble to get her hair fixed, her face washed, and get dressed for the service. Mama knelt there as calm as the plastic Elvis in front of her.

"Mama?" she said in a halting voice.

Mama shivered and turned her head. "Oh, baby. It's you." She held out her hands and Rhonda helped her to her feet.

"Thanks," Mama grunted as she gained her footing. "Did you get his phone?"

Rhonda opened her purse, slid a phone out and handed it to Mama.

"You did good, baby," Mama said. "And he's going to church?"

"Yes. He didn't want to at first, but I convinced him he should go."

"I bet you did," Mama said. "You're real good at convincing young men." She chuckled for a second. "And probably old men too."

"Mama, it's getting kind of late in Elvis' career. Have you given any thought to me being Ginger?"

Mama looked down at her feet as if she had something else to say and had left all the words on the floor. "We all have to make sacrifices around here. You know that."

"Yes, ma'am," Rhonda said, thinking, *Here it comes*.

"I know you've got your heart set on being Ginger. But right now, I'm kinda short handed in the Office."

"The Office?" Rhonda moaned, suddenly feeling as wrinkled as her skirt. She'd started out in the Office. But she escaped that drudgery by demonstrating her ability to recruit and perform as a member of the cast. Getting kicked back to the Office wasn't as bad as disappearing, but she couldn't help thinking that if she kept going backward she'd be washing pots and pans in the Kitchen before long.

"Well. What do you think?" Mama said.

"Think?" Rhonda said, thinking Mama didn't seem to be in a bad mood after all.

"About the boy."

"He was real good last night. All the Village seniors really flipped out over him. And they're not an easy audience."

"I'm not talking about his singing. We already know he's good. What I want to know is, how does he really feel about Elvis? In here," she said, poking a stubby finger in the middle of Rhonda's chest.

"Well, he looked kind of stunned when he saw the house. After he walked in here, I wasn't sure I was going to be able to get him out. He just stood here, gazing at the King's icon like he was in a trance or something."

"Wonderful," Mama said. "That was the spirit of Elvis trying to connect with him."

"Is he going to be the next one, Mama?"

"He could be, baby," Mama said. "From what I've seen and what everyone says, it sounds like the spirit is trying to move into him. But the question is, will he let it?"

"I don't know that," Rhonda said.

"Oh, I didn't expect you to know that, baby. I don't know either. We'll just have to wait. Hadn't you better be getting ready for church?"

"Oh, yes, ma'am," Rhonda said, her hand moving up to her unruly hair.

A lot of the things Mama said about the faith didn't make any sense if Rhonda thought about them very much. Especially how Elvis could die and at the same time be alive. And how his spirit could always be floating around somewhere, looking for a proper vessel to occupy. She often wondered how Elvis's spirit could hole up in one body, and be wandering around looking for another at the same time. But she was afraid to ask. Besides, if Mama said it, she believed it even if it didn't make sense. She believed it, casting aside all the pesky doubts that popped up in her head as if the lessons Mama taught her when she was a little girl had been transfused into her blood.

Sixteen years ago, she'd just been Rhonda Ann Price, living with her aunt Ceil in the Tin Can Village trailer park on the outskirts of Willow Ruth. She could remember being only mildly curious when a big truck hauled a battered old double-wide in the park. A small crowd of children gathered as men jumped out of the truck, jacked the trailer up on cinder blocks and left it there baking in the sun for more than a week without a sign of life stirring it. Rhonda and two of her girlfriends strolled by one day when the door sprang open and a moon-faced woman with a wavy permanent peeked her head out as if the old trailer had been an egg and the woman had been a chick who had just hatched out of it.

"Well, who do we have here?" Mama said. After no one answered, she said, "I've got it all cooled down inside. And I just made some oatmeal cookies. Would you girls like to have some?"

With the story of Hansel and Gretel etched firmly in their minds, the invitation to go inside the trailer by a suspicious old woman made Rhonda's friends scatter like frightened chickens. But Rhonda was curious, and on top of that, pretty hungry. She didn't care if this was one of those fairy tale witches from the story books, she really wanted one of those cookies. So she took one cookie from the woman while she stood beside the stoop. The cookie was so good, she gobbled down another and accepted the woman's invitation to come inside on the promise of more cookies as well as milk to go along with them.

"You're a skinny little thing," Mama said. "Are they feeding you enough at home?"

The truth was, they weren't, but Rhonda didn't say anything. She was so busy scarfing down a plateful of the cookies and washing them down with a tall glass of cold milk she didn't pay much attention to what the woman was saying, and she was looking around for something else to eat when she noticed there was music playing low in the background accompanying a man's deep voice asking if someone was lonesome tonight. While the woman rattled on about how she was looking forward to meeting everybody and giving them some kind of good news about somebody named Elvis, Rhonda enjoyed the chill from the airco on her skin and took a careful look around.

As ratty as the double-wide was on the outside, on the inside it was as neat as the fancy houses she saw on TV all the time. The tables were so polished she could see the reflection of the room in them. Unlike the scent of unwashed dishes and stale tobacco she was accustomed to, Mama's trailer smelled of lemon furniture polish and oatmeal cookies. And unlike the hard, worn plastic seating in her aunt's trailer, the couch she sat on was a soft blue fabric that just snuggled around her butt and made her want to sit there forever. Most of the pictures on the paneled wall were of a man with a pile of black hair in a flashy outfit holding a microphone so close to his mouth he looked as if he were trying to eat it.

"You're going to be my special little girl," Mama said. "But I can see that I'm going to have to fatten you up a little. The first thing I want you to do for me is to bring all your girlfriends back tomorrow."

After she brought her friends back the next day, Mama held the first of what she called "Sunbeam" classes. They had cookies and milk and learned about Elvis being born in a little house more humble than a Tin Can Village trailer. And she showed videos of him in concert while teaching the girls how to squeal, which Mama said was the only way for a female to properly show love for him once he returned.

She ate three meals a day at Mama's double-wide and sometimes spent the night there. When they moved to The Land of Grace, her aunt Ceil moved into a nice little cottage in the Village while Rhonda moved into a room in the Big House. When she wasn't going to school, she did odd jobs in the little white office building out back.

Mama saw that Rhonda had talent, and when Rhonda turned seventeen, she became the King's teenage girlfriend. After playing that part to perfection, she was promoted all the way to Priscilla. With her hair dyed jet black, she felt like the princess of this whole outfit. Red, Sonny and the rest of those redneck apostles had to take their marching orders from Mama through her.

She was pretty sure that was why that bunch of jealous, inbred shit-kickers had poisoned Elvis's mind against her. Where else would he get the wild idea that she was a nagging bitch? She had thought it over a lot and concluded she couldn't possibly be a nag just because she complained a few times about him spending more time with the apostles than with her. What girl wouldn't complain about that? Even her frequent mention of his weight gain had just been for his own health. And who could blame her for going a little ape shit about him going around the house all the time, stuffing his face with fried chicken and banana pudding? She wished she'd been a little more understanding after she overheard Red and Sonny say Dr. Nick had given him steroids because he wasn't getting fat fast enough. And she felt really bad that she had brained him with a brass ornamental lion after catching him naked on the Jungle Room floor with one of those slutty little nymphs from the Village.

Elvis was the King, and the King was exempt from everything, even a wife's jealousy. So unless Elvis forgave her, she still had some serious punishment coming. No matter how mad you get, you can't go around cold-cocking the King of Rock and Roll and expect to get away with it.

Rhonda needed to hurry, but Dr. Nick sneaking up the stairs froze her at the Music Room door. He always wore a black suit and swung a black leather bag at his side. If she'd never seen him before and only caught a glance of his smooth olive skin and shock of white hair on a street somewhere, she would have thought him a handsome, older man. But when she was twelve, he'd slid his hand under her skirt while he was supposed to be examining her ear and whispered in that strange accent of his, "You have wary nice legs for a little girl, you know that?"

Now the slow way he crept up the stairs made her think of a big lizard sneaking up on unsuspecting prey. After he'd disappeared beyond the landing she headed down the hallway to her room with an uncontrollable urge to wash the spot on her leg where his moist hand had once rested. She'd been scrubbing that spot for years, and it still didn't feel clean.

6

OUR LADY OF TAKING CARE
OF BUSINESS

Standing at the bathroom mirror with a towel wrapped around his waist, Doyle couldn't decide which he loved more, performing like Elvis or the ritual of becoming Elvis every day. After blow-drying and sculpting the last evidence of Doyle Brisendine away, he sucked in a deep breath and shared a little curling Elvis smile with his reflection.

When he stepped out of the bathroom, he thought it was a little creepy to find a suit as black as an undertaker's stretched out on the bed with a white shirt and tie on top. But he figured they just didn't want to disturb him. "Church," he said, shaking his head, rubbing his finger across the wool lapel of the suit. "If it's worth a few more bucks, why the hell not?" He slipped into the pants and found them long enough but loose in the waist. The shirt fit all right, but the coat was too snug to button.

He hadn't worn a tie since he was in the sixth grade, and that one had been a clip-on. So instead of worrying about how to attach the thing, he decided to check his email and his Facebook page for inquiries. After his agent dropped him a while back, he had taken a stab at promoting himself again. At first he'd done pretty well, revisiting venues where he'd been successful before and staying up nights researching new ones. But after three years, his efforts now barely kept him in fast food and gas.

After he didn't feel the familiar lump of his phone in his jeans, he emptied the pockets on the bed and found nothing but the envelope stuffed with cash and some loose change. Thinking he might have dropped it in all the excitement, he got down on the floor and pulled up the bed skirt. He was staring at a couple of formidable dust bunnies when the woman peeked into the room. "You decent?" she said.

"Decent?" he said, scrambling to his feet.

"Yeah," she said while moving cautiously into the room as if she'd never been there before. She seemed shy for some reason and looked old fashioned in her wide-brim straw hat banded by a blue ribbon that matched her plain shirtwaist dress. Under her arm she carried a hat box.

"I like this new look," he said. "And, guess what? Me and little Elvis are all rested." But when he reached for her, she danced away.

"Please. Don't," she said. "You've got to get ready for church."

"We really going to church?"

"We are really going to church." She dropped the box on the bed and opened the top. "Got a couple of things you need to put on first."

She held up a wig.

"What's that for?"

"You look too, uh, you know, Elvisey. We don't want people to notice you. It'll distract from the service."

"I'm not putting that shit on," he said.

She moved in close, and he got a whiff of that fragrance she wore as she pressed her breasts against him. "Please," she pleaded. "You do it for me, and I'll do something nice for you."

"Damn," he said, pointing to his hair. "I already went to all this trouble."

"That's my guy," she said as she pulled a chair from the dresser. "Have a seat."

After placing the wig on his head she helped him stick a black beard around his jaw line. She pulled a pair of glasses from the box and said, "Put these on, and let's see what you look like."

He already didn't like this church. In the dresser mirror, instead of a brooding Elvis, he saw a burnt-out college professor with a bad haircut. But he thought he had one consolation, and he stood and pulled her into his arms. "I'm kind of in the mood to take care of some business," he said. "You know. Like Elvis said—in a flash."

"It's Sunday," she said. "I'm not allowed to make love on Sunday."

"Hey, we're talking about Little Elvis here. He don't know it's Sunday."

She pushed herself away from him and said, "We'll have to get Little Elvis a calendar."

At the carport stood a black antique Cadillac limousine. A driver in a black suit and a black cap held the back door of the car open. "This?" Doyle said, almost breathless as he walked the length of the car. "We're going in this?"

"Yes, of course," the woman said. "Come on. You can look it over later."

Inside the big car, the woman snuggled against him in the back seat as they followed a narrow paved road through a thick clump of woods. The woods opened into a clearing, and they were on a hill looking down at the sun glinting from the roof of a metal building that dwarfed three buses unloading passengers in front. The front facade of the building was constructed of steel cut in the shape of a dome and riveted together. The dome was flanked by the image of two Gothic towers with the likeness of windows and ancient brown brick and mortar painted onto the metal. Behind the faux cathedral front was a rectangle of steel walls covered by a corrugated metal roof.

"Beautiful, huh?" she said.

"Uh, yeah," Doyle said, thinking if they'd added four big wheels, the thing would look like a humongous trailer.

Over the groaning of air conditioning units the size of automobiles, an army of rollicking voices rose up from inside, singing, "Down by the Riverside." He first thought the symbol towering over the building was a cross, but as he approached, he could see it was the Elvis logo, TCB over a jagged flash of lightning. "Taking care of business," he said.

"The name of our church," the woman said.

The people strung out across the clearing formed lines in front of the building. Men stood at the entrances, checking identification. After the driver stopped in front of the building, two men rushed to open the door. Once they were outside the big car, he started to find a place at the end of one of the long lines, but the woman grabbed him by the sleeve. "We don't have to wait," she said, tugging him along.

When they stepped into the building, he felt crushed by the singing, the hand-clapping and foot-stomping from the growing crowd. On a stage in front of the sanctuary, a man led the singing, swinging his hands so enthusiastically he looked as if he were trying to fly away. Behind the man, a band with two drum kits, keyboards, two guitars, a bass and a three-piece horn section rocked the room through two towering Marshall stacks.

The woman's lips moved, her voice swallowed by the surrounding sound. Doyle pointed to his ears and shook his head, so she motioned for him to follow her around the perimeter of the sanctuary to a ramp that led to a balcony. A thick velvet rope and a tall, broad-shouldered man with a crew-cut and a pair of narrow, unsmiling eyes obstructed the entrance to the balcony. The man wore a black suit and stood like a soldier at parade rest, legs apart, hands behind him until Doyle and the woman approached. The man bent over to unhook the rope, and his coat fell open to reveal a pistol holstered on his hip.

They walked to a railing overlooking the stage and stood in front of their seats, the woman clapping and singing, Doyle joining in, remembering all the lyrics to the song from his boyhood. As his lips moved, the chorus absorbed his voice into the mighty force that moved him to clap and sway along with the congregation.

Now close to the stage, Doyle had a good view of the bald man in the blue suit leading the singing. *Parker from the AMVETS*, he thought. *I'll be damned.*

By the time the song ended, the sanctuary rumbled with

the shuffling of the crowd dropping into their metal folding chairs. "All right! All right!" Parker said. "You're in good voice today. Now, who do you love?"

"The King!" the crowd yelled, the answer rising and falling around the room like an echo.

"Oh," Parker said. "You'll have to do better than that. Now, who do you love?"

He cupped his hand to his ear and leaned toward the audience who roared back, "THE KING!"

"I believe you do," Parker said, nodding, smiling broadly. "I believe you do. Y'all did such a good job on that opening number, I'm going to give you a little break and ask the rest of the TCB Quartet to come on out and help me do a number for you."

In the midst of whistles and cheers and an avalanche of applause, Red, Sonny and another man, all dressed in blue suits, joined Parker on stage, waved to the audience and launched into a four-part harmony of "How Great Thou Art."

"They're really good," Doyle said. The woman crossed her lips with her finger as tears welled in her eyes.

After the last note of music faded in the speaker, the crowd shuffled in their seats as the quartet stepped aside. A woman pushed back the curtain behind the band and moved toward the center of the stage. She was a fleshy woman whose hair was a salt and pepper arrangement of waves wrapped neatly in place and sprayed tight around her head like a helmet. The red robe she wore shimmered in the light, and as she approached the front of the stage the crowd took up the chant, "Ma-ma. Ma-ma," till she stood before the microphone, looking as if she were breathing in their voices.

"We'll be saved by the music if we accept it," she said.

The affirmation of, "Amen!" "Amen!" "Amen!" skimmed across the room like a flat stone across a lake.

"I know you think it's hard. You might even think there's some great, monumental effort you have to make," she said with a wide sweeping gesture of her arms. "But I'll tell you right now, my brothers and sisters, we're all like the poor woman in the book of Gladys, chapters fifty-seven through sixty-two. The book tells us that she stood on that dark, rainy afternoon with her nose pressed hard to the plate glass window of the Memphis Cadillac dealership, wanting a car that was impossible for her to ever afford. And He, not even knowing the woman at all, not caring that she was a drunken and promiscuous woman who had lost everything when her husband left her because of her sinful ways, He bought it for her."

She shook her head and chuckled. "He just bought it for her. As completely unmindful of that woman's dark sins as he is of yours or mine. And he didn't say a thing. Not one thing. Just walked out and dangled the keys of that beautiful automobile in front of her. And when she asked what she had to do for it, he held the keys up and said, 'All you have to do is reach out and take 'em.' And she took them. And it changed her life forever. The book tells us that she followed him wherever he was singing, and that she later became a devoted wife and mother."

The congregation shouted, "Amen!" and "Tell it, Mama!"

"And that's all we've got to do, you and me, just reach out and take his sweet salvation, and be swept away by the beat and the melody and the sweet lyrics that tell us of his love. When you do, he'll come to you as he did for me. He'll fill your heart as he did mine. As he promised in Omaha in June of 1977, 'I am. I was. And I will be again.'"

The woman lowered her head reverently and stepped back to stand by the quartet members who were standing in front of the band with their heads bowed. No one in the room spoke or even whispered, the silence penetrated by a smattering of coughing, the scuffing of a metal chair against the concrete floor and a low hum like an electric chant emanating from the tall speakers. Doyle sat with his heart pounding, crouched at the edge of his chair as though he were a runner awaiting a pistol shot to start a race. When one of the guitarists walked out and positioned the microphone stand in front of the band, a smattering of shrill girl-ish squeals erupted in the rear of the audience and spread across the room like a fire blowing through dry sedge.

The lights dimmed, and the white beam of a spotlight strafed the room, igniting a whole chorus of squeals that rose and fell in waves over the cheering of the men in the audience. Then a heavy pounding of tympani startled Doyle and he leaped from his chair and stood by the railing of the balcony to see where the spotlight was going to stop. Below, the audience knocked over chairs as they jammed in around the foot of the stage as heralding trumpets an-swered the percussion.

Unlike his own backing tracks, Doyle could actually feel the duel of trumpets and tympani winding him up in-side as it rose above the deafening cheers. Just as he thought he might scream himself from the tension of the music, the entire overture resolved smoothly into the familiar "That's All Right, Mama" vamp.

The guitar melody soared on high notes that taxed Doyle's ear drums, and the heavy beat from the drums joined the electric bass lines to accelerate the beating of his heart. But the music was completely obliterated by the cheers and screams when a tall, fat man in the '74 Arabian jump suit pranced onstage. The man's black hair glistened in the light, and he sported a pair of thick bell-bottomed sideburns along his cheeks. He held out a Sunburst cape like a pair of wings as he turned, showing the jumpsuit straining against his broad ass like a second skin.

He untied the cape from his neck, and one of the band members took it as though he were the man's personal va-let. He did a couple of stumbling karate kicks to the delight of the crowd. Then, with the band driving the music relent-lessly on behind him, he walked down the stage, stooping to clasp the hands of the hysterical women reaching out to him.

After the man trekked the length of the stage, a band member handed him an acoustic guitar. And with the gui-tar dangling from his neck, he moved toward the band and snatched the microphone to his mouth in one deft, aggressive move—just in time for his opening in the driving music, singing in a deep mellow baritone, "See, See Rider."

As he sang, he twisted his massive body and shook his chubby legs, sending spasms of orgasmic squeals shooting through the audience. At one point in the song, he went down on a knee, pulling the microphone stand along as though he were pulling the handle on a floodgate. When they saw him struggling to get up, Red and Sonny moved to each side of him, taking him by his arms and boosting him to his feet. All the while the singer clung to the microphone singing, "See, See Rider."

With the final notes fading in the speakers, he stumbled over the microphone chord, then gained his balance by leaning on the microphone stand. When he acknowledged the shrieking squeals and thunderous applause by bowing his head, a lock of his hair tumbled over his eye. "Thank you very much," he slurred in a deep, breathless voice.

As the band kicked into another fast rock tune, he dropped the guitar on the floor and shook his shoulders as if steadying his resolve and began singing, "Johnny Be Good." But his voice became scratchy, fading into a raspy whisper, and he waved the music to a halt. A murmur fluttered across the room as the man bent over, hands on knees, taking deep, gasping breaths and shaking his head. The guitarist who had set up his microphone handed him a bottle of water and a towel.

While the singer drank water and wiped his face, the quartet huddled in a conference, then Red stepped in front of the stage. "Ladies and Gentlemen, the King wants to apologize for this interruption, but he just can't continue. We tried to talk him into postponing today's service, but he wanted to sing for you folks so bad, we couldn't stop him."

A few groans erupted across the room, and Red shook his finger at them. "I know you're disappointed. But you're not half as disappointed as he is. And you've got to remember, it's your sins he's taking on that's causing this. Now while he won't be doing the full worship service this morning, he don't want to leave without performing the Ceremony of the Scarves because he knows how much it means to you."

The crowd applauded respectfully as the band played the introduction to "I Can't Help Falling in Love." The King took the microphone from the stand and trudged toward the front of the stage, crooning the song. One of the guitarists laid down his instrument and followed the singer while hands reached out from the audience, women shouting "Me!" "Me!" "Me!" Every time the King bowed his head, the guitarist placed a scarf around the King's neck. While the King sang, he wiped his face on the scarf and handed it to one of the waiting hands below.

"Wow," was the only word that would form on Doyle's lips as the singer handed out the last scarf. And *he* thought *he'd* been original with his three-phases of Elvis. But now he felt as if he had actually witnessed the King after he had gained twenty more pounds and tried to squeeze out one more show after that last TV performance in June of 1977 when he forgot lyrics and slurred his words all over the place. No doubt this guy had taken the art of Elvis tribute to the very edge. Nothing but pure genius could have made him think to take fat Elvis and make him even fatter, sick Elvis and make him even sicker, tragic Elvis and make him even more tragic. And when he lumbered off stage, Doyle could almost see a cloud of sadness hovering over the room. Finally, the musicians looked at each other, shrugged, then quit playing and abandoned the stage themselves.

Minutes dragged by with no one in the audience even offering to leave, and they stood, jammed in together, looking around at each other as though they didn't know what to do until Red's voice echoed through the speakers saying, "Ladies and gentlemen, Elvis has left the building."

7

THE TUPELO HOUSE

After the service, Doyle and Rhonda climbed into the limo and rode around to the back of the house. Their driver pulled in behind a second black limousine where Red and Sonny stood outside the open back door of the car. A scaffold lined with paint cans and brushes rose up to the top window of the house, and the sun shimmered on a fresh coat of white paint on the brick wall. Half of the green awning that stretched across the length of the house had either collapsed on the concrete walkway or was being replaced.

The driver hustled around the car and opened the door for Doyle as Mama stepped out of the lead limo and helped the men uncoil the King from the car. The King emerged at first showing only a pile of hair as black as the Cadillac. After he planted his feet on the ground and struggled to stand, he stumbled against Red. Finally, with his hair tumbled down over his eyes, the King gained his footing. He wrapped his arms around Mama and buried his face into her neck, his massive white jumpsuit with its sparkling cape quivering from heavy sobbing.

"That's all right, baby," Mama said. "Everything's going to be all right."

"Yeah," Red said, patting the King's back. "We got it all under control now, E. You gonna be just fine in a couple days."

Red and Sonny tugged at the King's hands, trying to tear him away from Mama.

"I'm sorry, Mama," the King said in a trembling voice as Mama twisted, finally freeing herself from his hold. "I couldn't finish."

Mama reached up and cupped his face in her hands. "I know you couldn't, sweetie," she said.

The back door swung open and a tall gray-haired man stood shaking his head. "Bring Elvis up to his room," he said. "I will need to examine him again."

"Come on now, let's get you in bed so Doctor Nick can take a look at you," Sonny said, now tugging on the King's arm.

"You go on with Sonny and Red," the woman said. "Get you some rest, baby."

The King wobbled into the house with Sonny and Red while Doyle thought, *He's really sick.* And he wondered if what they had in mind was for him to fill in till the King could get back on his feet.

Rhonda, standing beside him, rubbed the tears from her cheeks and when she swept the hat from her head, her face brightened. "You hungry?" she said.

"Hungry?" he said, now wondering how much this gig would pay.

"Yeah," she said. "I think Granny's fixing chicken and dumplings."

Doyle went back to the room, took off his wig and peeled away the beard. He caressed the fat envelope Parker had given him at the AMVETS, thinking he didn't care much for their costume, but he did like their money. "Just show biz," he said, shrugging at his image in the mirror.

After lunch only the big man with the simple round face remained at the table with Doyle. "I'm Charlie," he said "You know, like Charlie Hodge? I play guitar and hand the King his water and scarves during the ceremony."

"I saw you," Doyle said. "You did a good job."

"Thanks," he said, shyly dropping his eyes at the compliment. "E calls me Cholly. You can too, if you want to." After a moment of awkward silence, he said, "Why don't we go down to the TV room, watch a little Andy Griffith or something?"

"I'm not much of a Mayberry fan," Doyle said. "You got any idea what they have in mind for me?"

"Not in my job description," Cholly said. "I think Mama wants to talk to you about it when she gets free."

When they got up to leave the Dining Room, Cholly grabbed Doyle's arm and said, "Shh!" The white-haired man who had stood at the back door stepped off the stairs and walked through the foyer. Cholly stared as if he were looking at an oncoming train. After the man closed the front door behind him, Doyle asked, "Who was that?"

"Doctor Nick," Cholly whispered.

"Why are you whispering?"

"I don't know," Cholly said, shaking his head. "Something about him gives me the creeps."

"Think I see what you mean," Doyle said.

"Forget Doctor Nick," Cholly said. "Let's go watch some TV."

He'd seen the TV room in the basement of the real Graceland years ago, but he didn't remember it being so bright. The cobalt blue on the walls curved into lemon yellow in smooth lines to form cartoon shaped clouds. In the middle of the wall, jagged bolts of lightning flashed through the clouds under the letters, TCB.

A lemon yellow carpet covered the floor and the sectioned mirrors on the ceiling and the two remaining walls made the small space look like a sun-washed warehouse filled with cobalt blue furniture, stacks of old 45 records, a jukebox, and three vintage TVs whose gray screens gazed from the wall like ancient eyes blinded by the room's gaudy brightness.

Three men huddled together on the sofa with thick books in their laps. They looked up as Cholly and Doyle stood in the doorway. "We interrupting your lesson?" Cholly said.

"Nah," the tallest of the three said as he stood. "We were just getting to the end. Come on in. I'm Billy. This is Lamar, and this one's Joe."

"Joe?" Cholly said. "You a new Joe?"

"Not a new Joe," Billy snapped. "Just Joe like he's always been."

Cholly looked as puzzled as a dog hearing a high-pitched whistle.

"Sit down," Billy said to Doyle. "You might find this interesting."

After Cholly and Doyle dropped onto the couch in front of the other men, Cholly reached out to caress the huge white ceramic monkey on the coffee table. "Cholly, leave that damn monkey alone," Billy snapped. "One of these days, you gonna break it. And Mama's gonna be... " he shook his head and whistled through his teeth. "Boy, Mama's gonna be pissed."

Cholly released the monkey as if he'd grabbed a hot iron, leaving it teetering and rattling on the glass top of the table. The other men reached for it. Once the thing was settled on its base, the three put the books back in their laps and Billy began reading:

"'And every night the Colonel sat in Shreveport, wiping sweat from his barren head and swatting mosquitoes so gorged with his blood they couldn't even take wing in the hot, damp air. He cried out to God, saying, *Why hast thou forsaken us to the bowels of Louisiana?*'

"'And in the midst of the Colonel's despair, Elvis said, *Don't go checking in to Heart Break Hotel yet, Colonel. He'll take care of us. Has He not promised that He would?*'"

"See?" Cholly said. "E don't give up, man. He just don't give up."

"Try to hold it down till I open it up for discussion," Billy said, giving Cholly a narrow-eyed, threatening look. Then he dropped his eyes back to the book and continued to read. "'And he kept on singing through the heat and the sweat and the mosquitoes till one day God sent a man named Tino Barzi to the Louisiana Hayride to ask of the Colonel, *Would your boy be interested in going on The Dorsey Brothers' Stage Show behind a chimp act?* And the Colonel replied, *If it gets us out of Shreveport, he'll follow a snake and serenade a hound dog.*'

"'But Satan was present in the hearts of the show's musicians. And as Elvis and Scotty and Bill and D.J. rehearsed in New York City, the big band's members rebuked them, some falling off the bandstand in laughter, saying, *Don't these clowns know more than three chords?* And, *What's going on with all that hair? He dresses like a Harlem pimp.*'"

"Those bastards," Cholly said.

"Cholly!" Billy scolded.

"OK. Sorry. I get kind of excited."

"'The evil had even penetrated the heart of the producer, Jackie Gleason, who proclaimed, *I don't like this guy. He looks like he needs a bath. And he's shaking his legs so hard, he looks like he's been locked out of the bathroom.*

"'But the people of television swear as much by their Neilson ratings as a believer relies on The Word. So God placed his hand on the show's Neilsons. And those Neilsons plummeted so fast and hard, it caused the Dorsey Brothers to proclaim to Gleason, '*We're desperate, boss. We have to try something.*'

"'And so, it came to pass,'" Billy read, "'that on January 28, 1956, the whole world saw the King for the first time.'"

Billy rose and walked to the wall where he flicked on all three TV sets. Then he pushed another button under the center set. "Now, unlike all those stories about Jesus, we're not going to just read to you about this blessed event. We're going to show you."

"You seen this before?" Cholly asked.

"My first time," Joe said.

"I know you've seen it," Billy said, pointing at Doyle. "Heard you do a pretty good '56."

"I try to do him justice," Doyle said and the other men nodded their approval.

A blizzard of white sizzled across the three screens until the ghost-like image of a spectacled bald man appeared and spoke into a stand-up microphone, his voice at first garbled, then clearing as though the antique TV sets were receiving a wavering signal from a stage in some long ago time.

"He's coming out," Cholly said. "He'll be out any second."

"Cholly, can't you hold it down?" David said.

"I can't help it," Cholly said. "I just get all tingly."

"...We'd like you to meet him now," the announcer said. "And here he is—Elvis Prezzly."

Through the three snowy electronic eyes, a tall, thin, young Elvis bolted from the drawn stage curtains with an acoustic guitar dangling from his neck. He wore dark pants, a black tweed sport coat, and a black shirt with a white tie. His face trembled in a nervous smirk as he jabbed his right hand overhead before placing it over the sound hole of the guitar.

"Look at him," Cholly said. "It's like he just grabbed lightning outa the dadgum air or something."

"Cholly!" Billy scolded.

As the TV audience broke into muffled applause, Cholly said, "Listen! You don't hear any screaming cause they's not that many girls there. It was raining that night and they went out and gave a bunch of soldiers free tickets. Bet you already knew that, didn't you?" he said to Doyle.

Doyle nodded. He knew everything about the show. He'd seen them so many times he sometimes heard Bill Black's thumping bass and Scotty Moore's guitar riffs in his dreams.

They played three more performances of Elvis on the Dorsey Stage Show before Red and Sonny walked in. "These guys treating you okay?" Red said.

"Yeah," Doyle said. "Great. Only problem so far is, I seem to have misplaced my phone."

"Hell, you can use mine if you need to call somebody," Red said. "We got your van out in the barn."

"How about my stuff?"

"Got it all loaded and gassed up for you. Come on."

They walked out the back of the house through the carport, past the white office building Doyle remembered from Graceland, and onto a paved drive that led through a white swinging gate to a white barn that looked like the horse barn at Graceland. Red punched in numbers on a code box and the roll-up steel door rattled open.

Doyle walked in behind Red, breathing in a faint mixture of paint, gasoline and oil while his eyes adjusted to the dark. Dust motes danced in the light from the three windows on each side of the two long walls where lines of hulking vehicles rested in the shadows like a herd of hibernating beasts.

When Red flipped on all the lights, Doyle could see the tools hooked neatly to a peg board on the back wall and the hydraulic lift and grease bay toward the rear. There were three black limousines, an Eldorado convertible, and a couple of long Fleetwoods from the sixties with their fishy headlights and sharp finned tails. To his left, a maroon Seville perched on cinderblocks with a crushed driver's side quarter panel and rotted tires. Its hood yawned open and the pads slung over its fenders reminded Doyle of a trauma patient someone was trying to keep warm.

And there, among all the antiques, was his '96 Chevy Express, sparkling clean. "Damn," Doyle said. "I'd just about forgot the thing was supposed to be white."

"Yeah, it had some road on it," Red said. "I got the boys to clean it up for you. Hope you don't mind."

"No," Doyle said. "But you guys didn't have to..."

"Aw," Red said. "We had some guys not involved in the service this morning. They needed something to do. I guess Cholly told you Mama wants to talk to you."

"Yeah," Doyle said.

"She told me to apologize for her. She got pretty busy all of a sudden, the King getting sick and all."

"Sure," Doyle said, "I understand."

"Want to shoot some eight ball till she's ready?"

"Sure," Doyle said. And he followed him back into the house and down the narrow stairway that led to the basement, so distracted by his moving image in the overhead mirror that he missed one of the steps and had to grab onto the handrail to keep from falling.

Sonny came in after the game started and stood around watching. Doyle had always been a pitiful pool player, and after an hour of shooting eight ball with Cholly and Red, he was shocked when he won every game. When he finally dropped the eight ball after three misses, Sonny said, "Damn, Red. You think this boy might be a hustler?"

Doyle laughed at the absurd thought of him being a pool hustler and realized he was really having fun with these guys. He couldn't remember really ever having any male friends. Even in high school, everyone had treated him like a weirdo. Now, being treated by a group of guys as if he were the source of all the energy in the room felt pretty good.

Red's phone rang to the tune of "Heart Break Hotel." After he answered it, he stood with the thing to his ear, nodding and saying, "Yes ma'am. Yes ma'am. Yes ma'am."

He put the phone back in his pocket and said to Doyle, "Mama's taking a break, and she wonders if you've got time to meet with her a few minutes."

Doyle shrugged. "Sure," he said. "That'd be great."

Red led him back upstairs and outside to a waiting antique limousine.

"He'll take you to the Tupelo House," Red said as he opened the back door to the big car. "Mama's waiting for you there."

They drove behind an enclave of outbuildings where the woods stretched out for miles, dotted with hills scarred by old surface mines. In the distance, a road snaked through the trees and the sun glinted from a jumble of metal surfaces through a cut between two ridges.

"Hey," Doyle called out to the driver. "What model is this? '62? '63?"

"I wouldn't know, sir," the driver answered. "I just drive 'em."

On a hill overlooking the whole compound, a little

shotgun house gleamed glossy white on cinder blocks like someone's poor relative left all alone. A swing dangling from the front porch gave the place a homey look. And the pink Fleetwood that had brought him to this place sat in front as if it were keeping the little house company.

Doyle had the back door to the limousine open and two feet on the gravel drive before the driver could get around the car. "I would have got that door for you, sir," the driver said.

"I guess I'm not used to people doing stuff like that for me," Doyle said.

"They tell me you can get used to it with a little practice," the driver said.

The front door swung open, and Mama walked out on the little porch in a blue house dress. "Just look at you," she said. "They all said you was beautiful, but I had no idea you'd look this good."

"Why, thank you, ma'am," Doyle said, the heat of embarrassment rising in his face. "It's nice to meet you."

As he held out his hand, the woman opened her arms. "Honey, I don't shake hands," she said. "I hug." And she took him in her arms and squeezed him tight against the pillows of her breasts while he avoided contact with her hair, sprayed so stiff it looked as if one of those sharp waves might just take out his eye. When she released him, she patted his arms. "It's good to have you here, Doyle," she said with such passion, he believed it might really be good for her. "Come on in," she said. "You know what this place is?"

"Of course," he said. "It's just like the house in Tupelo where Elvis was born."

"Right," she said as he followed her in. "You got a really sharp eye. I like that in a man."

"I've been there several times," he said.

"I figured you had, baby. You couldn't perform like you do without truly feeling His spirit."

A single bed with an iron headboard and footboard dominated the living space with a threadbare padded armchair, a scarred dresser and a ladder back chair jammed in the corner beside a child-sized fireplace. Black and white pictures of Gladys and Vernon Presley with a little tow-headed Elvis adorned the yellow floral wallpaper around the room.

"Have a seat," she said, pointing to the armchair. He sat down while breathing in the scent of fresh paint and old fires. While he adjusted his butt around a stiff spring in the cushion, Mama pulled up the ladder-back chair close to him and eased herself onto it. "I like to come up here sometimes and pray and think," she said. "I do my best thinking here. I guess because this place represents where it all began so long ago."

"I enjoyed your speech," Doyle said.

"My sermon?" she said.

"Oh, yes ma'am. Your sermon."

"Well, thank you. That really means a lot to me. You know, Doyle, every time I walk in this little place, I think it's almost as plain as the stable where Jesus was born. Do you see what I mean?"

Doyle didn't, but he looked around and nodded just the same.

"You don't know the story about that first night, do you?"

"Guess not," Doyle said.

"No, you wouldn't know," she said. "Few people out-side of our little community really know. Did you know Elvis' daddy, Vernon, was given to drink and gambling?"

"No, ma'am," Doyle said.

"Well, to his shame, he was. And in a dice game one night, he lost his first born to the Devil hisself. 'Course he didn't know he was gambling with the Devil. He thought the bet was just a joke, but the Devil was as serious as a heart attack. He knew what Vernon didn't know—that the mother was pregnant with the King. And that old Devil was determined to get him.

"It just thrills my heart, thinking that the miracle hap-pened on a humble little bed just like that," she said, pointing at the bed. "The old Devil lurked over here in a corner while the blessed mother thrashed in the pains of childbirth. What the Devil didn't know was that The Lord placed another baby in the mother's womb. That baby was stillborn, according to scripture. Don't you know that ol' devil was boiling mad when he found out all his tricks had backfired on him, and all he won was a dead baby? A Jessie Garon instead of an Elvis Aaron?"

"Yes, ma'am," Doyle said. "I guess he was."

"You look a little perplexed."

Doyle knew he would have been a terrible poker player with his feelings forever broadcasting across his face as subtle as a neon sign flashing over a tittie bar. Now he feared some errant expression of doubt had insulted this nice lady, so he muttered, "Well, ma'am, I...I don't know, I guess all this is new to me. And I was just kind of wondering why the Lord wouldn't just refuse to pay off Mr. Presley's marker. Couldn't he have just told Satan when he came to pick up the baby, 'Dude, I'm boss around here. This is just not happening?'"

"Well, of course he could," she snapped. "He's God, for God's sake. But I can see what your problem is," she said, a little knowing smile wrinkling her chubby face. "You're new to this scripture and haven't had time to open yourself up to its wisdom yet. What you got to always remember is that God's got his own way of looking at things. And something that may not seem like a hill of beans to us might be necessary as all get-out to Him. Remember, from the gitty-up, that dice game was crooked as a dog's hind leg, and the Devil knew Vernon was just a ignorant laborer who wouldn't think they was any way in the world anybody would be able to collect on a bet like he made. Vernon didn't have a clue the baby growing in Gladys' womb was God's promise to unite all the Children and take away all their sins. And he sure didn't have any idea he was gambling with the Devil hisself.

"Now, they's a whole bunch of evil out there in the world, boy, and ever' dad-gum bit of it is created by Satan.

God knows that, and ever' now and then, He thinks it's necessary to show the Devil who's boss by beating him at his own game. You see?"

"Yes, ma'am," Doyle said, regretting that he'd bothered questioning this kind and generous woman. "I think I do."

"Good," she said, bringing her hands together and rubbing them in a brief frenzy. "Well, how are you enjoying your stay with us?"

"It's been really great. Everybody's been so nice."

"When's your next engagement?"

"Next gig I've got nailed down for sure is in Gonzales, Louisiana somewhere round the middle of May."

"That's a while off," she said. "What did you plan to do in the meantime?"

"Oh, I was kinda thinking about heading back home to San Angelo. It's been a long time since..."

"That's in Texas, ain't it?"

"Yes, ma'am."

"Got family waiting for you there?"

"Just an uncle and aunt is all. Only people I got left."

"They expecting you?"

"No, not really. It's been so long, when I get there it'll probably scare them all to death."

"Then why don't you stay on with us for a week or two? We all love having you."

"I don't know. I really ought to..."

"I was kind of hoping we could fit you into our family here in some way. But I figure that's really a two way deal, kinda like a marriage. We gotta like you, and, you gotta like us. I know you're anxious to see your folks and all, but we'd be willing to pay you for your time. Would...I don't know...would a thousand a week be enough?"

"A thousand...?"

"I know that's not a lot. But you'll be staying in the Big House. You won't have to buy any food or anything. I mean, if we can get together on something later on, I'll guarantee you, you'll get paid a heap more than that."

"I uh..."Doyle stuttered.

"Shoot, that old road to San Angelo ain't going nowhere. You can take that thing anytime you want to. Won't you stay with us just a little while longer?"

He couldn't help thinking how two or three more thousand would look stacked along with the six grand already in his pocket. And with the woman staring at him with the sad eyes of a calf that had lost its mother, he couldn't think of a way to refuse. Then he thought of the woman who brought him there. He did deserve a chance to redeem himself and show her his Little Elvis was for real. "Well," he said. "Yes, ma'am. That'd be real nice."

"It sure would," she said as she gathered him back in her arms for another breathtaking squeeze. "It sure would."

PART TWO

SURRENDER

8

SUSPICIOUS MINDS

Any time a conversation turned to politics, it wouldn't take long for Buck Waggoner to drift into the story of how he'd won his first campaign for sheriff of Reece County by five votes. "Five! Votes! " he would say, holding out the fingers of his right hand for his listeners to count. Then he would shake his head and stare across the room as if he could still see all five of those good citizens, standing in line at the door to cast their precious ballots in his favor. After he recovered from his reverie, he'd go on to tell how he'd won those votes by waiting patiently for the whistle to blast over the Willow Ruth Sock Mill where he shook hands and passed out campaign cards to its changing shifts of workers whom everybody back then called "lint heads."

It was Judge Elmer Haralson who first pinned the star on Buck's chest. Decades later, Buck was still wearing that same star when he served as a pallbearer at Haralson's funeral. It was a day he remembered well because they had barely eased the judge's hefty carcass into the ground when the Willow Ruth Police requested County help to guard the sock mill while its owners shipped the mill's equipment along with its fifteen-hundred jobs off to Mexico.

Through the years, the thick shock of hair over Buck's furrowed brow turned a majestic white, his waist size swelled into the fifties, and he had lost all interest in actual law enforcement. The job had become just a matter of getting re-elected anyway. So he kept a healthy crew of deputies out serving all the court papers and answering the domestic violence calls, investigating the burglaries and the occasional murder, and coordinating with the DEA to play whack-a-mole with the meth labs that kept springing up around the county like fire ant mounds. His only personal homage to policing these days was wearing that same old star pinned to his snug, brown uniform and lugging a Smith MP 45 holstered to his plaited leather belt. And of course, he took his daily tour across the county that he referred to in the office as his "after lunch digestion rounds," but that he privately called his "ghost patrol."

Today, as usual, he eased the County's new Dodge Charger past the old mill's acre of aging brick and shattered windows, noting the progress of the kudzu and trumpet creeper blanketing the west wall and snaking its way up the outside stairwell turret. He lingered in front of Reece County High School long enough to breathe in a few memories before pushing on to Willow Ruth. "Ghosts," he said as he parked the Dodge in front of the blank marquee of the old Willow Theater. "Got to where all I do is look for ghosts." As he looked down the street, he thought a ghost might actually be a welcome sight over all those old storefronts, their windows boarded with mildew-mottled plywood, black from yesterday's rain.

He closed his eyes and remembered that marquee flashing and the line of kids that snaked all the way down past the Western Auto at the edge of Main, waiting to catch the opening of *Love Me Tender*.

He and Carolyn Haney had gotten there early that night and waited two hours before inching along the sidewalk into the cramped little venue where they still had to stand.

The girls screamed all through the show so loud, he couldn't tell what the damn picture was about. His feet ached from all that standing. Worst of all, right in the middle of the opening credits, he had to piss like a racehorse. But his bladder was a lot more reliable back then, and he wasn't going anywhere because Carolyn kissed him a couple of times and held on to him as if he were the star of the movie.

In the past, he'd asked her at least a dozen times to go parking out at the chert pit on CR 41, but she always said no. That night, she not only agreed to go, when they got there, she crawled into the back seat of his '49 Studebaker Champion with him. No doubt, it was the King of Rock and Roll who got her all warmed up. Now, he looked down that empty sidewalk, all the way to the edge of Main, and, before he could catch himself, he sighed, "Goddamn, I miss Elvis."

Next, he planned to actually cruise out to the old chert pit, park in the very same spot and continue reminiscing about that night for a while, but before he could start the Dodge, Sarah Adkins' leaf blower of a voice squawked over the radio. "Sheriff, you out there? Come on."

"Shit!" he said before picking up the mic. "Sheriff here."

"Sheriff, you got some folks waiting for you outside your office."

"Who is it?"

"A woman named Adele Turner. Said she had an appointment? Been waiting since one."

"Tell her I got held up. Might be a while."

"Told her that already. She's got this lawyer with her. He said they'd camp out here all night if they had to."

Buck had never seen this Turner woman, but he remembered her name. When she came in before, he'd stalled and delayed till she got discouraged and left her telephone number and a note, saying it was "Of the utmost importance." He didn't make a habit of wasting hospitality on people who didn't vote in Reece County. So he'd shit-canned the note while thinking, *Important to you, Honey. But not important to me.* But coming back with a lawyer and a new dose of determination told him whatever this problem was, it wasn't going to get any better by ducking it. He looked wistfully in the direction of CR 41 and sighed, "Okay. Tell 'em I'll be there directly."

After a moment of silence, Sarah squawked, "That over and out, Sheriff?"

"Yeah," he sighed. "That's over and out."

Buck would have found the woman in the teal-colored pantsuit kind of semi-attractive if it weren't for those thick-framed glasses perched on a face so pale and gaunt it gave him the sudden urge to take her down to the Tastee-Freeze and feed her a couple of cheeseburgers, some fries and maybe one of those good chocolate shakes they whip up down there. And if the guy beside her *was* a lawyer, he damn sure wasn't one of those hired guns from a big Birmingham firm. For one thing, the woman didn't look prosperous enough to cover the hourly fee she'd be shelling out for one of *those* guys to sit around cooling his heels in Buck's outer office. And this guy had a stumpy neck and a set of squinty reptilian eyes that might be useful in scaring old ladies and little children, but they wouldn't fit in for a second with the button-down crowd of blood suckers that filed suit against Reece County a couple of years ago. Besides, the guy looked as if he'd spent most of his life in a gym, pumping up his chest and shoulders so he could squeeze them into a cheap brown sport coat a couple sizes too small for him.

"Buck Waggoner," Buck said, giving them one of his electioneering smiles and holding out his hand.

When the lawyer stood and scowled at Buck instead of shaking his hand, Buck dropped his arm and shrugged.

"My client scheduled this appointment to meet with you more than a month ago," the lawyer snarled.

"And your name is?" Buck said while twisting his head and arching his bushy eyebrow.

"I'm Morgan Crowley," the hulking attorney snarled. "I represent Ms. Turner."

"Ms. Turner," Buck said, turning to the woman. "I'm awful sorry for keeping you waiting. But unlike lawyers and such, sometimes a first-responder"—Buck had grown to like the term, first-responder, and dropped it into a conversation anytime the opportunity arose, hoping to conjure images of brave firemen and police officers charging into burning buildings—"Well," he shrugged. "Sometimes we just get delayed."

"Sheriff, you know why we're here, don't you?" the lawyer said.

"No," Buck said, shaking his head. "Can't say that I do."

"Sheila Barksdale?"

"Name don't ring a bell."

"If you'd read the letters I wrote," Ms. Turner said. "And the note I left for you the last time you stood me up."

"Ma'am," the Sheriff said. "If I stood you up, I'm awfully sorry. Sometimes this job won't let me keep to a regular schedule."

"Sheila Barksdale is Ms. Turner's sister."

"I see," the sheriff said. "Y'all come on in."

He led them into his office, pointed to the client chairs while he ambled around his desk and plopped down. "Okay. Now, something about your sister?"

"You know anything about the Our Lady of TCB Church?" the lawyer continued.

"A little," the sheriff said, turning to Ms. Turner. "But I thought this was about your sister, Ms. Turner."

"It is about her sister," the lawyer said. "Sheila and her entire family are being held captive by this TCB outfit."

"Oh, I'm sure you've got that wrong. I can't even imagine..."

The lawyer snapped to his feet and pounded two sheets of creased paper on the sheriff's desk. Buck opened his top desk drawer, extracted a pair of reading glasses and picked up the paper. It was a letter from this Sheila to her sister reminiscing about their childhood and all the family holidays they had enjoyed together. It's ending sentence, that someone had colored over with a yellow marker, declared, *we have seen the King and he gives us hope for the future in his resurrection, but he will not let us come home for the holidays this year.*

"I don't even know what this means," Buck said.

"Don't know what it means?" the lawyer snapped. "Ms. Turner's sister and her family disappear off the face of the earth. Suddenly Ms. Turner gets this letter. This is obviously some kind of a cult that's holding these people prisoner."

"You're jumping to all kinds of conclusions, here. And

cult is a pretty nasty word. Look, Ms. Turner, these TCB folks have been out there in the county for years. They've never been any problem. I've been here all the time, and I assure you, not one complaint has ever been lodged against them. It's my understanding that they're kind of a commune. You know, they provide a place for people to live and establish their own community and stuff. Now, I believe they *are* kinda what you would call faith-based. And personally, yeah, I think it's kinda weird. But a cult?" He shook his head. "I really don't think so."

"You know how much land this TCB outfit owns in your county, Sheriff?" the lawyer said.

"Not exactly," Buck said. "I think they got a pretty good spread, though."

"Pretty good spread? That what you call four thousand acres?"

"Sounds like you've been doing some homework, Mr. Crowley."

"Had a detective look into it," the lawyer said. "He even went out there. Said the place was surrounded by a couple of fences that would put Donaldson Correctional to shame. Said the inside fence appears to be electric. When he asked to see the Barksdales, an armed goon appeared and told him to clear out."

"Well," the sheriff sighed. "I'm not a lawyer, you understand. But you hadn't told me anything yet that sounded like a violation of any law I'm aware of. You see, we don't prohibit folks from owning property in Reece County, Mr. Crowley. In fact, hell, we encourage it. Now, if a home owner was to throw up a fence like that in the town of Willow Ruth, the zoning board would raise all kind of hell. But out in the county? Well, out there, a land owner can build a fence over the tree tops if he wants to. Long as he don't interfere with airplane traffic. And as far as a land owner or his employees guarding his property with guns—I know as an attorney, you're familiar with the second amendment."

"I've gone to the FBI," the lawyer said.

"The FBI," Buck said. "You took *this* to the FBI."

"That's right. They said this was in your jurisdiction, and if you don't do something with this, I was to get back with them, and they would look into it."

"Bullshit!" the sheriff said. "Pardon my French, Ms. Turner. But these days, after the Fed's little embarrassment at Waco, to get them to interfere with a religion, you'd have to have probable cause that somebody named Osama was living in that compound with Jimmy Hoffa tied to a nuclear device. What they probably told you was, you got yourself two adults who exercised their rights and absented themselves from their former home and took up residence somewhere else. These adults didn't ask anybody's permission because, as adults, they didn't have to. And they didn't visit relatives for the holidays because, as adults, they didn't have to."

"You mean the phrase, 'he won't let us' doesn't bother you?"

"No, sir," the sheriff said. "But I can tell it bothers Ms. Turner. Only way I can figure to give her peace of mind is to take her out there and let her talk to her sister."

"Wa...Well," the lawyer muttered. "That's all we're asking."

Buck stood, shrugged and pointed to the door. "After you," he said.

With Ms. Turner beside him and the muscle-bound lawyer squirming around behind the prisoner cage of the Charger, Buck drove through Willow Ruth and out into the county, half-listening to the tale of woe Ms. Turner had obviously been wanting to lay on him for months. "Sheila kept telling me how despondent Brad was after the plant laid him off," she said. "When the mortgage payment on their house almost doubled, they didn't know what to do. Then the bottom fell out of the market and they wound up owing more than the house was worth..."

"Um hm," the Sheriff said, his eyes following a flock of crows chasing a hawk into a thicket of pine.

"We offered to help," she said. "Honest we did."

"Yes, ma'am."

The pavement narrowed and cut through a copse of trees so thick, the Sheriff felt as if he were driving through a tunnel.

"They were just too proud," Ms. Turner continued as Buck drove on. "I got scared when I tried to call and found their land-line and Sheila's cell had been disconnected. Then I really got into a panic after I drove over there and found the key stuck in the front door, all their furniture and clothes still there, and a note on the dining room table in Brad's handwriting, saying, 'We are gone. You can have it all.' God, that really is a huge fence," she said as the woods gave way to an open field.

Buck stopped the car at the wrought iron gate, and an old man sauntered out of the gatehouse beside the stone wall. The Sheriff rolled down the window and the man leaned in.

"How's it going, Clyde?" Buck said.

"My name's Vester, Sheriff."

"Sorry. I can't keep that straight."

"What can we do for you today?"

"This young lady's got a sister she believes is staying here."

"Who is it?"

"What's the name again?" the Sheriff said to Ms. Turner.

"Brad and Sheila Barksdale and their daughter, Claire."

"She believes y'all are holding them against their will," the Sheriff said.

"What?" Vester said, backing away from the car as if he'd been shocked. "Against their will? Hey, Sheriff. Ain't nobody in here being held against their will."

"Well, you gotta understand, Ms. Turner don't know you from Adam's house cat, Vester. So you saying that don't give her no reassurance, if you know what I mean. So if you could direct us to where we might find the Barksdales..."

"Sheriff, nobody goes through those gates uninvited."

"Last time I checked, I was still the sheriff of this whole county. And I believe that includes the part on the other side of that wall."

"Yeah," Vester said. "But Sheriff, I don't mean to be quarrelsome or anything, but since this is private property and all, you'll need one of those whatchacallits to legally come in uninvited."

"You mean a warrant," the sheriff said.

"That's right," Vester said. "A warrant."

"He'd be able to get one if he showed a judge a letter indicating Ms. Barksdale's sister was in danger or a crime's being perpetuated beyond that gate," the lawyer said from the backseat of the sheriff's car. "Hey, this door doesn't have a handle."

"Who the hell's that?" Vester said.

"A lawyer," Buck said. "Well, a piece of one, anyway. He's got a point, though."

"Maybe so," Vester said. "Let me call somebody. See if we can work this thing out without getting lawyers and judges involved."

Mrs. Turner and her lawyer had gotten out to stretch their legs and had worn a couple of wide nervous circles in the gravel around the car when a black Cadillac limousine that looked long enough to be used as a rail car rolled up to the gate. The gate opened and the limo pulled up to the grill of the County's Dodge. A driver in a black outfit got out and opened the back door for a couple who looked to be in their forties and a blonde teenage girl who made Buck wish for the return of just a few minutes of his misspent youth.

Ms. Turner squealed, "Sheila," and the woman who'd gotten out of the limo squealed, "Addy" as they ran to each other. They hugged and swung around as if they were half-dancing/half-consuming each other for a few minutes. Then the man and the teenage girl got in on the hugging act as a husky red-haired man with a pointy red goatee got out of the passenger side of the limo.

"Sheriff," the red-haired man said, giving Buck a nod.

"Red," Buck said.

"Hear they's some kind of mix-up," Red said.

"We'll see," Buck said.

Buck introduced himself to Brad and Sheila Barksdale and their daughter Claire before saying to Brad, "Now, Mr. Barksdale. I just got one question to ask you. Are you and your family being held here against your will?"

"Our what?" Brad Barksdale said. "Against our will? You mean like prisoners?"

Buck shrugged. "Yeah, like prisoners or any other way."

"No, sir," Barksdale said. "We're here because we want to be."

"How about you, Ms. Barksdale?"

"Sheriff, I don't know what you're talking about."

"But Sheila, you wrote that somebody wouldn't let you come home," Ms. Turner said.

"I wrote that?" Sheila said.

After Ms. Turner showed her the letter, Sheila handed it to her husband and said, "I can see how she'd think that." She turned back to her sister. "What I meant was that the King needed us, and his love wouldn't let us go. I meant spiritually. We had to stay here and pray and that was what held us—not that anybody was actually keeping us from leaving. I knew what I meant, I guess I thought you would too. I can see now that you wouldn't have any idea what I was saying. Addie, I'm sorry to have caused you all this worry."

"How about you, young lady," Buck said to the girl.

"About me?" the girl said.

"Yeah, you being held against your will?"

"No," the girl said as if it were the strangest question she'd ever heard. "God no. I *never* want to leave here."

"I'll be glad to take you all back to Birmingham. You three can squeeze into my car here," the sheriff said. "Right here. Right now. And I'll guarantee you, nobody'll try to stop you."

"Not only that, Sheriff," Red said. "They can get back

in the limo, and Carl will take them anywhere they want to go. I mean, within reason. We'll even gather up their belongings and have them delivered to whatever address they give us."

Claire burst into tears and clung to Brad, burying her face in her father's shoulder. "I don't want to go, Dad," she sniffled. "I got my Coming Out this summer."

"Shh," Brad said. "We're not going anywhere, sweetie."

"You got any questions, Mr. Crowley?" the sheriff said.

"No," the lawyer said. "I guess not."

Red and Buck leaned against the limo while the lawyer stood with his hands in his pockets, watching the Barksdales and Ms. Turner talk. "Okay Red," the Sheriff said. "Tell me what happened."

"Well, Uncle Buck, it's an age old story. Mrs. Barksdale batted her eyes at one of our apostles and handed him a letter. Like a damn fool he stuck a stamp on it and mailed it for her, thinking there was a little poon-tang in it for him down the road."

"This kind of stuff happen often?"

"Nah," Red said. "Our folks pretty much behave theirselves. Our biggest trouble is building houses fast enough for all the people who want to come in."

"Well, that's good to hear. How's Mama doing these days?"

"She's amazing as usual," Red said.

"Yeah," Buck said. "That woman's always been amazing."

9

CONVERTS

Sheila had never spanked Claire in her life. And though she'd felt betrayed when she discovered that Claire had reported her for smuggling a letter out of the compound, she still hadn't been angry enough to actually hit her. But as she sat beside her in the limo she found herself struggling to keep from reaching over and slapping the smug, self-righteous expression from her daughter's haughty face.

She knew that Claire didn't feel as if she had betrayed her family at all. In fact, she had said she felt as if her mother had betrayed the family as well as the faith by communicating with the Others. By turning her mother in, she had only done her duty as a faithful member of Our Lady of TCB.

Sheila was hurt that Brad sided with Claire. But she shouldn't have been that surprised. Both of them had become so steeped in the theology of the TCB Church that they had developed a funny little gaze in their eyes as if they were always looking out toward the horizon at something Sheila could never see. Sheila tried to believe, and she did believe—sometimes. The Church had been so good to them that even when she had doubts she wanted to believe.

The Book of Gladys was clear on the matter. Unbelievers outside of the Land of Grace were the Others who would corrupt your heart if you fraternized with them in any way other than targeted recruiting. Sheila didn't care that her sister, Addy, was one of the Others, she couldn't stand the thought of being apart from her forever. So she wrote her a letter and got Joe Esposito to mail it for her by sort of hinting that she might sleep with him at some time in the near future. While it wasn't considered adultery for a wife to have sex with an apostle, she loved Brad too much to betray her wedding vows with any man.

Red sat across from them in the back of the limo, sucking in deep breaths and snorting them out his nose, his left eye twitching and his freckled face flushing into a brighter shade of red the longer they rode. He didn't seem to be looking at either of them in particular. It just looked as if he were taking them all three in with the same contemptuous glare. And no matter how many times Brad said, "We're sorry about this, Red," Red only responded by breathing harder and turning more red. "Sheila just missed her sister. You got to understand, they were real close growing up and all."

It hurt her to see her husband groveling on her behalf. Even to the chief apostle who would be influential in determining what would become of her for committing the horrible offenses of "unauthorized communication" with the Others and corrupting an apostle. She found it troubling that Joe had disappeared and another Joe had soon taken his place as if nothing had happened. At first Brad had agreed that it was a different Joe too, but he came back from a men's group meeting one night and explained to her that they had all been mistaken—this was the same Joe all along.

As they rode, she looked at Brad and Red and thought they could very well be members of different species. Brad was a big man but not quite as big or even close to being as hard-looking as Red. Just a few moments in Red's presence and she could sense a fierce storm roiling behind his green eyes, while in Brad's soft brown eyes she had never seen anything but kindness.

She and Brad had been high school sweethearts, deeply in love with each other since the ninth grade. But they did the smart thing by saving their money and postponing marriage until his third year in the Navy when they could afford a family. Right after Claire was born, Brad was discharged and quickly parlayed the skills he'd learned as a Navy machinist to land a good paying job with Rathmore

Refrigeration.

Years went by, Brad made foreman, and they bought a couple of cars and a house in the suburbs. Brad had done so well, she was not only able to stay home with Claire, they had even taken a Caribbean cruise and vacationed in Cozumel. They had no doubts that their careful planning and hard work had set them up to snatch this nice share of the American dream for themselves. After making love on leisurely Sunday mornings, they often had coffee in bed and talked about how smart they had been.

In the midst of all this good fortune, rumors floated around the plant of the company moving its entire operation to Mexico. But the bosses denied it, saying these stories were ridiculous because "RR" was too proud of their "Made in the U.S.A." stamp on all their equipment to ever move.

One Monday morning, Brad returned home from work after being gone for only two hours. He walked unsteadily to the den and collapsed onto his recliner, his face drained of blood. "Couldn't get in," he said, sounding as if he were choking on the words when she asked if he was sick. "When I got there, everybody was just standing around in the parking lot like a bunch of zombies."

She'd never dreamed how much being out of work could take out of a man. Every day Brad looked as if more and more of his substance had been sucked out of him. Sometimes when she listened to him calling a potential employer or one of the employment agencies, she thought his voice had taken on a defeated tone as if he'd come to expect rejection. He'd even taken to drinking a little too much on weekends. He'd never get mean, just more sad and pitiful. And he completely lost interest in making love. Which was just as well because she couldn't imagine sex with his hang-dog expression hovering over her.

She had gone to work at Macy's, a sales job that kept them in groceries but didn't pay nearly enough to make the payments on the cars, much less the mortgage. It was there that she ran into Mary Guin, a high school friend she hadn't seen in years. They swapped addresses and phone numbers, but she didn't dream that anything would come of it till Mary and her husband Roy knocked on their door one Saturday morning.

The Guins immediately understood their situation. "Same thing happened to us," Mary said. "Except we didn't lose our jobs to Mexicans. We lost them to robots. We thought all was lost until we found the answer to all our problems in our church."

"Well, I'm afraid we've not been very good Christians," Sheila said.

"Just as well," Roy said. "Going to most churches is about as effective as sending up smoke signals in the dark."

"Now, Honey," Mary said. "We don't want to put down other faiths."

"No, we don't," Roy said. "But the truth is the truth. And the government? Hell, they're damn sure not going to bring back our jobs. I mean, you listen to the Republicans and all you hear is tax breaks for the rich. And you listen to the Democrats and all you hear is rights for gays and immigrants. Nobody is saying anything about *our* rights and *our* jobs. That is, nobody but the Our Lady of TCB Church. I'm telling you, Brad, TCB'll give you work. I mean, meaningful work. And they'll provide you with a loving, caring community that won't abandon you for a second."

"And *our* King lives," Mary said. "Not just in our hearts but in the flesh. We see him onstage every week."

"Jesus?" Brad said. "You see Jesus onstage?"

"Oh, hell no," Roy said. "Elvis. We see Elvis."

Everyone got quiet for a moment. Then Sheila chuckled, shook her head and said, "I'm sorry, my mind had drifted off for a moment. I thought you said, Elvis."

"I did say Elvis."

"You don't mean, like, Elvis Presley, do you?"

"Exactly," Mary said. "The King."

Elvis was before Sheila's time. But everybody knew something about Elvis. She'd seen bits of his movies on

TV over the years. And once she'd seen his face on a post-age stamp. She thought the image of the side-burned singer in a flashy jumpsuit, banging on a guitar was as vivid an American image as Washington crossing the Delaware or Lincoln in a stovepipe hat. *But King?* "Wasn't he a drug addict?" Sheila said. "And besides, isn't he dead?"

"He was never a drug addict," Mary said. "The drugs they found in him was just proof that he was taking on our sins as the scripture tells us. And dead? Those sins do weigh heavy on him, but he keeps coming back. I've seen him myself. Make no mistake about it, he'll keep on com-ing back till he's finally taken in all of our sins and all the Children have come home."

When Sheila and Brad followed them out, Brad was taken by the antique Cadillac in the driveway. "Nice car," Brad said. "How long have you had that?"

"We don't own it ourselves," Roy said. "It belongs to all of the Children."

"The Children?" Brad said.

"Yes. All the people in the Land of Grace."

Once the Guins had gone, Sheila and Brad talked about how silly the whole thing sounded. They laughed about the Guin's hair and how they had dressed—Roy had worn blue trousers, a white shirt and a tan cardigan sweater. His hair was close-cropped and shined with some kind of product that kept it stiff and flat on top. Mary wore a blue and white shirt-waist dress and had her hair cut short and fixed in a stiff little permanent women used to wear. But Sheila ap-preciated the Guins understanding their situation and was impressed with the passion they had for their religion. She wondered if this kind of spiritual passion would help any-body through hard times.

The Guins came once a week, then their once-a-week visits became twice-a-week, and before long they came over every day, bringing along other church members with kids Claire's age—boys in tee shirts and jeans with the legs too long and rolled up to keep from dragging the ground, their hair cut short in flat-tops or long and swept back in duck-tails and pompadours; and girls in ruffled blouses, full pleated skirts cinched at the waist and their hair up in pony tails. Claire was having trouble making friends at her new school. Sheila had been worried about her, so she was happy to see her getting along so well with these kids.

Mary, Roy, and three other TCB members were there the day the foreclosure letter came. "Why don't y'all just come with us?" Mary said. "It just breaks my heart to see the way the Others are treating you."

"Oh, I don't see how we could," Sheila said.

"TCB will give you everything you need," Roy said. "Just leave everything like it is."

"You won't even need clothes. Once you get to the Land of Grace, you'll get new ones to go along with your new life," Mary said. "A life with some actual joy in it."

Some of the teenage girls from the Land of Grace had spent the night with Claire a couple of times, and Claire had already dropped a few hints that she was ready to move. "Let's go, Dad," she said. "Please! They all say it's wonderful there."

Brad looked down at the foreclosure notice, shook his head and said, "I don't see what we got to lose." And when he said it, Sheila could see hope in his eyes for the first time since the plant had closed.

Her first look at the towering fence gave Sheila a chill. It went on as far as she could see, then disappeared back in the woods. But in a clearing, far upon a hill in the distance, she could see that it continued on and on.

"Don't worry about it," Roy said. "A week from now, you won't even notice it's there."

"But why do they need a fence?" she said.

"It's there to let us know that no Mexican is going to come in here and take what's yours and mine," Roy said. "And it keeps out the corrupting influences, so we can live our lives in peace like they did back in the nineteen-fifties."

At the sight of the big house, she forgot about the fence for a moment. "Who lives there?" she said.

"That's Graceland," Mary said. "Elvis lives there. Haven't you ever heard of Graceland?"

"*I* have," Brad said. "My mom and dad went there one summer. But Graceland's in Memphis."

"Not this one," Roy said.

"How charming," Sheila sighed as they drove through the main street of the little village with its neat gauntlet of clapboard storefronts featuring: Rayburn's Drug and Sundries, Phillip's Hardware and Janaway's Clothing and Dry Goods painted in glossy yellow, gray and blue. And the flashing lights around the Willow Theater II marquee surrounded *Picnic* with William Holden and Kim Novak.

But she couldn't hide the disappointment in her voice when she saw the houses on Teddy Bear Lane. "They're..." she said.

"Kinda small, I know," Mary said. "But you'll get used to it."

"It's not that," Sheila said. "They're all shaped alike."

"That's the cool part," Roy said. "That way, folks won't be jealous of each other."

Some of the houses were blue, some green and others tan or white, but, compared to the two-story suburban affair they'd just walked out of, each one looked like a tin house trying to disguise its boxy shape with a pitched metal roof and an A-frame gable over a picture window that gazed out on a porch the size of the bed of a pick-up truck.

Brad fell into his work as if he'd always been there. "I think they're really glad to have me," he said. "Before I got here they've had to contract most of the equipment maintenance out to the Others. Now they've got me to keep everything running, and I can train some other guys."

She even grew used to the smallness of the house, the sameness of the neighborhood, the old movies at the theater, and the vintage shows on TV. And she never felt so much a part of a community as she did in the Land of Grace. There were ball games, picnics in the park and sing-a-longs. Her discussion group met at a different house every Tuesday and Thursday afternoon. She felt closer than ever to Claire, and after Sunday church service, both of them giggled about how their hearts were still pounding from the sight of Elvis onstage and how they'd screamed so much, their throats would still be sore on Monday.

They learned about The Coming Out a few weeks after they arrived at The Land of Grace. "Are they talking about teenagers having sex with the elders?" Sheila said.

"No," Brad said. "I think you misunderstood them."

But after three years of immersion into the scripture, she realized that having sex with the King or his apostles was a rite of passage all teenage girls had to endure before they could even date. Sheila wasn't buying it, but that glazed look had appeared in Brad's eyes, and he talked about it as if it were the most natural thing in the world. "It's like they say in the meetings—your old raising by the Others is interfering with your TCB thinking," Brad said.

"This is okay with you?" she said.

"Well, if it was with anybody but the King or one of the apostles, of course it'd be wrong. Bad wrong. But this way, see, she'll be purified."

"Purified," she said. "You believe that?"

"Of course," he said with a little bemused smile accompanying that faraway look of his. "Look, Sheila. I know where you're coming from. It's our daughter and all, and it goes against everything we were taught in the old life. But we were wrong. After all, it's in the book. It's the way things are supposed to be done. Besides, she's got to start somewhere."

"Don't you think it'd be better if she started years from now with someone she loved? The way you and I did?"

"Don't she love the King?" he said.

"Well, yes."

"If it happens she's not picked by the King," he said, "she'll be picked by one of the apostles. Aren't we taught to love the King's apostles?"

"I guess so."

"Well, see, what they do is not just sex. Well, it is sex,

kind of. But the sex is just the necessary part of the ritual. It's an act of love—true, spiritual love. Once she's experienced that, she'll carry it with her for the rest of her life."

It kind of made sense if she didn't think about it very much. After a little time passed, she got queasy over the whole thing all over again. For three years her friends at the ladies' discussion group told her, "If you let them, the Others' doubts will gather up and attack your brain like an invading army."

As time drew closer to Claire's Coming Out, Sheila had resigned to the fact that the invading army was occupying her thoughts. And the more she thought about it, the more she was determined that Claire's Coming Out wasn't going to happen.

All the way back home in the limo, Red still hadn't spoken to them. "I hope you're not blaming them for what I did," Sheila said while they waited for the driver to open the door. Red just stared out the window, his eye still blinking, his jaw working as if he were chewing on a tough piece of gristle. And he didn't say anything as they got out of the limo.

"You hungry, sweetie?" Sheila asked Claire. But her daughter ignored her and looked at her father instead.

"Dad, I've got to get to my class."

"I understand, baby," Brad said.

As Claire stomped into the house, Sheila said, "If they vote to shun me? Will you shun me too?"

"I'm praying every night that it won't come to that, baby," he said.

When Claire eased into the classroom, instead of getting slammed with an angry reprimand and an order to report to the principal's office for being late, she was met with a nod and a knowing little smile from Ms. Rogers. Her so-called friends, those silly girls who had once jumped at the chance to shun her when they first learned of her mother's transgressions, now stared at her, trying to hide their envy behind their simpering smiles.

What ever made her think these girls were her friends in the first place? She just knew Elvis would see how bogus they were at the Coming Out. Why, He wouldn't pick one of them to go upstairs with him in a million years. To get ready for her Coming Out, Sandra had spackled her face with makeup to hide the freckles that dotted her skin like little mud splatters. She had grown her stupid red hair down to her shoulders in an attempt to look like Ann Margaret in *Viva Las Vegas*. Claire couldn't help but giggle because every time that hair came into contact with even a hint of moisture in the air it sprang out like red wool. Then, instead of Ann Margaret, Sandra went around looking more like Larry in those Three Stooges shorts they played every Saturday down at the Willow II.

Brenda had styled her blonde hair long and copped the beauty contestant smile Linda Thompson used back in the seventies. To save herself for Elvis at Coming Out, Brenda channeled her passion into Moon Pies and Snickers. Claire thought about telling Brenda that her butt was starting to look like two big sacks of pecans wobbling together when she walked. But Claire was just too nice a person to say something like that, even to a phony like Brenda.

As if she were going to fool the King for a second, "Innocent" Millicent had dyed her already black hair even blacker to make it look more Priscilla-like. Now, it was so black, it looked purple. Cast against her pale skin, it made her look like a vampire in the sunlight.

Of course, Claire's dearest dream was being chosen by Elvis at Coming Out. She prayed every night that he would fall in love with her and want her to stay in the Big House with him as his queen forever. But just in case that didn't happen, she definitely had other prospects. She knew the boys couldn't wait for the girls to finally Come Out. As she slid into her seat, she found it too painful to even look at any of them. They were always preening and strutting down the hallway like peacocks in their muscle shirts, staring longingly at the girls.

There were a number of horny jocks with their let-ter-jackets and flat-tops who had their eyes on her. But Claire, like most of the girls, preferred the greasers. Bil-ly Sizemore, who won the school pompadour contest two years running, danced with her at all their heavily chap-eroned dances. While Elvis crooned "Don't" from the re-cord player during their last sock hop at the gym, Billy had pleaded with her to date him once she returned from her Coming Out. She whispered the most encouraging "may-be" she could, and she thought she was doing him a favor by rubbing her breasts against him while nobody was look-ing. That had been a horrible mistake because he became so excited, it took a couple of the chaperones to pull him away from her after the music stopped. It was embarrass-ing as all get-out, but it left her thinking that this boyfriend thing would be easy if her Coming Out didn't come out right.

Ms. Rogers' voice rose above a sudden crossfire of laughter. "Earth to Claire Barksdale," she said.

Claire's face burned from embarrassment. The giggles and amused faces of her classmates made her want to crawl under her desk. "I'm so sorry, Ms. Rogers," she said.

"That's all right, Claire," she said. "I know you've been distracted for the past month."

"Yes, ma'am," Claire said. "But that doesn't excuse my inattention in class. Did you ask me a question? Would you please ask again?"

"Yes," Ms. Rogers said. "Each of us was telling the Elvis childhood story that we thought most revealed His coming divinity. Do you have a favorite you'd like to share with us?"

Claire cleared her throat to give herself time to gather her thoughts before beginning. "Well, there are so many," she said, sighing. "But I think my very favorite is the birth-day guitar story."

"Ah, yes," Ms. Rogers said. "That is a good one. But why is that your favorite?"

"Well," Claire said. "I don't really know. I think it's because whenever that story comes to mind, I can just see the Holy Mother leading little Elvis down the Old Saltillo Road on their long trek downtown to the Tupelo Hardware to buy Elvis a birthday present. I can feel her embarrassment when Elvis asked for a rifle or a bicycle, and she had to reveal that she couldn't afford either of them. And then, in the midst of her despair and humiliation, the clerk reached behind the counter and pulled out an old guitar. He said, 'I think you can afford this, Mrs. Presley.'"

"On their trip back home with Elvis strumming on his new treasure, his mother apologized for not being able to afford the presents he wanted. And Elvis replied that his present was better than the bicycle and rifle put together. He told her that he wouldn't need a rifle because music would be his weapon from now on. And he had no need of a bicycle because the guitar would get him where the Lord needed him to go.

"Just think about it," Claire said. "It just had to be the hand of God that guided the clerk to offer the guitar to Elvis as a substitute gift. I mean, how else can you explain it?"

A smile spread across Ms. Roger's face. "That was wonderful, Claire," she said. "You know? I think that's my favorite story, too."

The boys stared at her with mixture of lust and admiration, and she could almost see green waves of envy rising from the girls. She thought that until she was chosen by Elvis at Coming Out, this would be the best moment of her life.

* * *

Red tapped on the door, nervously shuffling his feet on the porch while glancing at the green '63 Seville parked at the side of the Tupelo House. When no one answered, he took a deep breath and tapped again. Mama murmured something from the inside before the door swung open.

"Why're you driving that car?" he asked.

"That why you came all the way up here and interrupted my prayer?" she snapped.

"No, ma'am," he said. "I'm sorry for the intrusion. I guess I was just trying to break the ice or something."

"Well," Mama said. "Why don't we play like the ice has already been broke and you tell me what you want."

"Sheila Barksdale," he said.

"That's supposed to be a question?"

"No, I mean, what do you want to do with her? I can tell you right now, all the trouble she's put us through, bringing that lawyer up here, trying to get the law involved, she's just about got me pissed off enough to erase her ass. But it's your call."

"You need to remember where you are," Mama said.

"Sorry about the language," Red said as he stared down at his feet, feeling like a child in Mama's presence. "Didn't mean disrespect."

She slumped in the doorway and sighed, "Come on in."

After he followed her in, she pointed to the padded chair by the fireplace. He hated that chair with its loose spring that gouged at his butt every time he sat in it. But when Mama wanted you to sit, you sat.

"I'm not really upset with you," Mama said.

"Oh, that's all right."

"No, to tell you the truth, I was just thinking about her," Mama said as she sat in the ladder-back chair across from him. "Sheila, I mean. How did we come down to this, Red? All this harsh punishment and all. We started out to do good."

"We are doing good," Red said. "But remember, we figured out a long time ago that you can't keep on doing good if you let people go their own way. The Children talk. We can't keep them from doing that. Won't be long before it gets out that a person violated the rules and got away with it. Once they see that, how long before they see some of Our Lady's rules as a little inconvenient and decide to ignore them? You think our faith wouldn't fall apart? We're doing it for the Children."

"It just seems like it's one after another," Mama said, slouching down in her chair.

"Comes in bunches. That's for sure. I mean, we still got the matter of Rhonda. I know for a fact that people are still talking about how she got away with hitting Elvis."

"I know. I know," Mama said, holding her hand over her eyes. "You're not making this easy."

"Sorry," Red said. "I've talked it over with the Colonel and Sonny. There needs to be some consequences."

"There were consequences. She's no longer Priscilla."

"The Children still talk. They expect justice."

Mama nodded and stared into the dormant fireplace as if she were looking for answers among its white ashes. When she looked back at Red, her face brightened. She sat erect. "Mercy," she said.

"Mercy?"

"It is part of our faith, isn't it?"

"Yeah, but she hit the King," he said, pointing to his temple. "In the head with that big-ass lion. Uh, sorry for the language."

"Elvis is the source of our hope, and he's the source of our mercy. If that mercy came from him, it wouldn't be questioned."

"You like that girl, don't you?"

"She's been with us from the beginning. Without her, we would have had a hard time bringing the youth into the Land of Grace. She's been a great recruiter, and she was a cracker jack Priscilla. She just couldn't get it into her head that Elvis can do whatever he wants."

"So, how you want to handle it?"

"Everything will be all right if Elvis forgives her. He could demonstrate his forgiveness by accepting her in a new role as Ginger Alden. We'll get him to announce it when he recovers. Maybe at the next Coming Out."

"Okay," Red said. "Might work. But how about Sheila Barksdale? You know, it's not just the letter she sent and the fact that she corrupted an apostle. Her daughter tells us that she has doubts about the King that she keeps spouting around the house. The girl and her daddy pull her back into line, but I'm pretty sure she's going to be a big problem down the road."

"Whatever we do about her, we'll have to wait," Mama said. "Now she's got outsiders who might just come looking for her again at any minute. If they ask for her, we'll need to be able to produce her to show them everything's all right. We'll have to wait and make a decision about her later. Shunning her will have to be enough for now.

"The girl though," Mama said thoughtfully. "That girl. Claire, I think her name is. Now she did the right thing and demonstrated her faith by reporting her mother. We need to figure out a way to reward her in some way. She looks like she's old enough to have a Coming Out pretty soon."

"She's scheduled to be in the very next one, " Red said.

Mama nodded. "You tell the girl she'll be going upstairs with Elvis for sure. After her coming out, we'll find a part for her to play in the family. But tell her not to tell anybody. We don't want the other girls to think they don't have a chance to be picked by the King."

"Think you can get Elvis to go along with that program?" Red said.

"You leave Elvis to me," she said.

Red turned toward the Seville. "Where's the Mama car?"

"Couldn't get it to crank," she said. "Archie's got it down at the shop. He told me it was the solenoid or some such mess. And it's got something worn on the front end made him think it wasn't safe to drive. Whatever it is, he's got to order the parts."

"Just looks funny, you not in the Mama car."

"Well," Mama said. "The car don't make the person. You gotta remember, Elvis used to drive a Cadillac. But Elvis would have been Elvis if he was on a John Deere tractor."

PART THREE

REBORN

10

RESTLESS

*H*is days at The Land of Grace had been fun at first. Now they had fallen into such a boring pattern that the itch to get back out on the road gnawed at him from somewhere deep under his skin. It had been easy to fantasize that he was actually living in Graceland, but once the just being-there wore thin, his mind drifted back into his old favorite fantasy of playing in sold-out arenas crammed with hysterical women screaming and tossing hotel keys onto the stage wrapped in their panties.

He knew it was Sunday morning from the mumbling and shuffling going on in the hall outside his door. Lying in bed, staring up at the ceiling, he ignored the commotion outside as he drifted deep into a make-believe concert. He could see it all as if he were living it. He was wearing the skin-tight Egyptian jumpsuit with the Indian Head belt. In the middle of "Tiger Man" the crowd of women were squealing and crying, on the edge of experiencing a group orgasm. He wasn't about to let them have all the fun, so he let his hand snake down to his morning wood when the door cracked open and Cholly said, "Wakie, Wakie. Pee and shakie."

"What?" Doyle said, springing up in bed.

Cholly stood in the doorway, a smile stretching across his big, full moon of a face. "Hey, I didn't mean to interrupt anything important. I can come back later."

"No, I...come on in."

"I mean, I wouldn't bother you," Cholly said as he shuffled shyly into the room. "But it's Sunday and we need to get a move on to make it to church."

"I was just...I was just waking up."

"Yeah, I could see you was pretty well awake."

Cholly brought the usual suit and disguise and waited patiently on the bed while Doyle showered and shaved. After Doyle dressed, he let Cholly act like his personal valet, placing the wig on his head and sticking the beard around his chin. Then they trudged down to the Dining Room together for coffee, a biscuit, and a heavy dose of Granny's abuse. "You hadn't heard the man upstairs sing yet, have you?" the old lady said.

"I heard him," Doyle said. "The first morning I was here I heard him."

"Yeah, but he waddn't feeling good." She said as she plopped a plate piled with eggs fried as hard as Frisbees on the table. "You ort to hear him get after it when he's feeling his beans. Hell, what am I saying? Even with him sick as a dog, you still wouldn't qualify to be his piss boy."

"What's a piss boy?" Doyle asked Cholly later as they walked to the carport.

"Damned if I know," Cholly said. "Don't worry about Granny. She just loves her some Elvis."

"Yeah, I get it," Doyle said. "She loves Elvis and hates me."

"Hell, I think its just that she just loves Elvis and hates everybody else," Cholly said.

On his way outside, Doyle grumbled to Cholly about catching a ration of shit from Granny every time he saw her, about not getting laid since he'd been there, and the stupid disguise he had to wear every time he turned around. But after he remembered the thousand they paid him every Friday and thought about how he could actually use a couple more of those payments, he decided to be a little more grateful and just shut up. After he, Cholly, and other apostles loaded up in three black Cadillac limos, they rolled on to the church as if they were part of a funeral procession for a 1950's gangster.

At the church, the apostles went their own way while one of the armed ushers met Doyle at the limo and escorted him to his balcony seat. As he followed along behind the man, he thought that this is probably the kind of VIP treatment Elvis always got. He reared back in his seat, letting himself feel like a king as he watched the crowd milling in. His mind drifted to the unfinished business he had with Rhonda, and he crossed his fingers, hoping to see her walk in.

In the balcony across the sanctuary, the white-haired guy he'd seen skulking through the foyer took a seat. When he waved as if he were flagging down a taxi, Doyle thought he could be motioning to anybody. He didn't think the man had ever seen him and even if he had, he couldn't possibly recognize him in this disguise. He tried to ignore the guy, but now every time he looked in that direction the man's arm shot up, and, instead of waving, he pointed at Doyle, wagging his finger. There was no doubt he was pointing at him, and Doyle wondered what kind of message he was trying to relay. Was it some kind of display of recognition? Was it some kind of warning? Whatever it was, the little chill creeping up his spine told him he didn't want to know.

After a while, he completely forgot about the man when the band kicked into an up-beat intro. This morning the Colonel led the congregation into a deafening rendition of "Working on a Building." Doyle felt himself being taken away by the music, his voice and his handclaps swept up in the sound of the congregation like a breeze in a mighty hurricane.

After the service, Doyle made his way through the crowd behind the usher, feeling like some kind of fugitive under his disguise. But he understood everyone's concern about his Elvis-like appearance. Besides, as long as they kept paying him this kind of money, he would put on a wolf mask and howl at the moon. He was pretty sure they were going to offer him some kind of job. They were probably just waiting to see if he liked the place.

He walked through a side exit and found the limo with the driver standing at the back, holding the door open. "Red's riding back with us," the driver said. "He's going to be a few minutes. Anything I can get for you?"

"Uh, no thanks," Doyle said as he settled into the plush leather, still feeling unworthy to be the recipient of all this VIP treatment.

"Want some music?" the driver said.

"Sure," Doyle said. And he sat through Martha and the Vandellas' "Dancing in the Street," and Del Shannon's "Runaway," all the while thinking that with the King recovering like the Colonel said, he wouldn't really be needed around here after all. He figured the whole thing was too good to be true, anyway. The limo filled up with the vamp for "Marie's the Name of His Latest Flame." As he moved to the music, he could feel his throat forming that velvet baritone and see throngs of women screaming below him as he stood onstage, strumming his guitar and shaking his legs. He was looking down on his adoring fantasy audience with his lip curling into his Elvis smile when the limo door swung open. "Thanks for waiting," Red said. "Ready to go?"

"Uh, sure," Doyle answered, feeling as if he'd just been caught masturbating for the second time that morning.

They were quiet for a while, both of them staring pensively out the window at the pines whipping by. Doyle broke the silence by clearing his throat before saying, "Good service, today."

"Yeah," Red said. "But it ain't the same without the King,"

"Well," Doyle said. "No way it could be, I guess."

"Yeah," Red said. "You got that shit right. But I'll bet when you looked down that audience, you kinda got the urge to get up and rock out yourself."

"Oh, no," Doyle said. "I didn't...I was just happy to be singing along."

"Really?" Red said. "Well, I'm glad you enjoyed the service. You down for some softball this afternoon?"

"Sure," Doyle said. "If that's what the boys want to do." Then he got the idea to force the issue of his status. "Uh, hey, Red. I wanted to tell you that I've enjoyed my stay here, but I really need to be moving on down the road."

"Yeah?" Red said. "Where you headed?"

"Oh, I thought I'd head on back to Texas. Maybe take a little stock, see what life's got in store for me. Besides, as good as you folks have been, I don't really think this is going to work out."

"Has anybody done anything to make you mad?" Red said.

"No," Doyle said. "Hell no. Everybody's been nice. They couldn't have been nicer. I just..."

"Is it the money? Hell, I could talk to Mama about giving it a little bump."

"Oh, no. It's more than generous. I'm just..."

Red laughed deep in his chest. "Look, if it's our faith that's bothering you, I know all this hit you in the face kinda sudden. But don't let it worry you, man. We don't expect you to buy into something like this right off the bat. We're just humble folks who stay mostly to ourselves, trying to live what we believe. Tell you what. I'll show you something.

"Hey, Carl," Red called to the driver.

"Yeah, boss."

"Let's drive through the Village."

The limo circled around the church onto a narrow road that cut through a half-mile of pine and opened into a neighborhood of modular houses anchored in the middle of neatly landscaped lots on tree-lined streets with names like "Don't Be Cruel" Lane and "Hound Dog" Boulevard. In the middle of the homes sat a shady, manicured oasis, named "Viva Las Vegas Park," where families picnicked in the soft grass under a canopy of tall oaks, teenagers played volleyball and kids splashed in a swimming pool under the eye of a lifeguard.

"Not too shabby, is it?" Red said.

"Nice," Doyle said.

They rode beside a chain-link fence as high as a two-story building with a sign warning, *Danger. High Voltage.* The fence was topped with swirls of razor wire, and every mile or so an armed guard with a rifle slung over his shoulder waved to them as they passed. "They wanted security," Red said, pointing to the guard. "And we gave 'em security. Anybody commits a crime? Well, I don't even want to talk about what happens then.

"At one time Willow Ruth was the sock capital of the world till the Mexicans and Chinese took over and everything closed up. They had people sitting around for years unemployed, drawing food stamps and welfare, kids with nothing to do but tweak crystal, fight and fuck. We brought them all in here, and Elvis took on their burdens."

"Let me just ask you something, Red."

"Yeah?"

"Why did y'all pick me out to come here?"

"You got to understand," Red said. "We don't invite many outsiders in here, but when we do decide to share with someone, we're pretty selective. We keep up with the guys who do Elvis, and, believe me, we know the best ones. We picked you out to show you what we have here because we know you're such a serious student of Elvis, and we figured you'd get something out of it. Now, we'd like for you to stay with us a while, but if you need to be moving on, I understand. Hell, years from now when you're back in Bum Fuck, Texas..."

"San Angelo," Doyle said.

"Wherever. And you've got your grandkids around you, you'll laugh and tell about the bunch of crazy Elvis worshipers you met in Alabama."

"I won't laugh," Doyle said.

Red reached over, gripped Doyle's shoulder, and with his eyes narrowed into sharp slits said, "I know you won't."

Mama swayed on the front porch swing of the Tupelo House, her eyes narrowing, a scowl scrunching her jowly face as the limo stopped, the driver emerged to step around to the back door and let Red out onto the gravel. Her legs were crossed and her top leg swung like the tail of an irritated cat, faster as Red ambled up the steps.

"Can't be good," Mama said. "Or you wouldn't be interrupting my prayer time again."

"It's about the boy," Red said. "He's talking about moving on. I don't think we can talk him out of it this time."

"He's exactly what we've been looking for, Red," she said.

"He's that good, huh?"

"When our scouts raved about him last year, I flew out to catch his act in Enid, Oklahoma. I had to follow him over to Stillwater just to make sure I'd seen what I thought I'd seen. I swear, there was times during those performances, I thought I was actually seeing and listening to Elvis. But you can ask the Colonel. After the AMVETS show, he said he was the best he'd ever seen."

"He may look and sound Elvis-like," Red said. "But I think his heart's chocked full of dadgum worldly skepticism."

"Well," Mama said. "It's about time for him to be reborn."

"Whew!" Red said, smiling, giving his head a little twist. "I almost dread doing it again."

"Well," Mama shrugged. "Me too. I was just thinking the other night how easy its been for us to find people to act like Elvis. And it hadn't been all that hard to get people to accept Elvis as their King. All we had to do is just offer Him as an answer to folks who didn't have any other answers. But to make somebody believe he really *is* Elvis? To believe the spirit of the King has entered him? Well, that always takes rebirth."

"You're right as always," Red said. "It just gets a little messy is all I'm saying."

"That it does," Mama said. "But you gotta keep in mind—as blessed an event as birth is, it's not always the most pleasant thing to behold."

11

ALL SHOOK UP

*D*oyle had a lot of reasons for leaving—he didn't see where he fit into this operation at all. They damn sure didn't need an Elvis tribute artist because they already had the best he had ever seen. Rhonda had made herself scarce since church on the first day, and they hadn't bothered fixing him up with anybody else. The need for a little female attention had him a little itchy.

Yet, three days had zipped by since he told Red he was leaving, and he was still hanging around. Though he'd started feeling like a bum, he had to admit, their money was good. But he knew the main reason he stayed was dreading the loneliness of the road. All the time he had been there he hadn't been alone around the house for more than a few minutes. The boys kept him busy, playing softball, hiking or just hanging out. Sometimes they'd request that he sing some rockabilly and show off some of his 1956 Elvis moves. They always acted as if they were blown away by his performances. Still, he knew he needed to make some decisions about his life, and he figured the best move he could make would be to head on back to San Angelo and see what his options were. If he still had any.

He guessed Cholly had been tasked with entertaining him. And the chubby guitar picker was dedicated to the task. The minute Doyle's feet hit the floor, Cholly stayed on his hip like a loyal puppy, trailing him everywhere except to the bathroom. And even then, when Doyle came out, Cholly's face brightened as if Doyle were his long-lost brother he hadn't seen in ages.

Now Cholly looked heartbroken, and he apologized all over the place because he was going to have to leave Doyle alone for a few hours. "I'm sorry," he said. "I feel rotten just leaving you like this, man. But with E being sick and all, we keep having to put in different stuff to make the church service work. And on top of everything else, we're breaking in a new bass player. I promise, I'll be back as soon as we get it ironed out."

"Take your time," Doyle said, as he escorted him down the hall to the back door. "I'll be all right."

"You sure?"

"Hey, I don't need to be entertained every minute of the day. I've been keeping myself company for a long time now."

Doyle had come to like Cholly, but after he patted the chubby guitar player on the back and watched him climb into back seat of the limo, he felt as if someone had lanced a painful boil that had been torturing him for days.

He walked back into the house. Pans clanked from the Kitchen, and Granny turned loose a barrage of profanity on her crew that would make a porn star blush. But once that died down, the place was so quiet he could hear the air blowing through the registers along the walls. The quiet made him feel as if he were alone with the house for the first time. As far as he could tell, the building was a pretty good replica of the real thing. It was so real that he could believe he was actually living in Graceland with the Memphis Mafia and that Elvis might just step out of the shadows at any moment, order up a fried 'nanner sandwich from the Kitchen and take over the baritone part in one of the impromptu gospel quartets they put together late into the night.

Doyle wandered over the white carpet from the Dining Room to the Living Room. He hung out in the Music Room a while and fingered the keys of the piano before lighting a candle under the shrine. "I hope you don't hold it against me for imitating you all these years," he said to the life-sized icon. "I meant no disrespect, honest. It's just that you left us so soon, and your fans felt like they didn't get a proper chance to say goodbye. I guess what I've been trying to do all this time is to give them that chance. You know, a chance to say a proper goodbye and all." But of course, he knew that wasn't the reason at all. Every time he slipped that jumpsuit on he felt like Superman bounding from the window of a skyscraper. Before he left the Music Room, he looked around, feeling a little silly after telling a bald-faced lie to a guitar-toting plastic mannequin.

Walking out of the Music Room, he felt the same cold shiver he used to feel every time he caught a glimpse of a rattlesnake slithering across the barren lawn of his grand-parents' house on Julian Street. When he saw Dr. Nick step off the stairs, he ducked inside the door.

That damn Cholly's got me spooked, he chuckled, shaking his head. But he stayed hidden behind the stained glass peacock, waiting for the front door to click before wandering down to the basement.

He liked the Pool Room because its multi-colored fabric walls and ceiling, plus the muted glow from the Tiffany light over the pool table, made him think he was shooting pool in a 1900s New Orleans whorehouse. So he wound up in there, pretending to shoot eight-ball with the King. "Your shot, E," he said, and looked around to make sure no one had heard him. Then he shook his head after waiting a moment and said, "Not good enough. You may be the King of Rock and Roll, but you ain't no pool player." Doyle, being a terrible pool player himself, went on to shoot five or six shots, scratching a couple of times in the process before finally sinking a ball. "See, that's the way a master does it," he said to an amazed, imaginary Elvis.

He finally tired of shooting eight ball with a make-believe Elvis and decided to wander around the grounds by himself. He walked back up the basement stairs and out the back door. Beyond the yard, the barn door was gaped open and he thought it might be a good idea to check out his van. For seven years the van had been his only friend. He knew it was kind of sad, but he even talked to the thing on long stretches of lonely road. As he walked along the driveway, he rattled the keys in his pocket while thinking it would feel good to be behind the wheel again.

His van still sat among a huddle of antique Cadillacs. A rhythmic thumping rose from the front end of a '58 Eldorado convertible stretched over a grease pit. Doyle thought about announcing his presence after he saw the shadow of a man's head moving under the car, but he decided not to break the guy's concentration. Instead, he opened the back of the van and climbed in to find his signs, his lights, his speakers, his computer and his wardrobe box all arranged better than he could have done himself. He even had room to inch his way up to the driver's seat.

When he turned the ignition, the engine sounded eager, but before it could turn over, it gurgled and choked as if it were being strangled. After getting the same result when he patted the accelerator, he realized the only thing he was going to accomplish by grinding the ignition was to wear down the battery. He popped the hood latch and got out.

Other than checking the oil and coolant levels, he didn't usually know what he was even looking at when he raised the hood of a car. But anytime anything was wrong, he always raised it just the same and looked thoughtfully at the jumble of parts so he wouldn't look as helpless as he felt. This time, though, he thought he might just be able to diagnose the van's problem. The thing had actually demonstrated the same symptoms last year, and a service station mechanic replaced a fuse-like part for him. It looked like an easy operation that cost him a hundred bucks in labor on top of the cost of the part. He told himself that if this ever happened again, he'd know what to do.

He couldn't help questioning his judgment, but he was pretty sure that the fuse the mechanic had installed was missing. "Hey!" he yelled as he walked over to the grease pit.

"Yeah," the man under the Cadillac said. "Something I can help you with?"

"Got a fuse missing from my van."

"A fuse?" the man said. "Just a minute."

The man ducked his head under the Cadillac and walked up the steps of the pit, wiping his hands on a rag.

"What do you mean, a fuse?"

"You know," Doyle said. "The one that controls the gas."

"You mean, fuel pump relay?" the man said.

Doyle shrugged.

"Let's take a look," the man said.

The mechanic was tall and slim in a crisp blue uniform with *Archie* embroidered in gold over his shirt pocket. He followed Doyle over to the van, wiping his greasy hands with a rag. He looked under the hood with the curiosity of Sherlock Holmes investigating a crime scene before backing away and saying, "No shit. You're missing a fuel pump relay."

"Who would have taken it?"

"Damned if I know," the man said. "I'm in here every day, and I haven't seen anybody fooling around this van."

"Can you get me another one?"

"Probably so. Be tomorrow though." The man took his cell phone from his pocket. "This is kinda serious. We better get Red in on this," he said.

A limo pulled into the barn. The back doors to the limo swung open and Red and Sonny piled out, wearing tee shirts and faded jeans. Red carried a black object that he swung at his side as if it were a baton. "What's this about some kind of relay?" Red said.

"Fuel pump relay," the mechanic said. "Came up missing."

"Now, how does shit like that happen, Arch?" Red said. "I locked the damn thing myself. Doyle's the only one with the key. And the barn stays locked unless one of y'all are in here."

"Beats me. I told him we could get him another relay by tomorrow," Archie said.

"Yeah," Red said. "We'll do that, but we need to get down to the bottom of this."

"Yeah, we do," Sonny said. "Man, this sounds like some kind of Houdini shit."

"How'd you notice it?" Red said. "Was you planning to go somewhere?"

"Thought I'd take it for a drive," Doyle said.

"Just a drive?" Sonny said. "You're not leaving us, are you?"

"I wasn't leaving just yet," Doyle said. "I was planning to take off tomorrow, though."

"Tomorrow?" Red said. "Somebody make you mad or something?"

"No," Doyle said. "Honest. I'm not mad at anybody."

"We not paying you enough?"

"Oh, I told you before, I'm not complaining about money. If anything it's too much."

"You don't like the food, then?" Sonny said.

"The food's great," Doyle said. "Really. Well, everything except breakfast."

"Can't do anything about the breakfast. The man upstairs calls the shots on meals around here."

"The man upstairs?" Doyle said.

"Elvis," Red said. "He owns this whole thing, you know."

"No," Doyle said. "I guess I never thought..."

"Hey," Sonny said. "Show me where that relay thing's supposed to be."

"Well," Archie said. "It's supposed to be..."

"Don't you have some kind of work to do, Arch?" Red said.

"Yeah," Archie said. "I was just..."

"Then you'd better get to it, hadn't you?" Red said.

"Yes, sir," Archie said. He dropped his head and walked away.

"Now," Sonny said. "You was just going to show me."

Doyle glanced at the mechanic ambling off toward the grease pit. He shrugged, leaned over the front of the van and said, "It's supposed to go right here" when he heard the crackle of electrodes and felt something as hard a poker press into the small of his back. His body quaked, a white light flashed through his brain, and his legs turned to jelly. On his way down, his arms wouldn't respond in time to keep from careening off the fender of the van. His forehead smacked into the steel, and he was still struggling to raise his arms when his head bounced off the concrete.

* * *

"You killed him," Sonny said.

"What do you mean, I killed him? Hell, you could have caught him."

"Caught him? I didn't know when you were going to gouge him with that thing."

Sonny knelt over Doyle and rolled him over on his back. "He's not dead, but he's going to have a pretty good knot on his head."

"Mama ain't gonna like that," Red said.

"No," Sonny said. "She is not. Let's get him ready."

Red retrieved a box from the limo, and both men knelt over Doyle. Sonny wrapped a strip of duct tape across Doyle's mouth and pulled a blindfold over his eyes while Red fastened a set of handcuffs to his wrists. With Red holding his arms and Sonny his feet, they picked him up and shoved him into the back seat of the limo.

* * *

When Doyle woke, he was sure he had his eyes open, but everything was dark, darker than any dark he'd ever seen. Red and Sonny were somewhere near, talking, Sonny's saying, "What do we tell Mama?"

"Tell her the damn truth," Red said. "Sumbitch fell."

"Man, she's gonna be pissed."

"She's gonna be pissed whether we tell the truth or make up some shit. Truth's easier to keep track of."

Doyle felt as if he were moving, heard the low hum of an engine and felt the vehicle riding over an uneven surface. "That tooth's getting worse, ain't it?" Red said.

"No. No, it's all right."

"I see you rubbing on that jaw," Red said.

Doyle's mind formed the question, "What happened?" When the sound came out in a grunt, he thought he may have suffered a stroke or something. He couldn't move his hands. He was pretty sure his eyes were open, but he couldn't see. Feeling as if he were swallowed by a flash of panic, he gasped for air and thrashed around on the seat.

"He's awake," Sonny said.

A big hand patted Doyle's head. "You just had a little poke with a cattle prod," Red said. "You don't calm way-the-hell down, I'm going to give you another."

"What? Why?" came out of Doyle's mouth as grunts against the duct tape.

"Don't talk. Don't move." Red said.

The movement stopped. Car doors opened. A pair of big hands clamped on the flesh under his arms and dragged him till his lower body fell then landed with a crunch. He was pulled upright. Gravel crunched under his feet.

Doyle's panic combined with hot anger and he kicked in the direction of Red's voice, feeling resistance to his toe.

"Shit!" Red shouted. "Goddamn it! You got one coming to you, boy. You got a good one coming."

Doyle fought against being pulled. Someone grabbed his feet and he was hefted, the men doing the lifting huffing and puffing as they lugged him along. Feet pounded on wood. A door swung open, and he fell into space for a moment before landing on something soft that squeaked under him as he bounced. The men, breathing hard from the exertion, rolled him over, loosened the restraint on his wrists, then rolled him back over and clamped restraints on both wrists till his arms were outstretched. When they grabbed his ankles he kicked and twisted till Red said, "Move back, Sonny. He's asking for another jolt."

The sizzling sound froze him before he felt the jab and the jolt that turned his muscles liquid. While he lay immobile, the men fastened metal shackles around his ankles, and he lay spread-eagled on his back quaking from the shock.

"You don't resist. You understand?" Red said.

At the sound of the sizzling, Doyle grunted yes and nodded his head.

"Now you just lay back and think about how good you're going to be from now on. We might be back for you and we might not. Far as I'm concerned, you could just die of starvation."

Footsteps clomped across the floor. The door squeaked open and clamped shut, and Doyle lay there alone in the dark.

12

ARE YOU LONESOME TONIGHT?

*O*nce he was alone, every cheesy horror movie he had ever seen flooded into his head. He cursed himself for allowing himself to be lured into this place by a beautiful woman. Now he wondered why he didn't question why a woman like that would even give him the time of day. And the money. Who gives you that kind of money for hanging around singing songs, shooting pool and playing soft ball. He thought about how much fun it had been to pretend he was living in the middle of Graceland with the Memphis Mafia. But now he wondered if the people who lived here were just a bunch of gap-toothed hillbillies, getting ready to harvest all of his organs as if he were a wrecked F-150 in a junk yard. He was sure that some amateur surgeon would come in soon and remove both his kidneys with a dull scalpel. Finally his celluloid induced horrors were quashed by the real terror under the tight blindfold that made him feel as if he were sinking deeper and deeper into black water. He thrashed around in a drowning panic. As he jerked at his shackles, a chain of screams rose from deep in his chest and pushed through his raw throat only to crash silently against the duct tape and stack up inside him like angry traffic stalled on the interstate.

A wave of nausea tickled his stomach, giving him something else to worry about. With the tape across his mouth, he knew that if he didn't gain some kind of control of himself soon he might choke on his own vomit. So he lay as still as he could until his breathing calmed and his heart slowed to a manageable pounding thump.

His soaked crotch and legs told him that sometime during his struggle, he had lost control of his bladder. He fell into a fit of shame as he worried about Sonny and Red finding him on the wet bed like a child.

What the hell's happening here? he thought, now trying to sift through the steps of his abduction for any little sign of hope that he might just survive after all. *I don't think these bastards have any intention of killing me. If they wanted to take my kidneys or whatever, they'd just shoot me full of dope to quiet me down and take what they wanted. Wouldn't they?*

Don't they say blind people developed other senses? Hell, do I even have any senses left? And once he figured that he might actually have a few senses, he decided he would try to exercise them a little. He was definitely lying on a bed. There was a pillow at his head, and the mattress gave and springs squeaked under him as he rolled his shoulders and hips. He concluded the bed had a metal headboard and footboard that clanked when he jerked at his chains. Along with the scent of his urine-soaked pants he detected the soot of old fires. He rolled over again, stretching his body as much as he could. When he felt his hip at the bed's edge, he concluded the bed was small. Now, he was pretty sure he was at the little replica of Elvis' birthplace where he met Mama.

He didn't know how much time had gone by, but it was enough for his legs and shoulders to go numb and his bladder to fill up again. After a while he figured he was already wet, so he had nothing to lose by just letting it go. He lay in his own warm piss, his bladder relieved, but now he felt hunger gnawing away at his stomach, and his mouth felt as dry as if he'd been eating salty popcorn all day.

In the dark quiet that followed, he realized that he'd been alone before, but he'd never been alone like this. There *was* no other alone like this. On the road, he could at least play the radio. He could see the lights of the oncoming traffic, see the silhouettes of the drivers in the passing cars and imagine what they were talking about and where they were going. He might have been alone in a few motel rooms through the years, but he could at least play the

TV and see human faces however far away they may have been. He wouldn't know the couple next door or even know what they looked like. But he could listen to them arguing or making love on the other side of a thin wall and know he was not really alone.

He thought this dark silence must be what death is like. As time crept along he became certain that he was going to die all alone in the darkness, and he wept. The weeping was quiet at first, just a few sniffles, but graduated into body-wracking convulsions that threatened to make him sick. He sucked in a long chain of deep breaths, and in desperation, he strained to hear someone or something, even if it were nothing but the faint whimpering of a fellow creature, just to assure himself that he was still alive.

He'd come close to this level of desperate loneliness when he was a kid in the cramped little room in his grandparent's framed house on Julian Street. There he woke three or four times in the night to the squeak-squawk of his grandpa's wheelchair rolling down the hall to the bathroom. Once he had awakened, he'd struggled to go back to sleep after seeing the skeletal shadow of the cottonwood dancing on the wall as it moved in the breeze outside his window.

His grandmother told him that his mother left home right after giving birth to him. "Said she was going to Nashville," his grandmother said. "Gonna be a country singer." She shook her head. "That girl and her crazy dream."

"Gonna be a goddamn whore," the old man snarled from his wheelchair.

"You shut up," his grandmother snapped. "Don't you think you've done enough damage?"

The old man had burned all the pictures of Doyle's mother, but the old lady saved a school picture of a pretty blonde girl with lips stretched into a forced smile and eyes that looked as if she dreaded something she saw beyond the lens of the camera. "You carry this with you," she told Doyle. "And you know she wouldn't have left you for a second if she hadn't had to." Doyle understood. It was better to be a whore in Nashville than to live anywhere around the old man.

It seemed as if he'd spent an eternity of days doing nothing but staying out of the old man's way, trying to sleep in that house and trudging off to school where he felt like an invisible and mute alien, watching the other kids talking, laughing and playing while he wondered what they could ever be saying to each other. He grew up without friends, undistinguished in his studies and a miserable failure at all of the sports he tried out for. Without a grown man to take interest in him, he failed to acquire any of the skills expected of a male in the world. And it seemed as if talent in every form had passed him by till at fourteen, his voice cracked into a silky baritone, and he discovered he had an ear for imitating voices. "Like a gift from God," his grandmother sighed when he mimicked a few bars of "Don't Be Cruel" he'd picked up from one of her scratchy old 45s.

"Like a goddamn parrot," his grandfather snapped.

"Like a goddamn parrot," Doyle shot back in a close approximation of the old man's wheezy growl.

"Little bastard," his grandfather snarled. And with tears in his eyes, he leaned forward with his thin lips quivering, his gnarled fingers gripping the wheelchair arms as if they were around Doyle's throat and cast what Doyle thought was the worst curse the old man could inflict upon another human being, "I hope you wind up just like me," he snarled.

His back ached, the excruciating itches attacking his butt, his nose, his leg and the back side of his shoulder made him feel as if he were being eaten alive. All the darkness felt like nothingness and he gasped for air. After he calmed down, he remembered reading how Elvis hated to sleep alone. It was why he always surrounded himself with family and friends. He thought fear of this kind of horror would make you go out and hire some friends.

His grandmother told him she had fallen in love with Elvis after seeing him perform at the City Auditorium back in 1955. She stifled a giggle with her hand over her mouth like a shy school girl when she told Doyle that she ran away from his grandfather and followed Elvis to DeKalb. She almost saw him again in Austin, "But your grandpa caught up with me and beat my butt," she said. After Elvis died she collected supermarket tabloids and admitted to Doyle that, for the longest time, she believed in all the Elvis sightings, explaining, "It just didn't make sense that he was dead. I mean, how could Elvis be dead? He was Elvis."

She told him he even looked like Elvis after he crooned "Love Me Tender" for her one day. "Lot of people don't know he was a dirty blond like you."

"Lotta people don't know he was a freak like you," his grandfather said.

"Yeah, he was a freak all right," his grandmother shot back. "A freak who laughed all the way to the bank."

"All the dope they found in him, I'd be surprised he wadn't laughing all the way to the toilet," the old man said.

"Your mama sure loved Elvis," his grandmother told him when they were alone. And he felt as if his own love for Elvis must have been acquired through the genes passed on from the two women in his life—the one who raised him and the one whose picture he carried around in his wallet. "I always wanted to see Elvis again," his grandmother said. "But I never did. Then I hoped I'd at least get to see Graceland, but that don't look like it's ever going to work out either."

"I'll get a job and take you one day, Maw Maw," he said. "I promise."

"You're a good boy," she said, caressing his face. "You're a real good boy."

His uncle Brad gave him a hundred dollars for a graduation present. "You know, I been worried about you," he said to Doyle out on the stoop one day. "That old man in there's got some hard bark on him. He was damn sure more than your mother and I could take when we were kids, and he's our daddy. But I've got to hand it to you, you toughed it out. You thought much about what you're going to do after high school? It's not too soon to be planning for the rest of your life."

Doyle shrugged. After high school. The rest of his life. Two phrases that made him think of a thousand miles of dark road.

"You know, I'm the produce manager at Albertson's," his uncle said. "Yesterday I mentioned you to the store manager. He said he'd be willing to talk to you about a full-time job. That sound good to you?"

Doyle nodded, but it didn't sound all that good. He had no idea where life would take him, but he fantasized about show business. He didn't understand it, but it looked like a lot more fun than retail grocery.

The next day, he went down to the bus station, and when it was his turn at the ticket counter, he realized he hadn't figured out where to go. He blurted out "Nashville" after the lady behind the ticket counter got a little testy with him.

After riding all night, he did nothing but wander the Nashville streets, half expecting to run into his mother. In his mind, they would recognize each other immediately. They would stop and stare at each other in wide-eyed surprise before hugging and laughing about what an asshole his grandfather was and how good it was to escape San Angelo. Then she would invite him to move in with her.

He had been trying to visualize the kind of house and neighborhood she lived in when he thought how stupid the whole thing was. Even if she still lived in Nashville, she wouldn't be the same sad-eyed girl in the worn picture he carried. She would have aged. She would probably have gained weight, had her hair changed, maybe even be wearing glasses or something. And him, him, she hadn't even seen since he was a red, squalling newborn. If she had even taken a good look at him then.

He washed dishes at an Outback during the day and haunted the clubs at night, working every open mic and karaoke joint he could find. He tried out for a couple of bands, but the only call-back he got told him he sounded too much like Elvis. But when he saw Jake Wilcox, an Elvis impersonator, perform at The Palomino on the Murfreesboro Pike, he knew he'd found his niche.

"He sounds just like Elvis," one drunk woman swooned while Doyle thought the idiot didn't even sound remotely like the King. Oh, he had some of the inflection down, but his voice was too jerky on the fast numbers, and on the ballads he sounded as if he were trying out for the bass part in a gospel quartet. And when the woman said, "He looks so much like him, it's scary," Doyle wanted to slap her. Outside of the black hair, the imposter didn't look any more like Elvis than any fat man would once you stuffed his lard ass into a Stone Flame jumpsuit.

But the man covered his shortcomings with an amazing light show and the red neon E-L-V-I-S set behind him. His sound system sounded like an orchestra filling the room from backing tracks he controlled with a remote. Doyle thought that if he had all that stuff, he wouldn't even need a band.

The possibilities excited him. But the only jobs he'd been able to land just paid minimum wage. His excitement withered at the price tag attached to becoming Elvis.

He dreamed of taking up where Elvis left off. Unlike Elvis, he would separate his acting career from his singing, going on big, sold-out tours between Oscar-winning dramatic pictures. He knew it was a fantasy. But the fantasy helped him rationalize those first clumsy ventures into the world of street hustling. And when he became disgusted with standing on a street and being appraised by a parade of circling predators, he became the predator himself, taking the men's wallets and jewelry, sometimes leaving them bleeding in an alley when they resisted, knowing they had families and careers somewhere and weren't about to report a robbery and assault to the police after soliciting another man for sex.

There were nights when he thought he would die from

the shame. But after buying his gear, he smothered his shame by immersing himself in Elvis and rehearsing constantly for a month before returning to Texas.

As much as he looked and sounded like Elvis, his career would have fizzled out of the blocks if a reporter from the Killeen Daily Herald hadn't been bar-hopping with some pals on that Wednesday night when Doyle did the very first twenty minutes of his *King of Kings* act at Lois' Horseshoe Lounge outside of Belton. After sobering up, the reporter followed him to Sonny Jim's in Salado and Rocky's in Jarrell just to make sure he'd seen and heard what he thought he'd seen and heard. The resulting feature article, titled "Call Me Crazy But I Think The King Has Returned," landed him an agent and opened doors for Doyle to venues throughout the west. He even played to a sold out crowd at the American Legion in Las Cruces. But the dwindling excitement after every appearance told him that as good as he was, he was still just an imitator, an oddity that Elvis fans amazed at for a moment, then forgot as they planned their next pilgrimage to Graceland. His limited celebrity, though it may not have hoisted him to actual stardom, helped him believe that his life began on the night of his first gig as the King in Belton. And once he convinced himself of that, he could believe all the stuff that came before had just been a horrible dream.

13

A CHILD IS BORN

*D*oyle was awakened by a small, gentle hand snaking down to his crotch. "Just what I thought," Mama said. "He's wet hisself."

She hovered so close her breath tickled his cheek, and her hand lingered around his junk as if it planned to stay there for a while. When he tried to twist away, all he accomplished was a lot of clanking and aching from his raw, bruised ankles and wrists. His shout of, "Let me go, goddamn it. Let me go," snorting through his nose and leaking through the duct tape across his mouth in guttural pig noises.

"Look at him," Red said. "Still got a lotta smart ass in him."

"Aww," Mama sighed as though she were gazing at a pile of soft puppies. "I think he's just darling. You need to go tee-tee, again, sweetie? I'll bet you do. I'll bring you the potty. Then after I get you all cleaned up and in dry clothes, I'll fix you a nice breakfast."

Doyle thought, *"The potty? A nice breakfast? What the hell is wrong with these crazy people?"* And he answered by clanging about, trying to yell for help through the duct tape until Red said, "Stand back. I'm gonna give him the only thing he understands." The sizzle of electrodes froze Doyle's blood, then a quick touch to his thigh by the cattle prod rattled his teeth and sent his muscles into a tremor.

"Oh, dear Lord! Don't hurt him," Mama's gentle voice pleaded.

"He's gotta learn his lesson, even if it kills him," Red said. "You hear me, numb nuts?—pardon my French, ma'am. You could just die here. So what you need to do is whatever Mama tells you to do. We gonna take the tape off your mouth. Anytime I hear anything coming out of that pie-hole of yours except yes ma'am and no ma'am and yes, sir, no, sir, you gonna get some more of this stick. Now, nod if you understand what I'm saying."

Doyle managed a feeble nod, and when the tape peeled across his face, it sounded like the tearing of a page and felt as though his lips had been ripped off. "Ahhh!" Doyle yelled.

"Not so hard, Red," Mama scolded, her fingers now caressing Doyle's raw lips. "I'll put some Vaseline on 'em after I bring you the potty, sweetie."

"I can go to the bathroom by myself," Doyle answered.

His teeth rattled at the touch of the stick. And as he trembled from the aftershock, the bedsprings creaked from Mama's weight sinking onto the bed beside him. She cuddled his head to her pillowy bosom as she rocked. "You'll be all right, baby," she cooed. Doyle wondered if he was going to die after all. And for a moment he thought that maybe it would be better if he did.

"Yeah," Red said. "He'll be all right if he does like he's told. Yes, ma'am. No, ma'am. You understand, now?"

Doyle started to struggle, but realized his resistance wasn't getting him anywhere. "Yes, sir," Doyle said, deciding to play along.

"Just don't hurt this sweet thing," Mama said.

"He's a hardhead," Red said. "Like I always told you. Guy like him? Sometimes you just gotta 'splain it to him just right."

When Doyle stopped shaking, they unshackled him and removed his clothes. Then they attached the shackles to his ankles and sat him down on a hard, cold seat with his butt hanging through some space. He thought this had to be some kind of portable toilet since he hadn't taken more than three steps. He could feel Mama hovering over him again. She caressed his hair and cooed, "Having trouble going, sweetie?"

"Yes, ma'am," he said.

"My goodness. I can't wait to wash that purty hair of

yours," she said.

Heavy feet stomped away, then returned. "Where you want it?" Red said.

"Right here's good," the woman said. "You can stand up now, sweetie."

As he stood, he heard the gentle splashing of water. Then he felt the softness and warmth of the damp cloth on his face, then on his neck and shoulders. As she washed him, she gave him gentle instructions, "Turn around, now, sweetie." "Raise your arms, now, baby." When she ran the warm, soothing cloth across his balls, he could feel his cock rise up like the obedient soldier it had always been. "I'm sorry," he sighed, now bathed more in shame than soap and water.

"What did you say?" Red said.

"He didn't mean it," Mama said, her arms wrapped around Doyle's naked waist.

"I told him if he said anything but yes ma'am and no ma'am he'd get the stick. Now, Mama, we'll do whatever you say, but I think he needs another nice jolt from my electric stick."

"No!" she snapped. "He was just trying to be polite. 'I'm sorry' is 'bout the same as 'yes ma'am.'"

"All right," Red said. "I'm gonna let him slide this time 'cause you say so. But he better keep his mind on his bidness if he wants to keep away from this stick."

"He will. He's a good boy, I can tell right now."

"OK. You got this lady to thank for you not getting another shock. You understand?"

"Yes, sir," Doyle said. *I'm going to kill you, you son-of-a-bitch*, he thought, grinding his teeth.

She helped Doyle into dry clothes then led him across the floor, chains rattling, his bare feet slapping across a smooth surface. With the blindfold on, he felt like a blind man, stumbling through a dark world. He bumped his shoulder on what he figured to be a door facing, and a steamy heat mingled with the scent of biscuits baking surrounded him. Mama sat him down on a hardback chair, and Red handcuffed his hands behind him. Then Doyle sat as Mama shuffled around, banging metal, pouring liquid.

He could feel Red's presence in the room, could hear him clearing his throat and shuffling his feet. And in the darkness behind the blindfold, he imagined the flaming hair and the snarl twisting the ruddy goateed face. Anytime Red moved in close, Doyle's arms jerked up instinctively only to rattle the chains attached to the handcuffs.

"I got time to go out for a smoke?" Red said.

"Yeah, go ahead," Mama said. "I'll holler at you if I need you."

As Red tromped across the floor, Doyle imagined him hulking along, swinging his big arms as if he didn't know what to do with them if they weren't employed in hurting someone. Something clicked, then a door slammed and Mama said, "I'm sorry I can't undo your hands and take that old blindfold off. But I promise, I'll take good care of you. "

Doyle shifted his weight and felt the chair scoot along with him. He moved his arms and thought that if he stood, he might be able to clear the chair with his bound hands. But what would he do then? He could hear muffled voices through the walls and figured the men weren't that far away. He had no doubt that they would be on him before he could get to the door. A sizzling sound boiled up from somewhere close by as he breathed in the scent of bacon.

Mama tied a cloth around Doyle's neck and fed him scrambled eggs and grits with a spoon, followed by bacon and biscuits with her fingers. "It was hot, but I blowed on it for you, sweetie," she said. "Open up, now."

Trembling with a mixture of fear and hatred, he opened his mouth, then chewed as she dabbed his lips with the cloth.

"That's my good boy," she said. "Now I'm gonna give you some juice." He felt the straw penetrate his lips. Once he fell into the rhythm of the thing— the opening and the closing and the chewing and the swallowing, he realized that the food was wonderful, especially the biscuits that she had slathered in butter. He thought it was a hell of a lot better than the breakfast the cranky old lady cooked over at the fake Graceland.

After she stopped shoveling food at him and wiped his mouth with a wet cloth, she stood him up and led him to a padded chair with a spring that gouged his butt. Doyle sat as she rattled around, running water and making splashing sounds, all the time singing "Precious Memories" in a low voice,

The smell had changed where he now sat, the air heavier with the familiar scent of soot from the fireplace. He stretched his legs out, sliding his feet along the floor where the smooth texture changed to rough wood. After a while her small, steady steps approached him, she emitted a sigh, a heavy mass plopped and something skidded on the floor.

"I finally got through cleaning," she said, her knees now brushing against his. "Would you like me to read some to you?"

Read to me? Doyle thought. *As opposed to sticking me with a cattle prod?* But he knew the answer she wanted. "Yes, ma'am," he said.

"All right, then," she said, the zeal of a little girl sneaking into her voice. Something thumped, paper crinkled. Mama cleared her throat. "The Book of Gladys," she said, proudly. "Chapter one, verse one. 'Now, God commanded William Mansell to follow the warrior, Jackson, through the wilderness and across the waters of the Tennessee, the Coosa and the Tallapoosa. And there, they smote the Creeks with a mighty vengeance. And they killed them by the score...'"

Doyle's mind drifted to ways of escape. He would have to look for any weakness in their security and exploit it. He knew it was going to be pretty tough because they seemed to have everything covered. Tired from not sleeping much the night before, he dozed until he jarred awake when he remembered the cattle prod. Then he realized one advantage to having a blindfold on was, she couldn't tell when he was sleeping.

He woke every now and then to Mama droning on about God giving some guy land in Alabama and then taking it away when the guy shacked up with an Indian. The whole thing pissed God off so much, he laid one hell of a curse on future generations, telling the man, "'Your land will become so sterile that even the noxious weeds will not grow there. And your issue, which will be many upon many, will grow wild and given to strong drink and promiscuity. And they will abandon the land and wander to Gum Pond, Mississippi. And they will remain there with neither capital nor a trade to sustain them. And they will be despised among all men. And they will be called, White Trash.'"

But God told the guy that the curse would end one day. "'Long after you are one with the earth, in the west, the dust will rise up from the ground and become as rain from the sky. Men will leap from tall, pale buildings in a mighty city to the north. And the crops will not grow. And the chickens will not lay. In the midst of all this sorrow, a woman from among you will birth a boy child. And his song will shake the earth. And at the sight of him, and at the sound of his voice, and at the wiggle of his leg, women will scream and pull at their hair. And he will amass a great wealth. And he will gather your progeny into the Land of Grace. And upon those words, God became as the mist.'"

Doyle heard the book slam shut and Mama sucking in a deep breath. Then, after a long, quiet pause, she cleared her throat. "So, see," she said. "This tells us lotsa stuff…"

A tapping interrupted her, and she snapped, "What?"

"You ready for us?" Red called, his muffled voice coming from outside the door.

"I-will-call-you-when-I'm-good-and-ready," Mama barked.

"OK. OK," Red answered.

After another pause, her breathing calmed, and she began again. "One day soon, when you grow up, we'll discuss all this together, sweetie. But right now, I'm gonna just tell you the lessons you orta learned from this text. All right?"

"Yes, ma'am," Doyle said.

"The book tells us we supposed to overcome our weaknesses and obey God. But if we don't, we must ask forgiveness and not try to cover up our shenanigans. It don't do no good to lie to him anyway 'cause God knows all and sees all. You understand that?"

"Yes, ma'am."

"We're told God blesses us when we're obedient and will forgive us if we admit our sins. But he'll lay a curse on us in a minute if we don't follow that plan. You get that?"

"Yes, ma'am."

"But even if he curses us, he'll leave us with at least a smidgen of hope. See hope this time came in his prophesy of the coming of the boy child. You see all that?"

"Yes, ma'am."

"Good. Good," she said, the words, coming from deep in her chest, seemed to please her. Then she yelled, "All right, Red. Y'all can have him now."

Doyle thought nothing good could come of this as the door opened, and the hard soled shoes of several heavy men clomped in. Rough hands gripped Doyle under his arms and jerked him to his feet.

"I'm gonna have dinner on the table 'bout 'leven thirty," Mama said. "Y'all have him back by then."

"We will," Red said. "Come on, Hoss. We gonna take us a little stroll."

They cuffed Doyle's hands in front of him and pushed him across the floor, the chain rattling around his feet. Then they bumped him through a doorway, and he heard the screen door whap behind him.

Handcuffed to a bed, fed by hand and having Mama read to him from that bogus *Bible* was one thing, but traveling in this dark world, having to depend on the eyes of men he couldn't trust, ignited the same panic he felt last night. The sun warmed his face as big hands clutched his arms and helped him down four short steps. "Watch your step, now," one of the men said from far behind. Doyle had heard this voice before, but he couldn't put a face to it.

"Hope you gave your heart to Elvis in there," Red growled, " 'cause your ass belongs to me, now."

14

MAMA KNOWS ALL

Mud soaked through his clothes and caked across his face and over his head, forming his hair into thick, damp ropes. His skin felt wet and clammy under his clothes, but he could feel the sun now turning the coating on his face into a crust that cracked along his cheeks every time he opened his mouth. As he stood in front of Mama, handcuffed and shackled, he pictured himself as a gross and slimy creature risen from a stagnant swamp.

The men beside him had fallen silent. As hard as he listened, all Doyle could hear were crows cawing off in the distance, the men breathing beside him, and Mama's hard, angry pacing. From the sound of her steps, he figured she was above them, stomping up and down on the little porch with them standing out in the yard. When she stopped pacing, he thought he could feel her gazing down on him as if her eyes emitted rays of fierce heat.

He choked back a little chuckle, thinking of the bumbling trio beside him. Tough guys, he thought as he imagined them standing like the condemned, waiting for the firing squad to pull the triggers. Completely buffaloed by a fat, old woman. But he flinched as if he'd heard a volley of gunshots when she finally stomped her foot and shrieked, "I can't believe it. I just can't believe it."

"It's not exactly what it looks like," Red said.

"Well, let me tell you what it looks like to me, *exactly*," she said. "This morning, I had this boy looking like he just stepped out of a band box. Now, after just two hours with you three, he looks like he's been wallering around with the hogs. Is it any different than that?"

"Well, no," Red said. "If you gonna put it like that."

"Tell me how you'd put it, then," she said.

Feet shuffled through the grass beside Doyle for a few seconds.

"Well?" Mama said.

"He, uh…" Red said. "He called me a bad name, and I shocked him."

"You shocked him," she said. "He called you a bad name. Hadn't rained in a week. So you had to have picked out the only mud hole on this entire property and shocked him so he'd fall down in it."

"He was kinda already in the mud hole," Red said.

"He still have on his blindfold?" Mama said.

"Yes, ma'am," Red said.

"Then you're not saying this boy picked out the mud hole hisself."

"No. Joe was supposed to lead him around the mud hole."

"Joe?" Mama said.

"I told him to step up," Joe said. "But I told him too late. It was kinda my fault. I mean, him stepping into it in the first place and getting mud on his shoes and pants."

"But that don't account for that slop all over him," Mama said. "I swear! I don't see a spot on him that ain't covered in mud."

"It was then that he shrugged," Red said.

"Shrugged?" Mama said. "Thought you said he called you a bad name."

"Well, I uh shocked him the first time 'cause he shrugged."

"I see. Now, it's coming out. You shocked him twice 'stead of once. And you say he shrugged?"

"Yeah," Red said. "Like that. At Joe."

As the silence stretched out in the darkness, Doyle caught a whiff of food, something fried with onions and peppers mingled with the scent of apples and cinnamon.

"Boy, you shrug at Joe?" Mama said.

Doyle heard her, but with his hunger zeroed in on the food scent, he didn't know her words were aimed at him until a sharp elbow jabbed into his sore ribs.

"Uh, no ma'am," Doyle said.

"You didn't make any kind of motion aimed at Joe."

"No, ma'am."

"He's a lying little…" Red said.

"I didn't see him shrug," Sonny interrupted.

"Joe?" Mama said.

"He just kinda moved," Joe said, the words draining him of breath. "I didn't take it as a shrug."

"Then you shocked him," she said.

"Yes, ma'am," Red said. "But…"

"Then he fell in the mud," she said. "Was it then you called him a bad name, boy?"

"Yes, ma'am," Doyle said.

"And you admit you called him a bad name," she said.

"Yes, ma'am," Doyle said.

"I can see truth in what this boy says because he can admit when he done wrong," Mama said. "The whole thing's clear as a bell to me now. He stepped in the mud, and you got a little trigger happy with that cattle prod. Then he spoke out of turn 'cause he felt like he was being punished for something he didn't do."

She was quiet for a moment as if giving time for an objection that Doyle knew would never come. Then she said, "Sonny, you and Joe get them nasty clothes off him. Red, you come inside. I want to have a little talk with you."

While Sonny fiddled with the handcuffs, Joe said, "How'd she know what happened? It was just like she was right there with us."

"I'm telling you," Sonny said, "that woman's got powers they ain't even got a name for. Damn, I'm trying to unlock the handcuffs with the leg iron key. It's this damned tooth. Hurts so bad sometimes, I can't concentrate."

"I heard that," Red said. "Soon as Mama turns us loose, we're going to go get that thing fixed."

After his bath, Mama helped Doyle into dry clothes and called Red and Sonny to replace the handcuffs and shackles. Then she spoon-fed him pork chops, fried potatoes, collard greens and crisp cornbread pinched between her fingers.

"You don't like them old collards, do you, baby?" she said after he winced as a spoonful of the slime slid into his mouth.

"No, ma'am," he said with a shudder.

"Well, you eat 'em anyway. They real good for you."

After eating, she led him like a family pet to the same cushioned chair he sat in earlier, and the familiar coil spring gouged at his butt while music blared at him from somewhere in the room.

"That's the Blackwood Brothers," she called out as she rattled pots and pans. "They're one of my very favorite. Don't you just love them?"

"Yes, ma'am," he lied.

"Hear that J.D. Sumner on bass. He can really get down there, can't he?"

"Yes, ma'am."

After a while, the music stopped and he sighed as if he had just been relieved of a fierce tooth ache. "All right. All done," she said, her footsteps coming near. Then she scooted a chair in close, her knees bumping against his. "Got something for you," she said. "Lean forward and open your mouth."

When he leaned forward, he felt her hand close to his face as he breathed in the soapy scent of her fingers. "Open up," she said. He opened and she placed something on his tongue. As he chewed, he tasted banana and peanut butter and crispy butter-soaked toast.

"That's a fried 'nanner sandwich," she said. "Good, ain't it?"

"Yeb blam," he said, his mouth sticky with peanut butter.

"Let me give you a sup of milk."

After he finished the sandwich and washed the sticky down with milk, she wiped his mouth and caressed his cheek. "Want me to read some more to you?" she said.

"Yes ma'am," he said, thinking his passive little voice sounded as if it were coming from someone else's lips.

"All rightie, then," she said, pages rustling. "Where were we?" More pages rustling. "OK, Chapter Eight." She cleared her throat and began, "'And as the Lord had prophesied, the weeds and thistles grew up and smothered the wheat; and the corn tasseled out unto shriveled nubbins as if stillborn. When they ran out of buckets to catch the rain that dripped through the roof of the Mansell house, the floors collapsed. And William Mansell grew old watching his house rot, his cattle die and his children and swine drift off into the gathering forest...'"

15

DOCTOR NICK'S CLINIC

*R*ed had heard that Doctor Nick remodeled the clinic. He nodded approval to himself at the pictures of Elvis on the pale, green walls of the waiting room. He especially liked the huge blow-up of the King's iconic performance at the '56 state fair in Tupelo that covered the wall behind the reception desk. There were little clouds painted into the sky-blue suspended ceiling with the round bulb in the center casting out a glow like the sun. With all that bright light, he couldn't help noticing the place was spotless. After examining the floor closely, he couldn't see a single smudge or a grain of dust on the new beige tile. He breathed in a mixture of cloves and alcohol in the air, thinking the joint even smelled clean.

It was eerily quiet for the size of the crowd jammed in there. Only four adults sat in the eight rows of chairs, but with fifty or more school-aged children occupying the rest of the chairs and others standing with their backs to the walls like condemned prisoners waiting for a firing squad, he figured there should be some kind of racket going on even if it was nothing but whispers, giggles, and smacking gum. The only sounds he could hear were the air he sucked in past his deviated septum and the soulless, elevator version of "Heartbreak Hotel" wafting through the room on synthesized strings.

"Weird, huh?" he said. After getting no reply, he turned around to find Sonny nowhere in sight. He swung the door open and stepped back out into the sunshine to find his brother frozen at the bottom step of the clinic's entrance. "What the hell?" Red said.

"Hey, I think my tooth's all better," Sonny said.

"Bullshit," Red said. "A rotten tooth don't get better."

"No, it's...it's all better," Sonny said. "I...swear. It's a goddamned miracle is what I think."

"Look, I'm tired of hearing you piss and moan about that tooth. Come on in, and we'll get Doctor Nick to fix it."

"About this guy. This Doctor Nick. I don't get it. Is he a doctor or a dentist?"

"Both," Red said. "Mama said he couldn't get into med school right away, so he went to dental school. After he graduated from dental school, he got accepted into med school. She says we're lucky to have a guy who takes care of both."

"I don't know," Sonny said, twisting his head slowly. "Did the sumbitch study chiropractic and veterinary too? I mean, shit, I think I'd rather go to somebody who can make up his mind."

"Come on," Red said, clutching his brother's shoulder, "or I'll tell all the guys what a pussy you are."

He pushed Sonny inside and almost bolted himself when a scream rose from the door behind the reception desk, sending a shiver skidding up his spine. The kids around the wall twittered and looked around at each other in horror. Sonny tore himself away from Red's grasp and ran back through the door.

"Now, what the hell was that?" Sonny said after Red charged through the door and caught up with him outside at the foot of the steps.

"I've heard some of the girls who come here won't accept pain killers because they're afraid Doctor Nick will mess with them while they're out," Red said.

"Mess with 'em?"

"Yeah, you know, put his hand on their private parts."

"He does that shit?" Sonny said.

"There've been some complaints. Mama told me not to look too close into them because if I found anything I'd have to do something about it. He's the only doctor we've got, and he's supposed to be pretty good."

"I'm out of here," Sonny said.

"No, come on," Red said, grabbing Sonny's arm before

he could get away. "I won't let him hurt you."

Sonny trudged along with Red tugging at his arm. As Red pushed him through the door and down the aisle to the reception desk, a nurse in green scrubs stepped from behind a door with a clipboard in her hand. "Maria Ellis," she called.

"Hold up on Ms. Ellis," Red said as he walked past her, shoving Sonny along. The nurse nodded and followed them.

Doctor Nick, in green scrubs, stood at the door of an examining room beside a sobbing teenage girl. His thick white pompadour looked as if it had been sculpted to his head, and his pale blue eyes looked down on the girl as if he were going to take a bite out of her. "You will be fine," he told the girl in that slow, clipped accent Red had never quite figured out. "You make sure you scream like that for Elwis at the next serbice." He handed the girl a bottle of pills. "Take one of these erry three hours. For the pain." Red couldn't help noticing he whispered "the pain" as if he were saying a prayer. "The pain should be gone by tomorrow. If it isn't...you come back. Maybe I'll drill some more and help you practice your screaming."

Doctor Nick's cackling laughter echoed down the hallway as he placed his hand on the girl's shoulder. The girl, looking as if she were enduring some hellish misery, took the pills in her trembling hands and shuffled past Red and Sonny.

"Well, well," Doctor Nick said, still chuckling. "What hab I done to deserb the honor of a wisit from our great apostles."

"My brother's got a toothache," Red said.

"Well we can't hab our wonderful apostles going around with a toothache, now, can we?" Doctor Nick said. He motioned toward a room and said, "Right this way, and Doctor Nick will make that old ache go away before you know it.

"Right there in that chair," he added.

When his hand touched Sonny's back to guide him into

the dentist chair, Sonny slapped it away. "You don't put your hands on me," Sonny said.

"How can I examine you if I don't touch you?" Doctor Nick said.

"He's a little nervous," Red said.

"I understand," Doctor Nick said, nodding vigorously without disturbing a single hair in his heavily lacquered white pompadour. "People get nerwus when they go to a dentist or a doctor. And I'm both, so they get double nerwus when they come to see me. Would you like a nice Walum to calm you down?"

"Hell yeah, I want a nice *Walum*," Sonny snapped. "What was that little sister screaming about?"

"They are tough women, these Children we hab here," Doctor Nick said. "The women don't take pain killers any more."

"Well, *I* take pain killers," Sonny said.

"For my dental patients, I have Nowocain and Nitrous Oxide." Doctor Nick said.

"I want all that shit," Sonny said. "And anything else you got."

"Wery well," Doctor Nick said. He looked at Red. "You can wait outside if you like."

"Nah," Red said. "I'll wait here. Oh, and Doctor Nick?"

"Yes?"

"If my brother cries out in pain. I mean, if he even whimpers, I'll help you practice your own Elvis screaming. You understand what I'm saying?"

"I understand," Doctor Nick said behind a toothy smile.

"Hey!" Sonny said.

"Yes?" Doctor Nick said.

"Where's my fucking Valium?"

"I think in your case, I'd better put you all the way under," Doctor Nick said.

"That sounds like a good idea," Red said.

Sonny woke with Red, Doctor Nick and a nurse staring down at him in a glow of yellow light. "The unholy trini-

125

ty," Sonny mumbled.

"You all right?" Red said.

"Yeah," Sonny said. "I feel great. What happened?"

"I fixed your molar," Doctor Nick said. "You yust had a little cawutee with an exposed ner." While the nurse helped Sonny sit up, Doctor Nick scrambled through his medicine cabinet and turned, shaking a bottle. "I do not think you will hab further pain. But just in case, I'be got something really nice for you."

"What is it?" Sonny said, taking the bottle from Doctor Nick and holding it up to the light.

"Oxycontin," Doctor Nick said. "I don't want my faworite patient to experience pain. Well, my faworite next to Elwis of course."

When he patted Sonny on the arm, Sonny slapped his hand away. "What did I tell you about touching me?"

"I thought, since I yust had my fingers in your mouth, we were like family now."

"Let's get something straight," Sonny said as he stood, stumbling against Red. "You and me? We ain't no part of a family. You even hint to anybody that you had your fingers in my mouth, and I'll come back here and spell out my name on your skull with a ball peen hammer."

"Now, that's not nice," Red said. "Doctor Nick fixed your tooth and gave you some nice dope."

"Well," Sonny grumbled. He shrugged and said, "Thanks for the dope."

"My pleasure," Doctor Nick said. "Feel free to share it with your friends and tell them where you got it. Oh, Red, did you mention to Mama that little thing we were talking about?"

"What little thing?" Red said.

"About me becoming an apostle."

"Look, Nick, I told you. That shit ain't gonna happen."

"Why not? Am I not a trusted adwisor? Do I not help Elwis lead a pain-free life. And, after all, my woice is the last woice that Elwis hears."

"There ain't an apostle named Doctor Nick in the

book," Red said.

"You like all the nice drugs I hab, don't you?"

"You got some nice dope," Red said. "But the Doctor Nick in the book is just a doctor, and that's it."

"Can't the book be changed?"

"You're bullshittin' me ain't you?" Red said.

"No. I..." Doctor Nick said.

"The Blessed Mother wrote that book. She's up in Heaven. Now how is it gonna change?"

"I was just thinking..."

"Stop thinking and just be Doctor Nick. Let's go, Sonny."

Red led Sonny to the door with Doctor Nick following them to the reception desk. "What are all these kids doing standing around here?" Red said. "We got some kind of epidemic I don't know about?"

"Oh, no," Doctor Nick said. "Nothing like that. I just got a supply of medicine in, and it's time for waxinations. Most doctors have nurses waxinate the kids, but I'm a hands-on kind of doctor. I like to see the sharp needle puncture the little arms."

Feeling a little shaken by the doctor's last statement, Red's eyes followed the kids lined up around the room and shook his head. "How do you get them to stay so quiet?"

"Ah!" Doctor Nick said. "I will show you." He bent over and retrieved a hypodermic syringe the size of a bicycle pump. When he held it up, the gasp around the room sounded like a sudden gust of wind. "You don't have to worry. Ib yust had to use this one time, and no kid has spoken in Doctor Nick's clinic since. "

"You mean you actually..." Red said. Then he shook his head and said, "Oh, never mind. I don't even want to hear that shit,"

"Don't we need to get out of here?" Sonny said.

"Yes, we do," Red said.

"Oh," Doctor Nick said. "You should stay for the waxinations. It's amazing how I have trained them. When the needle goes in, they just stand there with tears streaming from their brabe little eyes. They don't eewun whimper."

"No," Red said. "I think I'll leave the *waxinations* to you."

And as he and Sonny walked through the waiting room, Red pointed to the floor, where puddles had collected under the feet of some of the kids. "Damn, they stood there and pissed on their selves instead of asking to go to the bathroom."

"That's fucked-up," Sonny said. After they stepped outside, he said, "Where'd Mama find that sumbitch, anyway? Transylvania?"

"I don't know," Red said. "But he knows where to find drugs."

"Yeah," Sonny said, rattling the Oxy. "He's creepier than a talking turd. But the boy does score some first-class dope."

PART FOUR

COMING HOME

16

ALL HER CHILDREN

After finally putting the boy to bed, Mama took the only remnant of her former life, her nightly glass of Napa Valley Cabernet, out to the front porch swing. The air was sweet with honeysuckle, a scent that always brought her home in her mind, no matter how far away she'd traveled. Fireflies rose from the boxwoods beside the steps. As she rocked, the squeaking chains of the swing accompanied the crickets serenading from the dark trees. Below, the glow from the big house and the little rectangles of light shining from the Village told her that her children were still awake. She took a sip of wine, thinking how they had essentially become her children, just as they used to be her daddy's.

Her daddy, R. J. Haney, had owned half the land in Reece County as well as the hosiery mill and controlling interest in the Willow Ruth Bank. And she, Carolyn Susan Haney, had grown up in a house that would have held Elvis' Graceland with a little room left over. The gaudy white edifice looked as if it had been modeled after her daddy's jowly face. It even had two dormers over the balcony that reminded her of her daddy scowling down on Maple Street through his smudged glasses.

There was little doubt that her daddy considered the workers at the mill to be his children, and as far as Carolyn could tell, they reciprocated by fearing him and loving him in pretty much the same way that she did. Carolyn realized that like his workers, the guiding force of her own life had always been to not disappoint R. J. And she didn't disappoint him for a minute till Elvis came along.

At the end of February in her junior year of high school, all anybody could talk about was this guy who kept coming on some television show on Saturday nights. Most of the kids didn't have television sets at home, so they hadn't seen him. But rumors of his performances rushed like ferocious waves lapping against the shore. Teenagers didn't actually have to witness the storm to know that something big had disturbed the waters. "Did you see that guy Saturday night?" they'd say. "Hey, did you see that guy?" "Oh, I didn't actually see him myself, but my cousin in Birmingham saw the show and said he made her want to uh. . . well, she said she had a hard time even breathing while he was singing." One of her girlfriends described him as the "dreamiest thing she'd ever seen" with "a pile of hair and sideburns down to here. And he hopped around like he was on fire or something."

She passed up a Teen Club dance so she and her friend Martha Simmons could watch the show everybody was talking about on the new twenty-one inch Zenith her daddy had bought. The two girls settled down on the floor together while her mama and daddy nestled behind them on the couch.

"Aren't they cute?" her daddy said as the show started with a brassy number from the band with a troop of chorus girls prancing through an intricate dance arrangement. "You *would* think so," her mother said, punching her daddy playfully on the arm.

Carolyn just wondered when they would ever quit all that silly kicking and bring on the guy with the sideburns. Martha sighed "Won't they ever just bring him out?"

Finally one of the old men hosting the show introduced a "young man with a provocative style," and her breathless, giddy feeling told her that something big was about to happen. With the TV being black and white and the reception a little snowy, she could only imagine the colors. But she could tell that the young man walking on stage, swinging a guitar from his neck, wore a light colored suit with a black shirt and white tie. His eyes were dark and brooding, and his lip curled into a rebellious sneer. Girls in the audience screamed, and Carolyn thought her heart would gallop out of her chest. He launched into a song about his blue suede shoes and how no one should step on them, all the while, shaking his legs as if the rhythm was gnawing at his insides. During an instrumental break, he hopped back beside the guitarist and bass player to dance, and Carolyn and Martha squealed along with the girls in the audience.

Her daddy jumped up and clicked off the television. "Nigger music," he growled.

"Daddy, please," Carolyn pleaded. "He was just..."

"No," her daddy snapped. "I won't have nigger music in my house. And all those gyrations were the most vulgar display I've ever seen in my life. I can tell you right now, you won't be watching anymore of this nonsense, Carolyn Sue."

But Carolyn didn't care what kind of music it was. She was already in love. Behind old R. J.'s back, she thought about Elvis all the time, bought all of his records and sneaked over to her girlfriends' houses to watch his appearances on *The Ed Sullivan Show*. Later that year, she lied to her parents, saying she was going to spend the night at Martha's while she went to the Willow Theater to see *Love Me Tender* with Buck Waggoner, a boy her daddy disapproved of only slightly less than Elvis.

Through her adult eyes, she could now see that Buck had been about as romantic as a six-pack of Pabst Blue Ribbon. And even though he had sported an Elvis-like pompadour of greasy black hair, he hadn't been all that much to look at either. Every time she thought about that night, and she thought about it a lot through the years, she liked to believe it was actually Elvis with whom she'd lain on the raggedy backseat of that old Studebaker. She'd always considered Buck Waggoner as just a convenient proxy.

In her sophomore year at the university she defied her father one more time by marrying a man whom her daddy dismissed as a "Yankee Jew" named Randall Cohen and moved with him to Connecticut. Early in the marriage she discovered that she wouldn't be able to have children, and Randall worked hard for the rest of his days, indulging her every whim to fill in the emptiness in her life. Over the years he took her to every Elvis movie and flew her out to Las Vegas fifteen times and Lake Tahoe twice to catch Elvis' shows. She still had the autographed dinner menu from the International for July 31, 1969 stored along with the first draft of *The Book of Gladys* in the Big House.

She couldn't recall where she had been when either Kennedy or Martin Luther King had been shot, but she remembered feeling as if her world had come to an end when the announcer on Danbury's oldies station reported that Elvis had died. Randall was working in the city, and she called his office in tears, only able to utter, "He died" through her burning throat. Randall, his cheerful voice melting into instant sympathy, replied, "I'm so sorry, Honey. I'll catch the next train out. If you can meet me in Brewster at six, we'll plan our trip on the way home."

"I'll already be gone," she said. "I hope you don't mind. I've chartered a private plane to Memphis."

"Memphis?" he said. "R. J. died in Memphis?"

"No, not Daddy," she said. "It's Elvis. He died this morning at Graceland."

She stayed in Memphis for eight days, through processions and candle-light vigils on Elvis Presley Boulevard. Randall finally came and talked her into going home. "Honey, don't you think it's time to go home and get on with our lives?" he said. "All this mourning's not healthy." But mourning wasn't what she and many of the people on the street were there for. They couldn't conceive of Elvis actually dying like an ordinary person and quietly believed that if they stayed on the street and prayed hard enough, he would return to them. She carried that belief back to Danbury. For years she returned to Memphis for vigils, and jerked copies of supermarket tabloids from the stand every time they ran a story of an Elvis sighting.

She always believed that Elvis would somehow reveal himself to her. And when years passed with no sign, she began following the impersonators in the hope that Elvis' spirit had entered some mortal vessel. Some of them were good imitators, but imitation was all they accomplished.

They lacked the charisma that came from Elvis' heart and shone from him like flashes of lightning in a storm. When Randall expressed concern over her obsession, she'd explained, "The Bible says some didn't believe anybody saw the resurrected Jesus, either."

Back in Alabama, her daddy had seen turbulence coming in the hosiery business and sold to a big clothing company a few years before foreign competition closed the mill. But he didn't live to enjoy his retirement very long. She was sure it killed him to see all his children wandering around Willow Ruth, unemployed and not knowing what to do next. At his funeral, former mill workers filled the pews of the First Baptist and spilled out into the parking lot and the street. They reverently moved aside for the family, and she could swear that as she walked by they stared at her as if they expected her to tell them how they were supposed to live their lives now that they didn't have the mill or the old man.

She had to return to Willow Ruth for more funerals during the terrible year that she lost first Randall and then her mother. It had been a long time since she'd been home, and driving into town in the rental car, she was sickened by the amount of litter strewn on the side of the interstate. Five miles outside of town, the landscape was scarred by a huge cluster of trailers that looked like a massive pile of garbage someone had cast across a treeless field.

Buck Waggoner, in his spit-shined boots and his badge shimmering from the pocket of his brown polyester uniform, stole glances at her all during the visitation at the funeral home. When she walked over to him, he blushed like a school boy. "Been missing you at our high school reunions," he said.

"I wanted to come," she said. "I was always too busy."

She made the mistake of asking about his life, and he nervously rattled off more than she ever wanted to hear about his wife, their three children and eight grandchildren, and concluded by asking her, "You never did have any kids, did you Carolyn?"

"No," she said. "Randall and I weren't able to have any. And Randall didn't want to adopt."

"Too bad," he said. "You would have been a great mother."

She knew he was trying to be kind, but it was the most depressing thing he could have said to her at this too-late time of her life. And she wondered if this insensitive bumpkin with a badge had actually been the boy she had given her virginity to back in 1956. But she let the remark pass and asked, "Buck, who lives in all those trashy trailers I saw when I drove into town?"

He shook his head, chuckled and said, "We call it the Tin Can Village. You remember Robert Goza?"

"How could I forget Robert? I went to the prom with him."

"I forgot about that. You damn-near broke my heart, too," Buck said behind a weak smile.

"He doesn't live there, does he?"

"Oh, no," he chuckled. "See, after they closed the mill down, the workers had to move out of the mill houses. Those who didn't move away mostly went on food stamps and welfare. Ol' Robert, always on the lookout for a dollar, got the bright idea to buy the Sanders farm, slap a bunch of ratty trailers out there in that field and move a bunch of those folks into them. I thought he was crazy as hell, but dad-gum if he didn't wind up getting the government to pay him rent."

"It sounds like a horrible place," she said.

"You don't know the half of it. We get called out there all the time for a shooting or a cutting or a wife beating. Anything gets stole around Willow Ruth? Well, that's where we go looking first. If things weren't bad enough, crystal meth hit that bunch like a smallpox epidemic. Then all those pills the drug companies crank out set 'em up for the Mexican brown heroin that's cheaper than a Snicker's bar. I'm gonna tell you, it's got so bad, I won't even go out there myself these days without a couple of deputies."

After the funeral, she went back to Danbury haunted by the image of the Tin Can Village. She wondered how there could be any justice in the world when her daddy's children had been tossed into a trash heap while Randall and her daddy had left her so wealthy she had to hire a whole platoon of accountants and lawyers just to calculate her net worth.

She had to do something. But how could she relate to them. Buck told her she sounded like a Yankee. Carolyn remembered from her days in Willow Ruth how the locals distrusted people from the outside. So she practiced for weeks with recordings of Appalachian women until she sounded a lot like a native again. She bought a wardrobe of simple house dresses and had her hair done in a cheap permanent. Finally, she bought a used double-wide trailer. Though the trailer's screw heads and seams were caked in rust, it still looked too nice to park in the Village till she had some men apply a few dents with sledge hammers and break three of the windows which she then had covered in silver duct tape.

But Buck insisted it wasn't safe for her to move in there alone. He recommended she hire his nephews, who had just lost their jobs at a bail bond service in Birmingham for being a little too rough with their clientele. "They ain't afraid of nothing," Buck said. "And both of 'em'll fight a circle saw."

Buck's description of the two didn't sound like much of a character reference, but she agreed that, given the reputation of the Village, a little security might be in order. While Carolyn moved into the Village, Eric and DeWayne Liddle took on the role of Carolyn's sons, and moved into a trailer next door to her.

Both men were tall with thick, muscular bodies. DeWayne's black hair was shoulder-length at the time, and he had a smug look in his eyes that seemed to be telling whoever he was looking at that he could take him with no problem in a stand-up fight. Eric had short-cropped red hair and a sprinkle of freckles on his cheek that would have made him look boyish if it weren't for the bent nose, the fierce look in his eyes, and the collection of scars across his face.

Both men immediately inhabited the roles they played as her sons, and consistently called her Mama from the day they moved in. They set up a weightlifting bench, a rack of dumbbells and a pile of iron plates outside their trailer, and spent most days drinking beer, listening to outlaw country and lifting.

Carolyn's next-door neighbor's son had become a terror in the Village. Carolyn relayed this to Eric and DeWayne while venting about all the problems she faced. Eric said, "Mama, I think that's one little problem we can fix for you purty quick."

"I wished you could," Carolyn said in her readopted Appalachian twang. "The Sheriff don't seem to be able to do nothing unless somebody swears out a warrant. And everybody's so afraid of him, they ain't going to do that for a second."

"Hey," Eric said. "He's probably a good boy. You know, just misunderstood and all."

"No, I think he's actually pretty dangerous," Carolyn said, slipping back into her Yankee accent. "Your uncle Buck believes he is."

"Naa," Eric said. "I'm sure he's not. All he probably needs is for somebody to take the time to 'splain things to him just right."

A week later, the boy disappeared off the face of the earth. When Carolyn asked Eric and DeWayne if they knew anything about his sudden absence, they looked at each other, shook their heads and shrugged. "Sometimes, people just vanish," Eric said. "Like that fellow we studied about in Sunday school. . . What was his name, DeWayne?"

"Enoch," DeWayne said.

"Yeah," Eric said. "Enoch. Disappeared into thin air. Now that's the Bible talking, not me, you understand. Maybe this Roger dude just got hisself Enoched."

As months went by, a number of other trouble makers had been Enoched. "Just got tired of being around," Buck Waggoner concluded after briefly investigating the disappearances. "Shoot, I don't blame 'em a bit. Other pastures wouldn't have to have much chlorophyll in them to be greener than what they had here. "

She was confident that even the bad people in the Village had come to fear her and her boys. But though fear was a useful tool in restoring order, she knew that she couldn't bring the children back without giving them hope. And giving them hope would require them to not just fear her but to have faith in her and love her as their parents had loved her father.

She had never been much of a Bible reader, but she bought one at the local Wal Mart, hoping to find inspiration. She saw the answer in the stories of the prophets. She didn't know whether God actually talked to Abraham, Isaiah and Moses, but what she found curious was that people believed them without any corroborating witnesses. After a few days of thinking, she had a revelation—all you really needed to be a prophet was what Randall always called, "chutzpah." You just had to find a bunch of people who really needed a prophet and the chutzpah to call yourself one.

Old-time religion had already been tried out on the Village, and it hadn't worked. These poor people felt as if everyone and everything had abandoned them. They needed a new-time religion with a new-time messiah. They believed in Jesus, but it looked as if Jesus needed some help. Why not Elvis? she thought. Back in August of 1977, hadn't she and the crowd on Elvis Presley Boulevard believed he was still alive? Hadn't she believed at one time that his spirit was out there looking for a home? Hadn't his life been a Christ-like miracle, rising from a hovel in Mississippi to unbelievable wealth and fame? What if he hadn't died?

They needed a text, some kind of holy scripture to lend authority to the new faith and give it structure. Since she would be leading the movement, she decided to make Elvis' mother, Gladys, the source of the scripture. After all, Elvis had been a mama's boy, and it just might be a good idea to have a Holy Mother. It sure worked for the Catholics. They were always seeing Jesus' mama in an old tree stump, an oil slick in a parking lot or a singed pancake down at the IHOP.

There was enough information on the details of Elvis' life to fill two Bibles. And, as she believed most religions had done, she cherry-picked the story, injecting just enough of the supernatural to give divine support to the narrative that she wove. The thing that really surprised her was that she wrote it so fast, she began to think that maybe the whole project had actually been divinely inspired.

For months, with Eric and DeWayne faithfully standing by, she conducted workshops on the text that she proclaimed the spirit of Gladys Presley had given her. Later, she produced pamphlets and trained a few of the more receptive Village residents to conduct discussion groups on the new belief. After her lawyers drew up the papers for the TCB Foundation, she deeded the foundation four thousand acres her father had left her out in the county and surrounded a huge chunk of it with a towering fence.

After a new village sprang from what had been nothing but abandoned mines among a tangle of scrub oak and pine, she led the Exodus from the trailer park. After that day, every time she felt a little blue, she recalled how the faces of the rag-tag refugees ignited in joy after she led them into the woods. Oh, she had them believing before they ever left the confines of their dilapidated trailers, but once they saw their new neighborhood with its neat modular homes set on tree-lined streets with parks for the families to enjoy, they really believed. The Village population was modest at first, but as economic conditions on the outside—in the Wilderness— worsened, she had to build more houses and employ guards to secure the fences.

The press had dubbed Elvis' apostles "The Memphis Mafia." She looked at Eric with his red hair, his ruddy complexion and penchant for fierce loyalty, and saw a perfect

Red West. She immediately renamed DeWayne, "Sonny" after Red West's brother, and before long they recruited ten others to fill the various roles of the Graceland denizens.

She'd promised the children the resurrected King, but she didn't have any idea where he would come from. "Got a million of them out there doing an Elvis show," Red said. "Why don't we just find the best one, and see if he wants to really be Elvis?"

The first problem of getting a prospect to Willow Ruth was solved by Robert Goza, who now managed the closest thing they had to a night club in Reece County, The Willow Ruth AMVETS. Carolyn could tell he still had a crush on her all these years by the way he continued to hang around the Tin Can Village long after she moved in. Like Buck, Robert had grown chubby, and every time she looked at him, she thanked God that she'd had better judgment than to get hooked up with him. But she'd found him useful since he had some rapport with the Children. He had a talent for public speaking that she remembered from high school, and he seemed to relish the idea of putting it to use as part of a new religious movement. "We'll just offer him a pile of money to perform at the AMVETS," he said when she asked him if he had any ideas on luring a messiah to Willow Ruth. "Hey, I could be like the Colonel."

But a performer who wanted to act like Elvis was light years away from him actually being Elvis. And to survive, what this religion needed was Elvis, not a cheesy imitation. All the other features of the religion could be accomplished with money and willing assistants. She was sure she had gone too far in offering the children a messiah. After all, there had been but one Elvis, and there would never be another. Still, she couldn't get the idea out of her mind that his spirit was out there floating around, looking for an appropriate place to land.

After moving into the newly finished Big House, she stayed locked in her room for days, actually thinking about burning the whole thing down. Eric and DeWayne banged on her door, but she ignored them. In her despair, she opened the Bible and read for hours until she became stuck on Mathew 18:3, reading it over and over— "except ye be converted and become as little children, ye shall not enter the kingdom of heaven."

"Become as little children," she said. "That's the answer." A few of the impersonators actually had the voice, the looks and the moves down. But that's all they were, just the appearance. But Elvis had much more than talent. He had a fire that glowed from somewhere inside him. It made people want to get close and be warmed by it.

But where had that fire come from if not from his childhood? She would find the most promising of the impersonators and make him into a little child who depends on her for his survival. Then she would raise him up as Elvis and replace his old life with that of a king.

To bring up her child into the world as Elvis, she had a replica of Elvis' Tupelo birthplace built on a hill overlooking the whole compound—the past overlooking the future. She now sat on the porch of that house, finishing her wine while thinking about her new child lying in gestation on the bed inside. She could hear him rattle the headboard and the footboard as he tried to roll over. Tomorrow, she would remove the blindfold and the chains, and he would really start being born again.

17

MAMA'S BIG BOY

*D*oyle no longer woke hoping the whole thing had been just a horrible dream. The darkness and the clanking chains against the headboard had become as familiar as sunrise and morning coffee used to be. He'd started out counting wake-ups to keep his mind active, but he'd given that up back when he gave up hope of ever waking up again. At least once a day, Red and Sonny reminded him that they could kill him at any time and just might if Mama didn't think things were going well.

The verbal abuse, the chains, even the cattle prod had become the rough spots in this dark life. Mama smoothed everything over with her calming voice and her touch that he looked forward to as much as her delicious food.

He had become accustomed to everything until the morning he woke gasping for air and rattling his chains with a cold hand resting on his throat. "Be still. Be still," a man's voice snapped through a thick accent as fingers pressed the soft spot under his ears. "Ummhum. Ummhum," the voice said. Without seeing him, Doyle knew it was the white-haired man he'd seen slinking through the foyer, and he thought he'd rather feel the shock of the cattle prod than to have these clammy hands touching him. After pressing what Doyle figured was a stethoscope to his chest, he fixed a Velcro blood pressure wrap around Doyle's arm.

"Well?" Mama said.

"He is fine," the man said. "Yust fine."

Doyle heard them moving across the room and out on the porch with Mama asking, "Did you look in on my baby this morning?"

"Elvis is coming along as expected. He's completely off his wite-imins so I don't recommend..."

They stepped out of the house, the door whapping shut behind them. Red had joined them on the porch, talking about "the boy doing good," in his boisterous voice. Something was different. First the physical exam, then the change in their voices. He couldn't quite hear it all, but it was "the boy this," and "the boy that" and something about the boy being ready. The door squeaked, and heavy steps shuffled into the room.

No matter how curious he was, he knew not to speak unless he was spoken to. He didn't care what it was as long as it didn't involve being touched by Doctor Nick. Hands touched his blindfold. "You need to keep your eyes shut, partner," Red said. "I'm going to take off your blindfold, and the light's likely to be too bright for you. The last thing we want is to hurt your eyes."

Doyle felt excited and frightened at the same time. He had been in the dark so long, he thought the skin might have grown over his eyes like those blind fish he'd heard of people catching in caves.

"Here, let me slip these shades on you, and then you can open your eyes," Red said.

The glasses were so dark all he could see was Mama's shadow hovering over him. And as the others unlocked his shackles, she said, "Hey, Baby. You hungry?"

"Yes, ma'am," he said.

"What would my baby like for breakfast this morning?"

He'd been limited to yes ma'am, no ma'am for so long the question was confusing. He wondered if he could even form any other sentences. *When did he ever get to decide anything?* And as he thought over the question, he considered the possibility that it was a trap. Maybe they were trying to see if he would reply with something other than the prescribed answers and punish him with the cattle prod. But something was different. Not only had they removed his blindfold, they weren't putting handcuffs on him. And he could sense the change in the air from the way Red's hand rested on his shoulder and the friendly tone in his voice.

"Would you like some egg gravy?" Mama said. "And a couple of Mama's big old cathead biscuits?"

"Yes, ma'am," he muttered.

"You can speak, Baby," she said. "You can say stuff other than yes, ma'am. Go ahead and say, egg gravy."

"Eh...guu," he said, cautiously approaching the answer while feeling as if his tongue were tripping over the roof of his mouth.

"Come on..." she said. "You can do it."

"Egg," he said. "Egg gravy."

She grabbed him and hugged him, rocking him back and forth as she squeezed. "That's my big boy," she said, and as she rocked, the shades tumbled off his ears. The light in the room made him feel as if he were looking directly into the sun, and he closed his eyes while Red picked up the shades and placed them back on his nose.

He had become so accustomed to the little tug from the shackles at the end of his stride that he stumbled a couple of times as he walked into the little kitchen. "Look at him," Mama said. "Look how my boy is walking."

After he sat at the table, Mama placed a biscuit in front of him, cut it open and poured the thick gravy over it. Without thinking, his mouth opened wide like a baby bird.

"No, sweetie," she said, putting a fork in his hand. "You're going to feed yourself today."

He realized that he'd been using forks for thirty years, but somehow the one he held now felt as if it weighed ten pounds.

After breakfast he stammered around until he was able to explain that he wanted to go to the bathroom. "You can go on out to the privy by yourself," she said, pointing out the back.

He wandered out the door, but Red watched him from the back door. After he returned, Red said, "Pretty bad, huh?"

Doyle nodded.

"You won't have to go out there many more times. I

think Mama's 'bout to move you over to the Big House."

Mama leaned over him as he washed his own hands in the sink. "We'll have our lesson after dinner," she said. "I think I'll let you go out and play with the boys now. Think you'll like that?"

Hell, no I won't like it, he thought, but blurted, "Yes, ma'am" like a recording.

Then she kissed him on the cheek. "I think you're eyes are getting adjusted. Got something for you," she said, and she exchanged his extra-dark glasses for a pair of regular sun glasses. Then she led him into the kitchen, placed a small red pill in his hand and poured him a glass of water from the pitcher she kept in the ice box. "You need lotsa energy, and this vitamin'll help keep you going."

He looked down at the pill for a moment, wondering what the hell she was trying to get him to take. Asking about the pill crossed his mind till she snapped, "You take it now," and he could almost feel the electric jolt that came from not following her instructions.

"Yes, ma'am," he said. He popped the pill in his mouth and chased it with a quick gulp of water.

"You know who you are, don't you?" she said.

"Yes, ma'am," he said.

"Who?"

"Doyle," he said.

"No!" she snapped. "That's not your name. And you're never to say that again. Do you understand?"

"Yes, ma'am," he said while making up his mind for the first time in his life to be Doyle Brisendine.

"You're my boy," she said, giving him a big hug. "My big boy. Now, go on with the boys, and be sure to get back here by eleven-thirty. We gonna have surprise company. You just make sure you get on back here on time."

"Yes, ma'am. I will," he said.

Red, Sonny, and Joe waited for him in the yard. He halted on the top step and looked the three over carefully.

He wasn't sure what a cattle prod or stun gun looked like, but neither of these men appeared to be armed with anything.

"What are you waiting on?" Red said.

"Oh, nothing," Doyle said. "Just getting used to the light."

"Well, let's get going," Red said. "We want to show you around."

He found himself lingering over small things that he knew he had seen before but had somehow forgotten. When he stopped off to pee in the woods, he found himself hypnotized by the deep green of a dogwood leaf. "Boy, what the hell you doing back there?" Sonny called.

Red chimed in, "If you shake it mor'n twice, you're playing with it."

"I'm coming," Doyle called back. When he joined Red, Sonny and Joe he said, "Thought I saw a snake back there."

"Snake?" Sonny chuckled. "Only snake you saw was that thing you had in your hand."

"Yeah," Red said, jostling Doyle's shoulder. "Like a hooded cobra getting ready to strike, huh Boy?"

The men slapped each other on the back and laughed way out of proportion to any humor in Red's quip. Doyle laughed too. Something had changed. They acted as if they liked him.

At the lake, overhanging willows shaded the murky water where a gaggle of fat geese fed on minnows in the shallows, and three scrub cows wallowed in the mud along the banks. Doyle reached the banks of the lake and looked down. Over the trees he could see the big house and the brick wall that joined to a chain-length fence taller than a man's head and laced with a swirl of razor wire. A van kicked up a cloud of dust on the road in front of the big house, then stopped at the gate to be greeted by the gatekeeper. Shadowy men with shouldered weapons stepped from the woods to take a closer look. With a wave of the gatekeeper's arm, the armed men stepped back into the woods, and the van rolled through the open gates.

As Red trudged on ahead, Sonny tapped Doyle on the shoulder and held up a paper bag. He smiled and reached into the bag and dug out a handful of breadcrumbs. As they approached the lake, he smiled and began tossing a trail of the crumbs across the water and on the ground as they walked along. The geese waddled up on the bank, then trailed close behind the men, pecking at the crumbs, stopping to raise their necks up to swallow.

"Hey, Red," Sonny said as he tossed a handful of crumbs toward Red. "You got an old friend back here wants to talk to you about something."

"What?" Red said, wheeling around. And when he saw the goose, terror flickered through his eyes. "Sonny, you son-of-a-bitch," he said as he took off running with the gander close at his heels, flying to catch up and peck at his ankles.

"Sonny!" Red called from the far bank. "Get this damn thing away from me."

Doyle, Joe and Sonny fell all over each other laughing till Red finally stopped. The gander flogged furiously as Red turned and grabbed the bird. After clutching the bird's neck and giving it a quick twist, he tossed it into the weeds. When Doyle and the other men caught up to Red, the gander was flopping around in a circle through the tall grass.

"Goddamn, Red," Sonny said. "You didn't have to kill it."

"Oh, he ain't dead yet," Red snarled. "But the sumbitch's gone wish he was."

He walked into the weeds and picked the wiggling bird up by the feet. "Boy, come on with me," he said, motioning to Doyle. "Got something you need to see."

Doyle followed Red to a trail that led into the woods, the goose flopping in his grasp. Sonny and Joe followed along behind. "What now?" Sonny sighed.

"Just going to show the boy the possibilities of this fence," Red said. Then he turned to Doyle and said, "You see that fence?"

"I see it," Doyle said.

"Just touching that damned thing'll make a jab from my little electric stick feel like you was getting massaged by a Japanese geisha." He swung the gander around his head and tossed it to the fence. As it hit the links, sparks burst around the bird and it crashed to the ground, the smoke rising from its singed feathers carrying a sickening smell.

"Hey, Red," Sonny said. "How much longer you going to mutilate that goose?"

"I think I made my point."

"Well I hope you did 'cause if we left right now, we'd be late."

Doyle, still staring down at the singed goose, jumped as a hard fist pounded his shoulder.

"You coming with us?" Red said.

"Yeah," Doyle said.

"I hate being late," Sonny grumbled.

"Won't be the first time," Joe said.

"Yeah, and won't be the last, either," Sonny said. "I just hate to get Mama all pissed. Fucks up my whole day."

18

THE BEST LESSON OF ALL

*M*ama waited on the porch as they approached the little house. Her arms were crossed tightly under her breasts, lips pouting like a child. "Where you children been?" she snapped, her voice seething with anger. "I got dinner getting cold in there," she said, pointing toward the door. "And we got company waiting. This ain't nothing but trashy behavior. And I won't tolerate trashy behavior for a second."

"We got kinda sidetracked," Red said.

"*Sidetracked*," Mama said, shaking her head. "You're always getting sidetracked."

"Tried to tell you," Sonny said out of the side of his mouth.

"We'll talk about all this *sidetracked* bidness later," she said. "Right now, the boy's got to come in and get washed up for dinner."

Mama stood on the porch of the little house, shaking her head as the trio loaded into a black Eldorado. "Don't you go taking after them," she said to Doyle. "Them three won't never grow up."

"No, ma'am. I won't," Doyle said.

From beyond the threshold, mingled with the odor of boiled collards and fried meat, a faint scent wafted into his nostrils, a sweet scent that triggered a vision before he even saw her, sitting there in the armchair, calmly smiling up at him, her sleek, black hair pulled back into a ponytail.

"Boy," Mama said after he stepped in behind her. "This is Dixie. She's come over to have dinner with us."

"I'm pleased to meet you, Boy," she said in a polite, girlish voice wrapped in a lilting diphthong that made Boy come out, Baw-wee. And she raised her arm and dangled her hand at the wrist as if she wanted it to be kissed.

"I can't believe you kept this girl waiting while y'all gallivanted around in the woods all morning. Now what you got to say for yourself?"

What do I say? he thought. *I say, You lured me into this place, now I want to wrap my hands around your neck and squeeze till those brown eyes pop out of your head and dangle down your cheeks.* But he wouldn't say anything. He would accept whatever Mama put in front of him.

"I believe he's kinda shy around girls," this woman who called herself Dixie said.

Figuring he would play along, he reached out for her hand. And when her fingers curled softly around his, he felt as if his skin held a memory of the last time he held her hand. Yes, it was the same woman all right, but Dixie wasn't her name. And what happened to her eyes? Instead of the flirtatious brown jewels he remembered silently promising sex to him from across the table at the AM-VETS, these looked up at him, blinking in some kind of calf-like innocence.

And what was up with this lame costume? In a prim, white blouse buttoned to her collar bone, hiding the peek-a-boo cleavage he remembered, she looked as if she had sprung from that upside-down flower of a blue skirt with its hint of white petticoat spread out across the chair. She had thin lace-top white socks turned down at the ankles and the shiny ballerina slippers planted firmly on the floor. The smooth curve of her knees were pressed together so tightly it looked as if it would take a crowbar to ever pry them apart.

But he got the message—Mama wanted him to act as if he'd never seen her before. So he cleared his throat enough to say, "Sorry I kept you waiting, Miss Dixie."

"Well, you should be," Mama scolded.

"Oh, they were just being boys," Dixie drawled slowly.

"If y'all will excuse me, I'm going in here and check on our dinner," Mama said.

"Let me help you, Mama," Dixie said, bending forward

with her hands clutching the chair arms.

"Oh, no. You two stay right where you are and get acquainted. I'll call y'all directly."

He and the woman stared at each other while the hollow clanging pots chimed in from the kitchen. The woman finally swallowed and said, "I been hearing a lot about you Boy."

"About me?"

"Well, who else am I talking about, silly?"

"Who'd be talking about me?"

"You know, Mama. And the main apostles—Red, Joe, and Sonny."

She blinked her eyes and curled her lips into a pouty smile as she looked down at the small hearth and the cold, gray ashes piled in the dormant fireplace.

"Y'all 'bout ready?" Mama called as if she were summoning them from the yard.

"Yes ma'am," Doyle called back. Then he looked down at Dixie.

"Well?"

"Well what?"

"What did they say?"

She smiled and shrugged. "Oh, they just said you're nice, and you've been studying the book really hard and all."

"Funny," he said. "They haven't said anything about you."

"No?"

"No," he said, shaking his head. "They haven't."

She glanced down at her lap and brushed her skirt straight, then looked back up. "To tell the truth, I think the boys are kinda jealous of you. And Mama probably wants to keep you all to herself. You know how mamas are sometimes."

"Think they've got anything to worry about?"

"Dinner's on the table," Mama said, now peeking her head from the kitchen.

Dixie reached out her hand and Doyle held it, helping

her to her feet as her lips parted in a smile and that sexual promise returned to her eyes. "Maybe," she said. Then, drifting back into character, she blushed and looked at the floor.

The three of them jammed in around the little table in the cramped kitchen. His hatred for the woman's part in his imprisonment was now being trumped by the fragrance she wore and the heat from her knee pressed against his.

"Dixie's going to handle your afternoon lesson for a change," Mama said. "Think you'll like that?"

"Yes, ma'am," he said, glancing over at the woman, giving her knee a nudge. "I think I will."

"This is sooo good, Mama," Dixie said in a breathless voice, ignoring Doyle's eyes as she pressed back against his knee and sawed dainty bits of ham, then scooped tiny morsels of sweet potato with her fork.

"Boy, you're not touching your food," Mama said. "You feeling all right?"

"I'm good," he said, now remembering the food steaming in the plate in front of him. She had cut him the corner piece of crisp, brown cornbread that he liked, and he picked it up and held it as he looked down at the greens, glistening with ham hock juice, thinking, *Yuck*!

"Boy, you better eat," Mama said. "You can't have no 'nanner puddin', you don't finish your dinner."

Mama's desserts were wonderful, and thoughts of creamy chunks of banana and soft vanilla wafers under toasted waves of meringue took his mind away from the woman beside him. He steeled himself to the task of choking down the pile of collards in front of him.

"Boy loves him some 'nanner puddin', don't you Boy?" Mama said.

"Ummhum," Doyle said around a mouth full of collards.

After they had eaten, Mama gave Doyle another vitamin. "It'll help you pay attention and learn more," she said, handing him a glass of water. While Mama cleaned the kitchen, Dixie and Doyle sat on the porch swing, Dixie with the big red book open in her lap. He thought Mama was right about that vitamin, this woman had his total attention.

"'It came to pass that when Elvis walked the halls of East Tupelo Consolidated, all eyes fell upon him,'" Dixie read. "'And idle talking and childish mischief ceased as if the children had been struck dumb by his beauty.

"'Now, Oleta was the eldest daughter of the man who bore false witness against Vernon, the father of Elvis, causing Vernon to be enslaved on Parchman Farm. And after she was appointed as the teacher of Elvis' class, Satan came to her in a dream, saying 'Watch how haughty and proud this Elvis child is. Bring him to the front of the class and ridicule him. The children will recognize him for the white trash that he is and rebuke him.'"

"What's rebuke, anyway?" Doyle said.

"Well, kinda like, voicing disapproval."

"I would never rebuke you," Doyle said as he considered leaning over and nuzzling the fine hairs on the back of her neck.

"Well, I would hope not," Dixie said. "But we need to get back to the lesson."

"You smell too good for rebuking."

"Moving right along. 'So upon commencement of the class, Oleta called Elvis to stand at the front of the room and asked, 'How can one so small and poor, whose father is disgraced, be so arrogant?'

"'And Elvis spake, saying, "My father is not disgraced. I am but a small servant bringing His kingdom to the Earth any way I can. 'And when he began to sing *Old Shep* all the children in the class were filled with the beauty of his voice.

"'Oleta, being much angered, clutched Elvis' hand and pulled him to the office of Principal Cole saying, 'When I brought this child to the front of the class to explain his arrogance, instead of answering, he defiantly sang a song.'

"'And standing in Principal Cole's office, Elvis sang,

Old Shep. Tears filled Principal Cole's eyes, and he beseeched Elvis to sing to all the children at assembly.'"

"What's beseeched?" Doyle said. He knew the meaning of the word, he just wanted to slow the story down.

"You know, like, begged."

Yeah, he thought, sucking in a deep breath of her as he looked out across the yard bathed in the warm sun. *I'm totally going to beseech your ass in a minute.*

"Let's see," Dixie said. "'Elvis sang *Old Shep* to all the school's children at assembly...'"

A mockingbird chattered and trilled from the trees as Mama stomped around the little box of a house, opening the windows while she sang. Then the growl of static from the speaker in the room and the muffled harmony of the Chuckwagon Gang singing, "The Gloryland Way" spilling out on the porch meant she would be bent over, scrubbing the scarred linoleum with that old mop of hers.

He thought about the possibility of Mama stalking out on the porch at any moment. But he thought, *I'm in the gloryland way myself.* Figuring this was worth the risk, he slid his hand over Dixie's thigh.

"Quit it!" Dixie whispered as she pushed his hand away, looking around as if they were being watched. "Mama'll get mad."

"Nah. She won't even see us," he whispered back, as he moved his hand back to her leg. "She's in there scrubbing that old floor. Besides, my hand's under the book. She can't see under the book."

"She sees everything," Dixie said, grabbing his hand and pushing it away again.

"Now where was I?"

"I don't know where you were," Doyle said, sliding his hand back on her thigh. "But I was right here."

She sighed and pushed his hand away again. "No," she snapped in a whisper. "She'll ask you about the lesson, and you'll get in trouble when you don't know anything about it. Then I'll get in trouble for not teaching you."

"You already know this stuff, don't you?"

"Yes," she said. "Of course."

"Then give me the short version. You know, kinda sum it up for me. Then we'll have time to talk."

"Weeell," she said, rolling her eyes, thinking for a moment. "It goes kind of like this—E astonishes all the teachers with his wisdom and songs. Then he walks and hitchhikes to the radio station and sings with Mississippi Slim. People call in and write in, wanting to know who this little angel is. And that's about it."

"She always tells me what the lesson is supposed to teach," Doyle said, chin pointing toward the house. "Damned if I can figure this one out."

"Well, silly," she said. "It's obvious that this one tells us that E was born with a godlike generosity and a wonderful voice. His voice, his charisma and his wisdom were all direct gifts from God."

"If you tilt your head this way a little more, I could just about kiss you," Doyle said, leaning into her shoulder.

"Somebody'll see us," she said, whispering again.

"Nobody's looking at us," he said. "Even if they were, we could hold the book up and hide behind it."

"Well, what makes you think I would want you to kiss me, anyway?"

"Ah," he said, smiling. "I can tell."

"Oh, you can?"

"Yeah. I can prove it to you. I bet you that if we hold that book up in front of our faces like we were totally into the story and all, then lean in close, you wouldn't be able to keep from kissing me."

"That's ridiculous."

"OK, let's try it, then," he said, clutching half of the book.

Together, they picked up the book and held it closely in front of their faces. "Now, watch," he said. "You won't be able to help yourself."

When he leaned in and pressed his lips to hers, she backed away with a gasp. "Not fair," she said. "You kissed *me*."

"You kissed back."

"Did not," she said.

"Let's try it again and I'll show you."

She didn't move when he leaned in and kissed her. After a moment when her lips surrendered and her tongue flicked against his, he wrapped his arm around her shoulders and pulled her close. Then he pulled away and whispered, "Let's go somewhere. My Little Elvis has got something to prove to you."

"No. We can't," she whispered back, releasing her grip on the book to peel his hand from her shoulder and push it away. "Besides, I don't know what you're talking about."

He'd forgotten all about the book, and it slipped from his hand and dropped to the porch with a hollow thud. Dixie scrambled from the swing and retrieved the book as the screen door swung open and Mama appeared in the threshold. "Y'all doing all right out here?" Mama said.

"Yes, ma'am," Dixie said, clutching the book under her arm. "I was just stretching a little."

"Y'all having you a good lesson?" Mama said as Dixie sat back down in the swing and opened the book.

"Oh, yes ma'am," Doyle said. "I believe this is one of the best."

"I'm glad you're enjoying it. Well, don't mind me, y'all get back to it."

"We will," Doyle said.

When Mama ducked inside, Doyle slid his arm back around Dixie. "Come on," he pleaded in a whisper. "Let's go somewhere."

"She'll catch us."

"She's not going to catch us. And if she does, we'll just say we didn't know we shouldn't."

"She knows I know better. You'd just get a shock from Red's cattle prod. They're already pissed at me, so I'd probably get something worse."

The thought of the cattle prod shriveled his erection for a moment. But when it stirred again, he knew he wanted Dixie even more than he feared Red's punishment. "Let's just step over to the side of the house," he whispered. "We could make out there. Nobody'd see us."

"No," she whispered back.

"We'd just make out. I swear. Nothing more. You know you want to."

"I know what's wrong with you," she said. "You've just got the Devil in you." She placed the book across his lap and whispered in his ear, "I think I know how to get him out."

"You do? You some kind of exorcist or something?"

"Something like that," she said. "Just look down at the book like you were really studying."

"What're you...?" he said as her hand slipped up his thigh.

"Shh," she said. "Look at the book."

When her hand pressed around the bulge in his pants, he closed his eyes, and his breath caught in his throat. "I... No. Let's..." he said, his chest rising and falling as if he'd just ran all the way back from the lake.

"Shh," she said.

He wanted to grab her, run his hands under that flower-shaped skirt and feel the soft flesh on the inside of her thigh. But all he could do was close his eyes, stretch out his legs and lean back stiffly in the swing, causing the chains attached to the stud over the porch to complain with a mournful squawk. And he froze there in exquisite torture with her warm breath tickling his ear and the whit-whit sound of her hand sliding back and forth over his denim to the rhythm of the The Chuck Wagon Gang blaring, "I'll Fly Away." Then a paralyzing spasm rocked him like a hard jolt from Red's cattle prod. And he collapsed into the swing.

When he sighed and opened his eyes, Dixie stood over him and took the book from his hands. Then she placed it in the swing beside him. She held her palm toward him and crinkled her nose. "See," she said. "The Devil came all the way through." And she smiled and blinked her soft eyes at him before wiping her hand on the knee of his jeans.

"I've gotta go, Mama," Dixie called.

"OK, baby," Mama called back. "Thanks for everything."

"Glad to help," Dixie said. "I think we really got somewhere today."

Mama appeared in the doorway, leaning against the mop she held in both hands. "I'm glad to hear that," she said. "I figure the boy can benefit from a different teacher ever' now and then, especially one close to his own age."

"I'm just pleased I could help," Dixie said. Then she turned to Doyle and smiled. "Now, don't you forget what we learned today, Boy," she said.

As he mumbled, "Oh, I'm...I." Dixie had turned and stepped off the porch. And before he could spit out an answer that made any sense, she'd hopped into the back of a black limo with her ponytail swishing behind her neck as if it were waving goodbye to him.

19

THE SHUNNED

Rhonda thought the driver acted a little grouchy when she got into the limo. For one thing, she had to open the door for herself. He grunted like a bear and shook his head when she told him she wanted to go back to the Big House. But she was having too good of a day to worry about one of the Children who was probably just having himself a *bad* day for some reason.

She figured she had at least two things going for her—she still had her room in the Big House, and Mama had picked her for an important assignment that she had pulled off pretty well if she did say so herself. She had to admit, she wouldn't have been her own first choice to play a 1950s teenager. She knew she was too old, well, too mature, for the part. The fact that there were hundreds of actual teenage girls in the Village who would crawl across a mile of broken glass to play the role told her that Mama might be amenable to work her back into the Big House cast despite the fact that she had knocked Elvis on his high-holy ass.

She had to admit that she had enjoyed the teenage role, especially the awkward, adolescent sexual encounter on the porch swing. She still felt the heat from the wild desire the boy had for her, and the command she had over him for that minute-and-a-half or whatever flash of time it was, sent goose bumps across her skin. For a second, she worried how good Mama's new prince was going to be if he was that quick on the trigger. Well, she was sure that wasn't her problem.

"Heard how the King's doing?" the driver said as he pulled the limo into the carport.

She didn't know if the drivers were under orders not to speak, but, as long as she'd been riding in limos in The

Land of Grace, the only words one of them had spoken to her had been, "Where to, Miss?" and "When should I expect you back?" and maybe a little, "yes ma'am" or "no ma'am" thrown in.

"Uh, last I heard, he was doing fine," she said.

"Know what's wrong with him?" the driver said.

She thought, *Duh! Too much Doctor Nick dope*, but, remembering the Children were never to hear anything negative about the King, she said, "I think it's the flu."

In the rearview mirror she could see the driver's black, short billed cap pulled down over his eyes, and the smirk that distorted his lips as if he'd gotten a whiff of a dead rat or something.

"Flu, huh?" the driver said. "Well, that's good. We were all worried he might have complications from that *concussion* he had a while back."

She waited for him to come around and open the door for her. But when he didn't budge after she counted to a hundred, she got out herself and slammed the door behind her. She had no doubt that this was the bastard's little way of telling her he wasn't about to forgive her for parting Elvis' shiny black hair with that ceramic lion.

After changing into jeans, a white top, and putting up her hair, she stomped through the Big House, still a little pissed at the driver. As she stepped out of the back door she could see apostles Jerry and Lamar loitering outside the Racquetball Building. Hoots rose from some big game they had going on inside. Jerry yelled "I got next," so loud they probably heard him over in Willow Ruth.

"Apostles," she scoffed, shaking her head, thinking they acted more like children than children. They went around telling everybody they were interpreters of the scripture and advisors to the King. But their job seemed to be nothing more than playing all the time and trying to keep Elvis amused.

The woman standing by the office door in a pale green shirtwaist dress didn't look like one of the custodial staff, and she definitely wasn't any member of the Kitchen crew that Rhonda remembered. Since she had that 1950s' blond hair flipped-up on the end, Rhonda figured she had to be one of the Children, probably a housewife or teacher, completely unauthorized to be here.

"Can I help you?" Rhonda said.

"You Rhonda?" the woman said.

"I am," Rhonda said as she slipped her key into the office door.

"My name's Shelia Barksdale," the woman said.

Rhonda had never seen this woman before, but she was known throughout the Land of Grace these days as *The Slut Who Corrupted an Apostle*. She thought the last thing she needed was to get caught anywhere around this bitch.

"Hold it right there," Rhonda said. "You're not supposed to be here."

"I guess this means you heard about me being shunned."

"Well, you've got to admit, you are pretty damned shunable."

"How about you? Aren't you being shunned?"

"Me?" Rhonda said as she opened the door. "I don't know what you're talking about."

"I hear everybody talking about how you almost killed the King with a..."

"Now wait right there. Let's get this straight. That was a big misunderstanding that was blown way out of proportion... Are the Children still talking about that?"

"When they're not running *me* down," Shelia said.

Rhonda leaned on the door facing, squinting her eyes as if she were trying to see through the skull of this woman—this woman who was obviously attractive despite the red eyes and the worry lines wrinkling her forehead.

"You're just going to have to leave," Rhonda said. "I can't afford to be caught talking to you."

"Please," Shelia said. "Just a give me a few minutes. God! Listen to me. I've gotten so lonely, I've stooped to begging people to talk to me. I think...I think I'm going crazy sometimes."

Rhonda looked behind the woman at Jerry and Lamar standing guard at the Racquetball Building. The apostles knew Mama was busy and the King was upstairs at the Big House flat on his back. So without anything to do, they were probably up to their usual apostle pastimes—playing games, drinking beer, and passing a bong around.

"Come on in before an apostle sees you," Rhonda said. When Shelia walked in, Rhonda closed the door and locked it.

"Now, what are the Children saying about me?" Rhonda said.

"They're all pretty much pissed that you haven't disappeared, been horse-whipped out in the Village square or something. They think you're some kind of witch who's put Mama under a spell."

"What? That's the craziest thing I ever heard."

"I'll admit, I was right along with them till they started shunning me. Shunning! Can you imagine? I didn't even know that was really a thing."

"They actually think I'm a witch, huh?"

"I thought all this shunning would blow over after a while. But then, my husband and daughter moved out. While I'm standing there trying to make sense of the whole thing, Brad, my husband, walked right by me like I wasn't even there and stuck a note on the fridge telling me they were moving out. Wouldn't say a word to me. My own husband."

"Wonder where they got the idea about a witch," Rhonda said, moving across the room, her eyes wandering around the pictures of Elvis on the walls.

"I've just been sitting around waiting for them to come for me," Shelia said. "You know, make me disappear like they did apostle Joe. They say they come in the middle of the night. Do you know anything about that?"

"It's ridiculous," Rhonda said. "There's not one word about witches in the *Book of Gladys*." She wheeled around and walked back to the door and opened it. "Well, witch or not, I'm not going to improve my reputation by talking to you. You need to leave."

"Please, just a few more minutes," Shelia said. "Let's talk about something. I don't even care what it is. You can curse me. Tell me how sorry I am. How much you hate me. I swear. After all this shunning, just hearing a human voice that I know is directed at me is better than sex."

"No, I'm required to shun you," Rhonda said as she peeked out to see if anyone was looking. "Get out."

"Think about it for a second," Shelia said. "What kind of power do these people have if they can convince two people who are being shunned to shun each other? I mean, how crazy is that?"

"I don't know what you're talking about. I'm not being shunned. I got a lot of people to talk to," Rhonda said.

"Really? Who do you talk to?"

"Well, Mama. The apostles..." She hesitated, remembering that the list really stopped at Mama. The apostles just spoke to her to receive or convey messages to or from Mama. They all looked at her as if hearing her voice was like taking a dose of bitter medicine.

She didn't really even talk to Mama all that much these days. Mama made it pretty clear that her communication with the boy was to be limited to recruiting him, getting him to go to church and giving him his lesson today. Other than that, she had ordered her to stay away from him. Even the girls in the Village whom she'd known as children acted as if they were ready to spit on her anytime she walked by them. "Uh, I was going to make some coffee. I guess you could stay long enough to have a cup. But then you're going to have to get out."

While Rhonda made coffee, Shelia sat on the couch, rattling on as if a year's supply of words had been dammed up inside her and were now bursting free, concluding, "Agreeing to come to the Land of Grace was the biggest mistake I ever made."

The coffee finished dripping, Rhonda poured two cups. She gave Shelia a cup and sat down behind her desk.

"Let's get something straight," Rhonda said. "You

were blessed when you were chosen to join our church and community. Our Lady of TCB was the only hope you had for salvation. Your experience in the Wilderness is just another example of the Others dangling the sweet life in front of you only to jerk it away. They'll do it every time. It's written in the book."

"I had a sweet life promised to me here, too. But it's been jerked away."

"That's all on you, honey, " Rhonda said. "It was you who communicated with the Others. It was you who tempted an apostle."

"I just wanted to see my sister again."

"The only sisters we have live in the Land of Grace."

"God," Shelia said. "You're more brainwashed than my husband and daughter. How long have you been here?"

Rhonda was calculating how long she had been there when the doorknob twisted and someone shoved on the door. Granny's shrill cry of "Open this fucking door!" accompanied a banging that rattled the windows.

"Shit," Rhonda said, looking around as if she were trying to find somewhere to run. "Get under that desk," she whispered, pointing to the metal desk that faced the door.

"What?" Shelia whispered back.

"Believe me," Rhonda said. "You don't want this bitch to catch you anywhere around here."

With Shelia curled behind the desk, Rhonda took a deep breath and patted her hair before swinging the door open.

"What took you so long?" Granny snapped.

"I spilled some coffee, and I was in the middle of cleaning..."

"Bullshit," Granny said as she stalked into the room. "Why you got the door locked in the first place?"

"I didn't know it was locked till you started banging on it," Rhonda said.

"Who else was here?"

"What are you talking about?"

"Got two cups of coffee," Granny said, pointing at the desk.

Rhonda looked down at the cup Shelia had been sipping on. "Oh," she said. "I poured that for myself and...and I noticed it had lipstick on it. It kinda grossed me out, so I poured another."

Granny examined the lipstick smear on the lip of the cup, then stared at Rhonda through her tight little reptilian eyes. "You're up to something," she snarled while sniffing the air and looking around the room.

"I'm not up to anything," Rhonda said. "Now, I'm pretty busy here. What can I do for you?"

"That eye's still out on that goddamn range," Granny said. "I put in a work order for it two weeks ago."

"I've called the people in Benton Harbor, Michigan," Rhonda said. "You know, they haven't made that model since the 1950s. So, we're having to look all around the Wilderness for it."

"Well, I need the damned thing right now. Every time I cook for a bunch, I need every eye on that stove and two or three more if I can get 'em."

"I don't know what else I can say. You're just going to have to wait."

Granny looked hard at Rhonda while twisting her tight, thin lips. "You're up to something. I hadn't figured it out yet, but..." She pointed her forked fingers at her eyes, then toward Rhonda. "I got my eyes on you."

"Whatever," Rhonda said, shrugging. "You see the sign on the door that says, 'No Loafing in office. Strictly for employees only'? It says 'If you have business here, please take care of it and leave.' That says it comes from Vernon, but we know it actually it comes from Mama. So you took care of your business. Now all you need to do to comply with that sign is to leave."

Granny glanced at the sign, and nodded. "Just remember. I got my eyes on you," she said as she backed out the door.

"Don't come out yet," Rhonda said after Granny slammed the door. "That old bitch is tricky." She cracked the door and peeked out. "Okay. You can come out now."

"I can tell that woman doesn't like you one bit," Shelia said as she straightened up and brushed off her dress.

"No. She doesn't love anybody but her Elvis. She just loves him because he brags about her cooking and calls her his Dodger."

"Dodger?" Shelia said.

"Don't ask," Rhonda said. "You need to get out of here."

"Listen," Shelia said. "I was just thinking. Could you talk to Mama for me? Tell her I wasn't thinking right when I wrote my sister. Tell her I now know it was a mistake and I'm really, really sorry for what I've done."

"I will," Rhonda said. "But you can't come back. You being here just makes things worse for both of us."

"I understand. But you'll talk to Mama for me, won't you?"

"Sure," Rhonda said. "I'll talk to her. But you need to go. The apostles won't be playing racquetball all day. Some of them may be wandering around up here any minute now."

Rhonda stumbled when Shelia threw her arms around her and squeezed her. "Thank you," Shelia said, her breath tickling Rhonda's ear.

"Yeah," Rhonda said as she freed herself from the awkward embrace. "Now get on out."

"You'll talk to Mama..."

"Of course I will."

"Think she'll forgive me?" Shelia said.

"Umm, she might," Rhonda said. "You never can tell. Now, go on."

As Shelia backed away, a sad smile quivering her lips, she looked as if a glimmer of hope had brightened her eyes. But the little reassuring pat Rhonda gave her shoulder was only meant to get her gone. She had no intention of sharing this little conversation with Mama because she was trying to overcome being *The Bitch Who Cold-Cocked Elvis*. It wouldn't help her cause to have Mama think she was associating with *The Slut who Corrupted an Apostle*.

20

LEAVING HOME/GOING HOME

*E*very evening, when dusk settled over the little house, Mama put him to bed. But now, instead of clamping his wrists and ankles in shackles, she sat him up at the headboard and gave him a cup of hot chocolate. "This'll help you sleep," she said. And it did. Once he finished the drink and she tucked the covers around his neck, he sank into a sleep so deep he didn't remember moving till he found himself sitting on the side of the bed with the morning sun streaming into the little window and Mama handing him a vitamin and a glass of water.

Once he swallowed the vitamin he felt as if a film had been peeled from his eyes, and so much energy came boiling up from inside him he wanted to jump and run somewhere. He thought it was a good thing he had the vitamins because the apostles played hard. They liked to hike the hills around the compound like soldiers on a forced march and toss a Frisbee or a football around for hours before he returned to the little house for his lesson.

One morning he woke with Red sitting beside him on the bed.

"Where's Mama?" he said.

"She's got something else to do this morning," Red said. "Stick out your tongue."

Why? popped up in his mind, but he knew better than to let the question leave his lips, so he opened his mouth for Red to place one of the vitamins on his tongue. "You look like you could use a couple of these things. Swallow it on down and get dressed. You're moving into the Big House today."

A limousine waited outside with a driver holding the back door open. They climbed in and rode down the hill without talking. Looking back at the little Tupelo House, something caught in his throat and tears welled in his eyes. When he remembered the torture and deprivations he had suffered, he wondered why the hell he was feeling so sad about leaving that dump. He knew it was crazy, but as the little house grew smaller behind him, he felt as if he were watching his childhood fade away.

With the Big House looming ahead, he wondered what they had in mind for him there. Though he'd stayed there, things had changed. He thought they might even have some super-sized torture waiting for him.

When they stopped at the back of the Big House, he started to open the door, but Red stopped him. "Man's got a job," he said. "Let the man do it." And he waited for the driver to walk around and open the door.

He followed Red into the big house with all the caution of someone expecting a trap door to yawn open and swallow him. "Come on in," Red said, impatiently beckoning him. "Nobody's going to hurt you. In fact, I'd be willing to bet nobody's ever going to hurt you again. If they did, they'd have to answer to me and Sonny."

From the Dining Room, a chorus of deep laughter erupted, then subsided into a rumble of men's voices accompanied by the ticking of forks and knives against china. Someone said, "Hey, Red" when he led Doyle in. The six men at the table turned their heads toward the door, and all the sound in the room evaporated as if someone had punched a mute button.

"Reckon we can find a place for this boy?" Red said. "I don't think he's had anything to eat since breakfast."

The men sprang to their feet. A goblet tumbled from the table and shattered against the marble island, splattering tea and ice across the white carpet.

"He can have my place," a couple of them said in unison. "Yeah, right here," Cholly said, motioning to the chair that he had pulled away from the table.

"You sure, Cholly?" Red said.

"Oh, yes," Cholly said, chuckling, patting his belly. "I

shoulda quit on the second plate anyway." Then he turned his head toward the Kitchen.

Three women scrambled into the Dining Room, one clearing the plate and wiping the table where Cholly had sat while another set out plates and silverware. By the time Doyle sat down, the third woman had dropped to her knees on the other side of the table, scrubbing the brown stain in the carpet as if she were trying to dig a hole in the floor.

"Can I leave him in your care, Cholly?"

"Oh, sure thing," Cholly said, now standing behind Doyle, patting Doyle's shoulder. "I'll take good care of him."

"If you can take care of that, Cholly," Red said. "Me and the boys got a lot of work to do."

"What y'all got to do?" Cholly said.

"Well, we got to get ready for the big night tonight."

"The big night?" Cholly said, breathless. "Is E coming down? Are we going to have a Coming Out?"

A smile spread across Red's face, bunching some of the freckles into the scars on his nose. "Can't slip nothing by you, can we Cholly?"

* * *

Mama swung the office door open and stood in the doorway, leaning on the facing as if she'd been standing there all day. The little twinkle in her eye and the smirk straining against the deadpan expression she wore told Rhonda everything was finally all right. Rhonda stood slowly, afraid to really believe it, but certain it was true. "I'm in aren't I?" she said.

"Now, how did you know?" Mama said, smiling now as she walked in. She met Rhonda in the middle of the room and swooped her up in her chubby arms.

"I could tell by your face," Rhonda groaned through the little air that hadn't been squeezed from her lungs by Mama's hug.

"Can't hide nothing from you, can I, baby?"

She twisted from Mama's embrace and said, "What did he say? Tell me everything."

"He said, 'okay.'" Mama said, shrugging.

"That was it. Just, okay?"

"Oh, when I told him I wanted you to be Ginger and said I wanted him to announce your engagement tonight at the Coming Out, he looked at me for a minute like I was speaking in an unknown tongue. I showed him your picture, so there was no mistake who I was talking about, and he looked off into space kinda addled. But you've got to understand, now, the boy's been sick. I mean, real sick. But he finally said, and I think these are his exact words, 'Okay. Anything you want, Mama.'"

"So what does this mean as far as the Children are concerned?"

"Why, baby, it means everything. If Elvis forgives you enough to ask you to marry him, what choice do they have but to forgive you too?"

Relief came over Rhonda so quickly, she almost slumped to the floor. But then doubts began pecking away at her brain. "But his career is almost over, isn't it, Mama?"

"Sadly, it is, baby," Mama said, shaking her head. "There's nothing we can do about that. It's all in the book."

"It's sad to lose him and all. And I hate to be selfish. But where does that leave me?"

"Well, first of all, you'll be almost like a widow. It would take a hard heart not to sympathize with grieving fiancée."

"But that only lasts for a few days," Rhonda said. "What'll I do after the Resurrection? Let's face it, I'm not right for the teenage girlfriend any more. The Children won't accept me as Priscilla again..."

"You know, actually I've been thinking about adding you to the service for a long time. I just hadn't figured out exactly how to do it. I think it might be a good idea to start with a few little things at first. Maybe a reading here and there to get the Children used to your presence on stage. If that works out well, I might just let you take over the Colonel's spot. I ain't been too happy with his performance lately. I mean the whole thing kinda drags when he's talking, don't you think?"

"I've been thinking that for some time," Rhonda said. "I was just afraid to say anything."

"Well, I keep my eyes and ears open all the time," Mama said. "You can bet on that. The main thing I've been thinking about is that one day I won't be here, and somebody's gonna have to slip into that red robe of mine."

"Mama," Rhonda gasped. "You don't mean..."

"Who else?" Mama said. "You've always been my little girl."

"I'll make you proud, Mama. Honest I will."

"I know you will. But don't get in too much of a hurry. I ain't gone yet. Now, I'll lock up this office so you can get ready. You've got yourself a big engagement to announce."

21

BLUE HAWAII NIGHT

All afternoon Cholly stayed in such a manic state of excitement he kept jumping up during *The Beverly Hillbillies*, *Gunsmoke*, and *Bewitched* to pace the floor of the T.V. Room. They went into the Pool Room to shoot a little eight-ball, but Cholly was so distracted he ripped an L-shaped slash in the felt table. "Boy, you won't tell anybody I did that, will you?"

"Well," Doyle said. "Not unless they accuse *me* of it."

"Man, they won't care if you did it," Cholly said.

"They won't?"

"Shoot no. You can trash this whole place, and they'd probably apologize to you for not having more stuff to trash."

"You gotta be kidding," Doyle said.

"If I'm lyin', I'm dyin'," Cholly said. "You and E got it made. You met E yet?"

"No," Doyle said. "I saw him perform once."

"He's amazing, ain't he? Sometimes he sings something at the Coming Out. You know, to get the girls all stirred up for the night ahead. Then, he'll pick him one out, take her upstairs and screw her into another dimension."

"Is Mama going to be there tonight?"

"I don't know. Sometimes she is and sometimes not."

Something about that answer wounded him a little. He had to admit that he missed the old lady. It seemed like forever since the last time she'd brought him his hot chocolate and tucked him in.

"Oh, shit!" Cholly said. "Red gave me two jobs to do, and I almost forgot the second one. Will you be all right here by yourself for a little while?"

"I don't know," Doyle said.

"Yeah," Cholly said, patting Doyle on the arm. "You'll be all right. Just rack 'em up and play like I was here. I'll be back before you can sink the eight-ball."

As soon as Cholly charged out of the Pool Room, Doyle moped around the table, gathering the balls into the triangle of the wooden rack. He wondered where Mama was. Had she forgotten him? In one hard stroke of the cue, he broke the cluster of balls so hard the cue ball hopped off the table. The balls scattered, clicking into each other, banking off the side while three of them plopped into the cushioned pockets.

A chill trickling up his spine distracted him from all the violence on the pool table. For a moment he thought he saw the multi-colored fabric walls inching toward him over the blue carpet. "That's crazy," he said, shaking his head. He recalled a time when he didn't mind being by himself. But now he felt stranded as if he were the only person in the world. He told himself that it wasn't anything like being alone in the darkness of the little house, wondering if he would starve or worse, wondering if he would die from the torture of being alone in all that darkness.

The door was open, and he breathed a little better when he heard a crowd gathering somewhere upstairs. So he wasn't exactly alone. And he damn sure wasn't in the dark. The Tiffany lamp over the pool table had the room lit up. Still, he was so glad to see Cholly burst into the room, he didn't even care if he was holding out a shirt that looked like a fruit salad had been spilled all over it.

"Look," Cholly said. "We'll be like twins."

After seeing that Cholly wore a duplicate of the shirt, Doyle asked, "What's with the wild shirts?"

"Blue Hawaii Night," Cholly said. "You know. Like the song and the movie. It's the theme of the Coming Out tonight in the Jungle Room."

Doyle took the shirt.

"Well," Cholly said, "to tell you the truth, it's always the theme of the Coming Outs. I guess it's because Hawaii is one of E's favorite states. It reminds him of the show he

did. You know— *Elvis: Aloha from Hawaii via Satellite*."
Man, more than one-and-a-half billion people watched him
from around the world that night."

Doyle slipped into the shirt and shrugged. "Well, let's
go," he said.

"Oh, no." Cholly said. "You gotta put on your wig and
beard. We've got a bunch of the Children in here tonight."

Doyle had forgotten about the disguise. And he wondered why they couldn't just introduce him to the Children
and tell them that though he might look a lot like Elvis, he
was just a tribute artist. He shrugged and began placing the
beard across his chin. These people had long ago stopped
entertaining any of his questions.

The moment they stepped out of the Pool Room he
could hear music and the crowd buzzing from above.
When they got upstairs, they pushed their way past men
in Hawaiian shirts and women in hula skirts who filled up
the hallway and spilled out to the Dining Room, into the
foyer and the Living Room, talking, laughing and holding
drinks. "Coming through," Cholly said. "We're supposed
to be in the Jungle Room."

Just inside the Jungle Room, the woman Mama had
called Dixie sat with a white flower in her hair and a black
and white sarong split half-way up her tanned thigh. On her
neck, she wore a lei of white flowers, and she sat so erect
in the long-back totem chair, Doyle thought she looked like
a Polynesian princess surveying her subjects from a pagan
throne. Doyle waved to her. When she just looked at him as
if he were invisible, he figured she either didn't see him or
didn't recognize him in his wig, beard and Hawaiian shirt.

He stepped up beside her as she waved off a drink offer from one of the staff. "You really amaze me," he said.
"What the hell happened to you?"

"Excuse me?" she said, looking at him as if he'd
stepped on her foot.

"Boy," Cholly said. "This is Miss Ginger."

"Pleased to meet you, Boy," she said as if she didn't

really mean it.

"What?" Doyle said. "Ging...Hey, my name's not Boy. "

"Well, whoever you are," she said. "You need to move because I'm expecting someone."

"Yeah," Doyle said. "I'll excuse you."

"Anything I can get for you, Miss Ginger?" one of the serving women said.

Doyle eased around the apostles and their girlfriends and wives gathered in the Jungle Room till he found himself standing alongside Cholly at the back wall.

He leaned into Cholly's ear and asked, "Why is everybody calling her Ginger?"

Cholly shrugged. "That's her name. What else we gonna call her?"

Speakers in the corners of the fabric-covered ceiling piped a slow, twangy Hawaiian music onto the crowd below. One of the staff walked through the room every ten minutes or so, spraying the air over everyone's head with an atomizer that smothered the odor of tobacco and whiskey with the sickly sweet scent of gardenia and piña colada. Where Doyle stood, water trickled from the ceiling, glistening the shelf of flat brown stones striped with sprigs of green ivy. Cholly told him this was supposed to be an indoor waterfall, but a shallow lighted pool full of sand and smooth round pebbles along the floor was the only thing that kept it from looking like the result of a bad leak in the pipes.

As he stepped around the little pool, he felt water squishing under his feet. "Kinda messes up the carpet, don't it?" Cholly said.

"For real," Doyle said over his shoulder. "Shouldn't we tell somebody?"

"Nah," Cholly said. "They change out the carpet around here all the time. Ain't no biggie. 'Sides, can't turn it off. E won't set foot in here unless the waterfall's on."

Sonny and Joe stepped into the room. "Clear a hole," Sonny shouted as he made a motion like a breast stroke with his hands. "Virgins coming through."

Two of the wives rose from the huge chair with the creepy wooden monkey face looming over its backrest. And as the crowd parted from the center of the room, four teenage girls in short white sundresses paraded in, taking up stations in the monkey chair, three crammed into its broad seat and one perched on a padded arm. One of the girls on the seat got up and plopped down on the hairy ottoman in front of the monkey chair.

"E loves his girls," Cholly said.

"Hey, Cholly," Sonny shouted over the clamor. "E wants you to bring his supper upstairs."

"Hear that?" Cholly said, gripping Doyle's arm. "I get to go upstairs. I bet E asked for me special."

After Cholly left, the crowd was so charged up in anticipation of the arrival of the King that during most of the next hour, a smattering of squeals rose up from the girls and the people around Doyle sucked in their breaths every time someone returned from the Kitchen or the bathroom.

He maneuvered himself around to the doorway as girlish squeals rose up from the foyer. Red and Sonny walked through the crowd, motioning with their hands for everyone to be quiet. Then behind applause and soaring squeals, the King stepped into the doorway. A rope of black hair dangled over his right eye and he stood with his legs spread wide apart, his head tilted forward as he took in the room over the top of his eyes. He wore a tight silk turquoise jumpsuit with a high backed collar, the lace-up front untied and gaped open all the way down to his swollen belly. Cholly stood at his side, smiling like a proud papa.

When the King stepped into the room, Dixie/Ginger stood, removed the lei from her neck and held it out for him to duck into, but he completely ignored her and walked over toward the monkey chair where the girls now gathered in a nervous clump. "Y'all sit back down," Red commanded. "So the King can get a good look at you." And the girls, giggling and squealing, resumed their positions on and around the monkey chair.

The King nodded, smiled and winked at the girls as he

examined each of them as if he were picking out a tomato at the market. Still looking down at them, he crooked his finger at his side and said, "Red," and Red snapped to his side with a military obedience. Though a cacophony of voices filled the room, Doyle stood close enough to hear The King say over Red's shoulder, "Red, get me that blonde in the monkey chair. Not that skinny one on the ottoman, now. I don't want that one. I want the one with the nice chubby butt hanging over the armrest."

"Now, wouldn't you rather have the other blonde?" Red said. "She's prettier than the chubby one."

"Did you hear what I said?" the King said. "I stutter or something?"

"No, sir. It's just that Mama kind of wanted you to pick the other one."

"Does Mama pick the virgin or does the King?"

"You do, E," Red says. "It's your prerogative, man."

The girls flapped their arms as if they were going to fly away in ecstasy squealing, "Pick me! Pick me!"

"While you're at it, Red," the King said.

"Yeah, E?"

"Might as well get me that one with the jet black hair. I do love me some black hair."

"I know you do, E. But since you're getting two, wouldn't it be better to have two blondes? Wouldn't that be twice the fun? You know, like the chewing gum."

"Read my lips," the King said. "I don't want the other blonde. I don't want to hear any more about that blonde." He turned to walk away, then wheeled back around, making the girls scream as if the floor had dropped out from under them. He smiled another curling smile, nodded and said, "Might as well go for the trifecta. Get me the little redhead, too. She's kinda pale for my taste, but I got to thinking that little bush of hers probably looks like its on fire."

"I bet you'll have that thing smoking before the night's over," Red chuckled, nudging the King's shoulder.

"You damn right I will," The King said loud enough for everyone to hear while looking straight at Dixie/Ginger, his eyes opened so wide there was no mistake that he was really talking to her.

"You just got one left, E," Red said. "Might as well take her, hadn't you?"

"Now, what did I just say?" the King said.

"It might hurt her feelings to be the only one not picked."

"Y'all can have her," the King said. Then he turned and stomped out of the room with Cholly following along like an clumsy puppy.

Red said, "Hey, Sonny. Better get Mama. We're going to need her to do some damage control." He gathered the chosen while leaving the lone reject to be comforted by her consoling father.

"It'll be all right, Claire," Brad Barksdale said.

"They promised me," the girl shrieked. "They promised."

Even with the party breaking up, Dixie/Ginger still stood by the totem chair, her fingers thumping its carved wooden back as she trembled and hissed through her clenched teeth.

When she slammed the lei onto the floor and stomped it, a couple of women, still elated that their daughters were going upstairs with the King, turned their heads, mouths gaped in shock.

"Getting an eyeful, bitch?" Dixie/Ginger snarled. "Why don't you just take a picture while you're at it. It'll last a lot longer."

Doyle had never seen a woman this pissed off, damn few men for that matter. He thought if she stood in the right light he might just be able to see some of that anger rising from her skin like waves of heat off asphalt. As Dixie/Ginger stood there, threatening the women with her eyes, he thought it might be a good idea to get out of there himself. It was about bedtime, and he wondered if Mama would bring his hot chocolate tonight. Before he could get to the door, Dixie/Ginger grabbed his hand and tugged him toward the hallway. "Come on," she snapped. "Time to turn in for the night. You'd like that, wouldn't you?"

"Well...Hell yeah," Doyle said.

* * *

As Claire and her father followed the Apostle Sonny along through the carport to the little white building behind the Big House, Claire's anger and disappointment felt like a dull saw blade, gnawing away inside her. Anything she tried to say came out in a pitiful whimper. Her tears clouded her vision, but she didn't care where she was going. She had been rejected by Elvis himself. Her life was practically over anyway. Her dad walked beside her, patting her back, trying to wrap her arm around her. "You'll be all right, baby," he said.

But Claire kept pushing her dad away. She kept seeing herself sitting on that damned ottoman like a fool all by herself. She was sure everyone was talking about how she'd been rejected.

The apostle knocked on a door and a woman's voice inside answered, "Come on in."

He held the door, letting Claire pass in front of him, but then said, "Just the girl."

"But I need to..." her dad said.

"No!" the apostle snapped. "You need to stay out here with me. Like I said."

The door closed and Claire felt as if she had walked into a dream with Mama's smiling face rising like the moon from behind a brown metal desk. "Come on in, baby," she said as her smile dimpled her jowly cheeks. She walked around the desk, held her arms out wide for Claire and said, "Come over here, baby, and give Mama a hug."

Claire had only seen Mama in the church service or special occasions. Instead of her red robe, she wore a loose-fitting house dress. She wondered how she could actually touch Mama. She had come to think of her as a saint who could only be seen from a distance. Someone to admire but not touch. To actually touch her, well, that seemed out of the question. She trembled as Mama wrapped her up in her fleshy arms, and held her there. "You calm down now, baby. Everything's going to be all right."

And Mama squeezed her, squeezed her as if she were trying to squeeze the hurt right out of her like the last of the toothpaste from a withered tube. She thought it had to be a miracle the way her sorrow and anxiety melted away while she breathed in Mama's sacred scent of lilacs, sweat and hair spray. "Now, why don't you sit down and tell me what troubles you," Mama said after she released Claire from her hug.

They sat on a brown vinyl couch in front of the desk with Mama holding Claire's hands. "You don't need to feel sad," Mama said. "You don't need to worry about a thing. Remember, Elvis has a plan for all of us."

"He doesn't have a plan for me," Claire said. "He hates me. Apostle Red promised me I would be picked in the Coming Out, but The King picked everybody *but* me."

"Baby," Mama said, smiling, patting Claire's hand. "Don't you see? Why, that's where His plan comes in. See, Elvis works in mysterious ways. Did you see how fat he is?"

Claire sniffled and nodded tentatively, afraid to say anything negative about The King.

"Fat as a butterball. Honey, that's because of all our sins that he's took on hisself. Those old sins have just about weighed him down. Soon he'll be gone from us."

He may have rejected her, but the prospect of Elvis dying brought on sadness, and she began to sob again. "Why does he..." she sobbed. "Why does he have to die? Couldn't he like, go on a diet or something instead?"

"It's in the scripture, baby," Mama said. "Nothing we can do about that. Don't be sad though. You've never been around for Elvis Days, have you?"

Claire shook her head. "No, ma'am," she said. "I've read about it and studied about it in Sunday school."

"We gonna have one coming up. The ceremonies start off real, real sad, but they end up as jubilant as all get-out with everybody having a big old time. You know why everybody's so jubilant?"

"Because everybody knows he's coming back?"

"That's right. We all become happy because we know that by the end of Elvis Days he'll come back to us. And when he comes back, he'll be slim and beautiful and full of life. Not fat and tired and grumpy. In the new resurrection he won't yet be full of our sins, so he'll be fresh and new. That's his plan for you, darling."

"Really?" Claire said.

"Absolutely," Mama said. "When Elvis saw you sitting there in the Jungle Room, he wanted to save you for the new resurrection instead of using up your eligibility now."

"So I'll have another Coming Out?"

"You won't have to have a Coming Out," Mama said. "You're going to be Elvis' girlfriend." She caressed Claire's hair and shook her head. "You're hair's so pretty. I'm thinking of you as maybe Linda Thompson to start with."

"Do you mean it?"

"I mean it more than anything. The only thing holding you back is that mother of yours."

"She knows she did bad," Claire said. "I think she's sorry."

"She's not sorry," Mama said. "You know what would make Elvis happy?"

"No, ma'am."

"It would make him happy as a clam if you was to come over here to live at the Big House and be my girl. I can be your mama like I'm his mama."

"But what'll Mom do?"

"Oh, she'll be punished for her sin. I don't have anything to do with punishment. That's God's jurisdiction. Usually what happens is, folks who break the law just go away somewhere."

"I'm mad at Mom for breaking the law and all, but I don't want her to go away," Claire said.

Mama stared at Claire for a moment, smiled and nodded studiously. "You know something?"

"What?"

"When you get a little older, we could darken your hair, and you'd be a perfect Priscilla."

Claire's breath caught in her throat. "Priscilla?" she said. "Really? I could be Priscilla?"

Mama wrapped Claire in her arms again. "You sure could, baby," she said as she gave Claire a big squeeze. "I can see it all now."

* * *

Back in his bedroom, Dixie/Ginger slammed the door behind them. "Shit!" she screamed as she kicked off her shoes, bouncing them against the wall.

"What are you so pissed about?" he asked.

"His royal fat-ass highness was supposed to walk into the Jungle Room, thank everybody very graciously for coming, then announce our engagement before he picked one of the little so-called virgins to go upstairs with him."

"One?" he said, his mind for some reason stuck back on the virgins. "He took three of em. Wait a minute. Your engagement?"

"He was just showing off," she scoffed, frowning, shaking her head. "Trying every trick he knew to embarrass me and that little girl he left behind."

"Man, those girls looked awfully young," he said, shaking his head. "Did you say engagement?"

She sat down on the bed and chuckled. "Well, before you get overly concerned about those sweet little things, he's not going to do much damage to any of them. Believe me, Honey. In his shape? Pfizer doesn't crank out enough Viagra to make his little pea pod stand up."

"Looks like that information would be kinda bad if it got out," he said.

"What information's that?"

"You know, about him not being able to get it up."

"It wouldn't be good."

"Won't the girls, you know, tell?"

"Tell?" she said, snickering. "Are you kidding? They'd

be afraid to tell. It's against the law to say anything bad about Elvis. Besides a night with him or one of the apostles means from now on, they're officially women. They can now have boyfriends, get married, and whatever. They'll come down in the morning," she said, changing into a girlish voice as she waved her arms over her head. "They'll be all 'it was totally paradise. Just paradise.' And talking about what heights of ecstasy he took them to. When really all they did was curl up around his hairy ass like a litter of puppies around a ratty old cushion while he kept them awake snoring and farting all night."

"What are y'all going to do about him?" he said.

"Do about him? You don't do anything about Elvis. Elvis is the King. He can do anything he wants. The question is, now that he's rejected me as Ginger, what are they going to do about me? I bet he still resents me for hitting him in the head with that lion back when I was Priscilla."

"You hit him with a lion? Wait a minute. What's this Priscilla shit?"

"It was just a brass lion," she said as she sprang from the bed and headed for the bathroom. "I'll be right back."

The dark, leather lump of her purse seemed to call to him from the dresser. *Who is this bitch, anyway?* he wondered. He walked over to the dresser and unzipped the top of the purse while watching the bathroom door. "I'll be damned," he whispered after scooping out her wallet and finding an Alabama driver's license with her picture on it, issued to Rhonda Ann Price—Route 1, Willow Ruth, Alabama. When he put the wallet back in he felt a key ring. He slipped the ring out, twisting the keys around till he saw the one with the Cadillac emblem. He slipped the key off the ring and dropped the ring back in the purse.

When she swung the bathroom door open and said, "Miss me?" she startled him so badly he dropped the key on the carpet.

She was standing there naked with her hair loose and her smile saying that she enjoyed the expression on his face. "You like what you see?"

"I do," he said.

"Why don't you take that stupid shirt off?"

As he unbuttoned the shirt, the only thing he could think of was that about this time every night he got some hot chocolate. He chuckled at how he'd picked up a taste for the stuff. He'd just sort of wanted it a few minutes ago, but now that want had ballooned into a hunger that made his hands tremble.

"You seen Mama today?" he said, draping the shirt over the back of a chair.

"Mama?" she said. "God, you are just like Elvis. You have a woman standing in front of you naked and all you can talk about is your Mama." She stepped back into the bathroom. When she came back out she was wriggling back into her dress as if she were angry at the garment.

"Hey, what are you so upset about? I was just thinking about getting some of her hot chocolate. Don't that sound good? Then we could..."

"Good?" she said. "You idiot. A couple of sips of that stuff and your Little Elvis? Well, honey, your Little Elvis will shrink up the size of five nickels. And you'll be dead to the world. As far as I care, you can stay and wait on your mama all night. I'm out of here."

After she charged out of the room, he entertained the idea of going after her, but his thoughts drifted back to the hot chocolate. He was even thinking about wandering down to the Kitchen and see if he could whip up a cup of it himself when the door swung open and Cholly strolled in with a steaming mug in his hands. "Mama told me to make sure you got this before you went to bed," he said. "Was that Miss Ginger that came out of here?"

Doyle snatched the mug, sloshing some of the brown liquid on the carpet.

"Hey, be careful," Cholly said when Doyle raised the mug to his lips. "Man, you'll scald your gizzard."

22

BREAKFAST WITH THE KING

A hand gripped Doyle's shoulder, gave him a shake, and he rose to the surface of a deep, hazy sleep, thinking the round face hovering over him was Mama till he heard, "Wakie, wakie. Piss in lakie."

Cholly pulled him up to the side of the bed and stuffed a pill in his mouth. "Hurry up! Hurry up, now!" Cholly said as he slipped a straw in Doyle's mouth.

Doyle downed the pill with a mouthful of water, and the room brightened. Cholly laid fresh clothes on the bed while Doyle shook the remainder of the sleep out of his head and said, "What's the rush?"

"Man, E's in the Dining Room," Cholly said in a breathless voice, his eyes widening as he spoke. "And we're missing it."

The moment they opened the bedroom door he could hear the commotion rumbling down the hall from the Dining Room. "Hear what we missing?" Cholly said, clapping his hands like an excited child. "Let's go. Man, they's always excitement when E comes down."

As they got closer, Doyle heard the King say, "I'm not gonna let you bullshit me no more, Red. I'm telling you, now." And Red answered in the lilting voice adults use to placate a child— "Nobody's bullshittin' you, E."

The King sat at the head of the table. Behind him, the blue drapes over the window had been drawn wide like the curtains of a stage. Red and Sonny sat on either side of the King, and all the apostles jammed in around the table, which looked as if it had grown since Doyle last saw it. With its added leaves, it now covered the length of the island of black marble and stretched far out onto the surrounding white carpet.

The sun streaming in through the window behind the King glinted across the mirrored table and sparkled the crystal spears in the chandelier overhead. It shone fiercely over the King's head and around his shoulders, transforming the King's face into an eclipsing moon that made Doyle's eyes hurt when he tried to stare directly at him.

"Come on in, little buddy," the King said. "You're the only one in this whole goddamn house I can trust."

"Aw, E," Cholly said. "I ain't the only one, and you know it."

"I ain't talking to you, you chipmunk-looking toad," the King snapped. "I'm talking to that good-looking young cat trailing along behind you there. Somebody get this boy a chair."

"I'll get it," Cholly said.

"Yeah, you go get it, you kiss-ass toad," the King said.

"Now why you wanna go and badmouth poor ol' Cholly like that, E?" Sonny said. "You might hurt his feelings or something."

"To hell with his feelings," the King said. "And to hell with yours, too."

"Don't mind E. He don't mean nothing by it," Cholly said as he hustled breathlessly back into the room, lugging a couple of chairs under his arms. Cholly placed one against the wall, then he dropped the other chair under the table and sat down in it.

"Oh, hell, no," the King said. "You get your dumb ass over there against the wall, and ever'body scoot down one. I want my little buddy to sit right here," he said, patting the table in front of Sonny.

Sonny looked over at Red. Both of them shrugged. Sonny stood and motioned for the guys on his side of the table to move down. The apostles moved down and continued to look at each other, chuckling nervously whenever the King spoke as if they were afraid he might tell a joke that might somehow go un-laughed at.

"Come on over here, little buddy," the King said.

Doyle felt nervous about the whole thing, but when he

glanced at Red, Red chin-pointed toward the chair next to the King.

As he drew closer, Doyle could see a thumb-sized smear of gravy and a couple of dots of ketchup on the lapel of the tan coat the King wore. The coat was bordered in chocolate brown under the arms and down the sides in a vain attempt to make the fat man look slimmer, and its collar and that of the pumpkin orange shirt underneath stuck up so high and stiff, they looked like double neck braces for a whiplash victim. Gold framed sunglasses with amber lenses the size of drink coasters hid the King's eyes. And Doyle thought the big man had enough gold chains wrapped around his neck and dangling down his bare chest to tow one of those Cadillacs a couple of blocks.

"There you go," the King said, patting Doyle's shoulder after he sat down. "I can tell you right now, me and you gotta stick together in this den of rattlesnakes." Then he yelled, "Let's get this boy a plate in here. "

"Call us a den of snakes," Red said. "When every one of us is as good to you as we can be. And you know it, E."

"Good to me?" the King said, dropping his sunglasses down his nose and staring over them at Red with narrowed eyes. "All that dope you been feeding me."

"Oh, E," Red said. "Man, I wish you'd quit it. That's just some bad dreams you had when you was sick. I'd never do that to you."

"Bad dreams, my ass," The King said. "If you could see how they've treated me," he said, looking at Doyle, "you'd think I was a redheaded stepchild."

"We treat you like a dadgum king," Red said. "Because, man, you are the King. Ain't that right, boys?"

"Yeah! Yeah!" The apostles all said, nodding, smiling, some of them with full mouths.

"You the King, E," Joe said. "The number one cat in charge of taking care of bidness."

"TCB, baby," an apostle named Ricky said from the other end of the table.

Granny stalked into the room followed by one of her

helpers, a middle-age woman so thin the stained white apron she wore over her frayed jeans wrapped around her twice. A frown crinkled Granny's leathery face when she saw Doyle. "Oh, it's you," she said, her voice dripping with disappointment as her helper put a plate and some silverware down in front of him.

The King scooted over and wrapped his arm around Doyle's shoulders. "This is my main man, here, Dodger," the King said. "I'd like for you to roll this boy up some fresh breakfast. Eggs you got there beginning to look like a pile of dried up cow flops."

"He don't eat eggs," Granny said.

"You don't eat eggs, little buddy?" the King said, talking to Doyle in the same tone he might use for a puppy.

"Well, yeah," Doyle said. "Sometimes. But not like that. I like em sunny-side up."

The King dropped his arm from around Doyle's shoulders as his nose crinkled and his lips curled into a grimace. "Don't ever say that again, little buddy," the King said, his huge frame shuddering. "Man, I don't even want to be in the same house with a runny egg."

"See, I told you, smart ass," Granny said, punching Doyle on the shoulder. "This one don't eat nothing for breakfast but a measly biscuit."

"Well, then," the King said. "Couldn't we get some biscuits? We need something to tide us over till the chicken gets done, anyway."

"What's wrong with them?" she said, pointing to the mound of biscuits in the center of the table.

"We need some hot ones," the King said.

"Well," Granny said, pinching the King's cheek. "Whatever my sweet baby wants."

"How soon you gonna have my chicken done?" the King said.

"You gotta hold your horses, sweetie," Granny said. "It'll be a while."

"Be a while?" Red said. "Hell you'd think she had to wring their scrawny necks, gut 'em and scald their stinking feathers off in an iron pot in the back yard."

"My baby don't want them chickens fried up the way ever'body else does it. He wants 'em the way *I* do it. Don't you, baby?" Granny said.

"Yes, ma'am," the King said. He looked at Doyle and shook his head in amazement. "Nobody can burn a gospel bird like Dodger can."

"All right then," Granny said. And with a little proud toss of her head, she turned and strutted into the Kitchen.

Doyle sopped at a puddle of syrup with the last of his massive biscuit when three of Granny's helpers paraded into the Dining Room holding silver platters laden with golden brown chicken. Granny leaned against the china cabinet, wiping her hands on her greasy apron as the King's lip slowly curled into a smile.

Granny nodded as the women placed the platters in front of the King, who had pushed his chair back. "Dodger," he said, shaking his head. "This ain't nothing short of a masterpiece. I just don't know how the hell you do it."

"Ah," Granny said, shrugging. "You get as many miles on you as I got, you just naturally pick up a little trick or two along the way." But Doyle could tell the old lady thought she had done something extraordinary by the way she stood there with her arms crossed, her eyes narrowed and her lower lip poked out over her upper one.

Across the table, Red shook his head and said, "That is a hell of an accomplishment, ain't it, Sonny?"

"Yeah," Sonny said. "Specially by somebody who spent her girlhood riding bitch on a Harley and pulling a train of greasy, long-haired bikers ever' day."

"Hey!" the King snapped. "You don't talk to my Dodger like that."

"Aw," Granny said. "Don't mind those two. When they handed out manners, they thought they said 'nanners and headed off to the fruit section." Then she shouted, "Now, where's that sweet tea?"

Granny's helpers, who were ogling the chicken themselves, shuffled obediently off into the Kitchen.

"Dodger can mix up some sweet tea, too," the King said. "You wouldn't think they was much to it. But getting it just strong enough with just exactly the right amount of sugar blended in so it's just right when it hits a glassful of ice is like...hell, it's like goddamn chemistry or something."

"We better dig into that chicken before it gets cold, hadn't we, E?" Sonny said.

"What's all this *we* shit," the King said. "This is *my* chicken."

"Now, E," Red said. "I know you got a man-sized appetite on you, but even you can't eat *all* that chicken."

"My little buddy's gonna help me out," the King said, tossing a thumb Doyle's way. "When we've done all the damage we can do down here, I'll get Dodger to sack it up for me, and I'll eat the rest of it tonight."

"And y'all gonna eat it all and not give us any?" Rickey said.

"You got that shit right," the King said.

"E," Red said. "Man, that's so many kinds of wrong, I can't even start listing 'em."

"Yeah," Sonny said. "The way you been raised around here, I'm surprised you don't know what bad manners it is to eat chicken in front of people, knowing they want some. Mama'd be disappointed as hell in you if she was here, and you know it."

"See?" the King said, pounding his big fist on the table, rattling all the plates and silver around him. His outrage turned to whining "They gonna tell Mama on me. Can't have nothing of my own in this goddamned place."

"Can't have nothing?" Red said, spreading his arms out. "Man, *aaall* this shit's yours."

"Not mine," the King snapped. "Ain't none of it mine." He struggled to his feet, leaning with one hand on the table, winded from the simple act of standing.

"This shit?" he gasped, gripping the gold chains on his neck. "Not mine either." He jerked the chains. Some of them broke at the clasps and he tossed them on the table with a clunk.

"Be careful now, E," Joe said. "That's stuff's kinda valuable, you know."

"If the shit was mine," the King said, "you wouldn't care how I treated it."

"It's just that ever' time you break it, E," Sonny said, "you put us to a lot of trouble, going around and getting it fixed and all."

"See?" the King said to Doyle. "They try to make it look like they work for me, but the truth is, it's me that's working for *their* asses."

"Aw, E," Red said. "Why you want to get like this?"

"Hell," the King said. "If I can't even have my own special chicken by myself, I might as well cut out all this King bullshit and wait on you. Y'all call me the King, but I ain't no better around here than the damn kitchen help.

"Pick up that tray, would you, little buddy?" he said, glancing at Doyle as he pointed to a tray of chicken.

"What the hell are you up to, now, E?" Red said.

Doyle picked up the tray and followed the King behind Sonny's chair. "Here's you a drumstick, *Mr.* Sonny," the King snarled, plucking a drumstick off the pile of chicken and dropping it on Sonny's plate.

"Thanks, E," Sonny said. "But I'd rather have me a little of that white meat there, if you don't mind."

"You'll take the drumstick and be damned glad you got it," the King said. "And I hope you choke on it." Then he moved down to Joe.

"And who the hell are you supposed to be?" The King said.

"Joe."

"Joe? Hell, you ain't the Joe I know."

"Now, E, he's the same Joe he's always been," Red said.

"See, little buddy," the King said. "Just some more of their bullshit. Tell you what. I'll call you Bullshit Joe. Here's the backbone for you, Bullshit Joe. If you're as big a chickenshit as the other Joe, it'll be the only backbone you had in your miserable life."

"They's no talking to him when he gets like this," Red said, shaking his head.

"Humph!" the King said, moving on, giving a thigh to one of the apostles named Marty and a wing to another named Lamar. After they walked around the table, the King lifting chicken pieces from the tray and as he dropped them on each of twelve men's plates, he called out their names and the piece of chicken served. When he had gone around the table, one small brown lump remained on the tray. "Looks like you get the gizzard, Red."

"The gizzard," Red said. "*I* get the fucking gizzard?"

"Yeah, I was going to save you the asshole, but it's attached to that backbone I already gave to Bullshit Joe. You can see, he's kinda partial to it. Just look at him gnawing on that thing. Hell, look at all of them," he said waving his arms around the table where the apostles held chicken to their faces as they severed crusty flesh from the bones with their teeth. "See there, little buddy. They's only two things in this room that I have anything in common with—that's you and that chicken. See, they feeding on that burnt bird like they been feeding off me since I've been here."

"You need to be careful what you say, E." Red said. "Hell, we're all used to you, but that boy there might take you serious."

The King sneered down at Red. "He needs to take me serious. Ol' Bob Dylan used to say, 'You don't have to be a weatherman to know which way the wind blows.' Well, I can tell you right now, you don't have to be an Old Testament prophet with a long, white beard to know that one day, all you assholes gonna double cross me. I mean *ever'* *damn* one of you," he said, now pointing his finger at each one in turn.

"We'd never double cross you, E," Red said.

"No!" "No!" The apostles said, shaking their heads, their mouths not far from the chicken they held.

"Hell, we love you, man," Red said. "Now, come on, sit

down, and let's eat us some serious chicken."

"Here," the King said. "Have you a delicious gizzard."

As he dropped the gizzard on Red's plate, one of Granny's helpers brought in a pitcher of iced tea. "Get 'em all some glasses," the King said. "I want you to have you a big ol' time, so when you shoot me full of dope and leave me on the bathroom floor to die like a beached whale, you can remember how on this day, you not only ate up all my special chicken, you drunk up all my sweet tea like you was sucking my blood.

"Come on, little buddy," the King said, now waddling toward the Jungle Room.

"Where y'all going, E?" Red said.

"Down to the TV room and watch a little *I Love Lucy*."

"How 'bout the rest of this chicken?" Red said.

"You damn vultures can have it. I already lost my appetite."

23

THE KEY

Of all the members of the Big House, Rhonda hated to see Granny the most. It was no wonder. The old lady had a face that only a troll could love, and Rhonda was pretty sure that those flinty little eyes and that disapproving sneer would revisit her in her nightmares if she gazed on them for too long. But it wasn't just her appearance. Back when Rhonda had been Priscilla, the old lady had eavesdropped through every keyhole and around every corner and reported every little spat she overheard between her and Elvis to Mama. And she never missed a chance to fire off one of her backhand comments like when she caught Rhonda coming down the stairs one day and said, "Pretty dress. I mean I kinda admire the way you don't care that the real Priscilla wouldn't have been caught dead in something like that. But it's still pretty. You know, if you look at it in the right light and all."

"Why does she hate me so much?" she asked Mama after Mama questioned her about some harsh comment she'd made to Elvis that Granny had reported.

"Oh, she don't hate you, baby," Mama answered. "She just wants the best for Elvis. And ain't that what we all want?"

What Rhonda wanted was to stay away from Granny as much as possible. But Granny was in charge of the Kitchen, and Mama had said the old crone's initials had to be on every grocery order. Every time she saw her, it was some kind of confrontation. Today, to make matters worse, Rhonda had to walk through the gauntlet of apostles loitering outside the Jungle Room and the Dining Room along with the pungent scent of marijuana permeating the air.

"Hey, Baby." "Hey little sister," The apostles called

out. She could feel one of them breathing on her neck as she squeezed by. One of the bastards even patted her butt. "I know Elvis don't love you anymore, but you could be comfortable sitting on my face," Sonny slurred.

"In your dreams," she said as she ducked into the Kitchen. Four of Granny's helpers turned when she closed the door behind her. "Where's Granny?" Rhonda said. One of the women pointed toward the Dining Room.

The crystal tumblers were smeared with greasy fingerprints, and all the chicken bones spilling off the plates and littering the white table cloth made the place look like the sight of a recent massacre.

"What's going on out there?" she asked Granny, who was leaned against wall looking at the palm of her hand as if she were reading her own fortune.

"Mama's out of pocket, and they're going ape shit as usual," the old lady said with a shrug. "But the real question is, who does this belong to?" She held up a key between her thumb and forefinger, a crooked smile quivering her tight, thin lips.

"Where...uh...where did you find that?"

"One of my girls found it in the boy's room this morning. Got any idea where it came from?"

"No," Rhonda said. "How would I...?"

"Oh," Granny said. "I just thought you'd know. Y'all being so close and all. I'm thinking about going down to the TV Room and have a little fun before I turn it over to Red."

Rhonda handed the grocery order to Granny. "You forgot to initial this."

"Always trying to catch me in a mistake, ain't you?" the old lady said as took the pen Rhonda offered her.

"No, it's nothing like that. You know Mama's a stickler for procedure."

The old woman scratched out something that resembled initials on the order before looking up at Rhonda and saying, "Want to go see Red with me?"

"No," Rhonda said. "I've got to get back to the Office."

"I didn't think you would," the old woman said. "You probably don't know any more about the key than you do about that little handjob the boy got from a certain somebody a while back."

"How did you...?" Rhonda said.

Granny pointed two fingers at her eyes and said, "I always had these eyes on you girl. When I ain't had my eyes on you, I had my friends watching you. Some of my friends drive limos."

"I don't know what you're talking about," Rhonda said.

* * *

Doyle followed the King down to the basement. "Shut that door, little buddy," the King said when they stepped into the TV Room.

Doyle closed the door as the King eased his broad haunches down onto the couch. The moving reflections across the sectional mirrors on the ceiling and the wall around the fireplace always startled him when he walked into this room. Now he felt as if the jigsawed pieces of a dream flickered all around him.

"Little buddy," the King said, shaking his head so hard the entire front of his hair tumbled into his eyes. "Man, I been wanting to talk to you since I heard you was here." He swept the hair back with his hand, his words quivering from his lips, tears welling up in his eyes. "Goddamn! I been in denial for so long it's ridiculous."

Doyle dropped down onto one of the matching blue ottomans in front of the mirrored fireplace, wondering what he would do if the King started blubbering. Well, he knew one thing for sure, he wasn't going to hold him in his arms, pat him on the back and say, "There, there," and shit.

"I should've seen the writing on the wall some time back when my belly first lapped over my belt and my ass started busting outta my jumpsuits all the time," the King said. "You know what I mean?"

Doyle nodded while trying to come up with some excuse to get away from all this whining.

"Sometimes," the King sniffled, "Hell, sometimes, I'd look in the mirror and see a dude so weird, I thought that Spanish cat, Picasso, might have painted him. I didn't know it, but they had me going around all the time with at least a middle-grade high. So usually, I was so high, I'd just shake my head, and suddenly I'd see the same handsome face I always remembered. Red, Sonny and the boys made sure I got whatever little toys I wanted, let me act like a kid, throwing tantrums all over the place, let me win all the games. Man, they made me feel like such a big hero, I'm ashamed of myself. And when I started busting through my britches, they'd just buy me bigger clothes.

"And women?" he shook his head. "Damn. I still had women screaming and yelling, trying to get down and worship this fat ass of mine. Young chicks, too, boy, fighting each other every night like alley cats just to see who'd be the first to gimme a blow job. Little buddy, you can imagine, it's pretty easy to forget you're a fat slob with that kinda shit coming down."

The King dropped the dark glasses down his nose and examined Doyle's face through a pair of hollow eyes with loose blue skin hanging under them like bruised fruit. "I'm telling you," the King said. "I should have listened to 'em. They was telling me all the time, and it just flew over my head like a bird—the apostles with their faith lessons, Mama with her sermons on how Elvis would die and rise again and again. It's even written down in the book how Elvis died, consumed by the sins of the world. But I didn't know that shit applied to me till I got sick and accidentally heard the sumbitches talking about how they'd over-done the pills and that damned hot chocolate they was giving me at night. The bastards weren't afraid I was going to die. They were afraid I was going to die too soon."

A chill rippled up Doyle's spine, and he sprang to his feet.

"Where you going, little buddy?" the King said. "You not leaving me, are you?"

"No," Doyle said. "Just needed to move around a little."

"You know you're here to take my place, don't you?"

"What?" Of course he knew it. Becoming the King was the message Mama and the apostles had been preaching to him all along. He'd just not thought about it involving someone else dying.

"I'm telling you, they been watching you," the King said. "Probably for years. Had your ass staked out like they had mine."

"Why me?"

"Why?" the King asked. " 'Cause, like me, you're probably a dead-on Elvis act."

"I guess I was pretty good," Doyle said. "But there are a lot of good Elvis acts out there."

"Yeah, but most of the good ones get steady gigs around Vegas or their hometowns. Some of them might be good, but they don't take it serious. They have a regular life with a day job. You know, they just do the Elvis thing for shits and giggles. Another thing, I don't have no family to speak of. How 'bout you?"

Doyle shook his head.

"You know they're not going to let you go, don't you?"
Doyle nodded.

The King shook his head. "I bet you spent your little time with Mama in that Tupelo House, didn't you?"

Doyle nodded again.

"And those pills? Make you feel on top of the world, don't they? But let me tell you, those damn things got a sharp hook to 'em, little buddy. It was the pills and the shit they put in that chocolate that damn near wasted my ass."

As if he'd suddenly lost interest in the whole conversation, the King pushed himself up from the couch. "Damn," he said. "I wish I hadn't shot my mouth off and left all that chicken back there on the table."

"Want me to go get you some?" Doyle said.

"Nah. With that bunch of hyenas? We'd be lucky if they was even any bones left. Hey, there might be some Butterfingers over there behind the bar."

"I'll look," Doyle said.

Behind the padded yellow bar, Doyle prowled through a couple of drawers before he saw the candy. "Got one Butterfinger, three Snickers and a couple Reese's," he said.

The King ambled over to the bar. "Good! Give 'em all here," he said, holding out his pudgy hand. "And check the fridge and see if we got any Pepsi."

The King had already gnawed halfway through the Butterfinger when Doyle opened a cold can of Pepsi and set it on the bar.

"I stay hungry as a bitch wolf all the time," the King said. "Along with all the other stuff, I'm sure the bastards are slipping me steroids to fatten me up." He took a hard slug from the Pepsi, then attacked the wrapper on one of the Snickers.

Through half a mouthful of candy, the King said, "You want to know how much I didn't want to believe my own ears? I actually sold myself on the idea that I had misunderstood them. I guess I liked being treated like royalty too much. But I finally put all the denial aside and just knew they was out to get me when Mama said she wanted me to marry this chick she called Ginger, and she wanted me to announce our engagement at the Coming Out last night."

"I know exactly who you're talking about," Doyle said.

"Yeah?" The King said, his eyebrow lifting into an arch. "Well, Mama showed me a picture of her so I'd know which one to pick." He dropped his eyes, then drew in a deep breath. "I swear, it was the same bitch who told me her name was Dixie when I first come here. Then she said her name was Priscilla. We even got married, or they told me we got married. I don't remember much about the marriage, but I do remember her raising holy hell when she caught me butt naked with one of those chicks from the Village." He rubbed the side of his head. "I still got a scar where she went upside my head with that big-ass brass lion in the Jungle Room.

"Man, I wanted to do what Mama asked. I mean, I'd

do about anything for that woman. You know what I'm saying?"

Doyle nodded. He knew exactly what he was saying.

"But the name Ginger was what finally raised the hackles on the back of my neck. Anybody who knows anything about Elvis knows that when you get down to Ginger, you've come smack-dab to the end.

"If that wasn't scary enough, I overheard Red tell Sonny that if they kept on going at the rate they was going, they were going to have to expand the Meditation Garden. You ever been to the real Graceland?"

"Yeah," Doyle said. "Twice."

"You see the Meditation Garden?"

Doyle nodded.

"Well, I've been all over this place except the Meditation Garden. The main reason I haven't been there is, I just couldn't think about Elvis lying in the ground. Besides, I didn't think they had one of those damn things here since I was still alive and all. But they got me to wondering what could be out there. I thought since you can move faster than I can, maybe you'd slip outside and check it out real quick."

"I don't know. Maybe."

"If you'll go out there and take a look, I'll watch the doorway and say I was just taking a look at the sunshine if they come along."

While Doyle and the King sneaked upstairs, it sounded like a party going on in the Dining Room. "Buncha hogs in there, eating all my chicken," the King snarled. He lumbered toward the noise, but Doyle caught his arm.

"We've got a little something to do, remember?"

"Oh, yeah," the King said. "Let's go."

With the King watching the door, Doyle made it down the walkway under the green awning and the trellis to a brick wall at the corner of the house. He could hear water splashing, then silence, then splashing again in a slow rhythm. He waited and listened for a while before peeking around an arched entrance.

Behind the wall lay a courtyard where a fountain rose in the air before splitting into the shape of a starburst and splashing into the circular pool below. Around the main fountain, five baby fountains spit up circles of water. A black wrought iron fence encircled the pool, and a stretch of turf surrounded the fence and three man-sized marble slabs.

Gold leaf boarded each rectangle slab with TCB engraved over a golden lightning flash. The gold inscription of the slab to the far left read, *The King.* And inscribed under it, *August 16, 1997.* The one in the center read, *The King, August 16, 2002.* And the next one read, *The King, August 16, 2007.*

The King had to have seen the fear on Doyle's face because he looked even more alarmed when Doyle slipped through the threshold and let the door ease back. "What is it?" the King said. "What'd you see, little buddy?"

"Let's get out of this hall," Doyle said.

Back downstairs in the TV room, Doyle told the King what he'd seen. The news set the big man pacing the floor. "Oh shit," he said. "You sure it's 2012 already?"

"Absolutely," Doyle said.

"What month?"

"I played at the Willow Ruth AMVETS on the Twenty-eighth of March. I don't know how much time's gone by. But it's pretty hot out there, so if it's not August right now, it's pretty close."

The King was still catching his breath when the door swung open and Granny stalked in. "What're you two up to?" she said.

"Nothing, Dodger," the King said. "Just fixing to watch us a little TV."

"I don't know what the hell all these people think they're doing," Granny said, shaking her head. "But you two are not supposed to be alone together under any circumstances. I'll swear, Mama turns her head for a second and that whole bunch winds up in the Dining Room gobbling down chicken and passing a joint around while y'all are down here plotting and scheming like a couple of A-rab terrorists."

"Well, we ain't up to nothing, Dodger," the King said. "Honest."

"Can't tell me this piss-poor excuse for an Elvis tribute artist ain't up to something," Granny said. "Y'all been messing around outside, haven't you?"

"We ain't been nowhere, Dodger," the King said.

"Bullshit. He's got you lying for him now. I saw him go out the door." She dangled a key out in front of her. "Know anything about this, big star?"

"What is it, a key?" Doyle said.

"What is it, a key?" Granny mimicked. "One of my girls found it in your room and brought it to me."

"Well, I don't know anything about it," Doyle said.

"Okay. If that's the way you're going to play it. Guess I'll have to go get Red and let him get to the bottom of this," she said.

"Let's talk about this for a minute, Granny," Doyle said.

"Nothing to talk about," she said. "Not gonna be much of a loss. Like I told you that night at the AMVETS, you wouldn't make a pimple on the King's ass."

She gave him a sneer, wheeled around and headed for the door. After a quick survey of the room, Doyle came face to face with the huge white ceramic monkey on the coffee table. If the old lady told Red about the key, he was sure he'd be in for a round with the cattle prod at the very least. Through a surge of anger and fear, he hefted the big monkey with both of his hands. "I'll show you a pimple," he said. And before Granny could reach the door, he was behind her, swinging the big monkey. The statue crunched into the base of her skull and slammed her face into the wall, smashing a section of mirror. Her neck whipped back with a snap, and her face slid down a jagged shard of mirror, leaving a slick of blood all the way to the floor where she slunk to the carpet. She quivered a couple of times like a wire being drawn taut before becoming as still as the huge white monkey Doyle had dropped beside her.

Doyle knelt where she lay on the carpet with her mouth gaped open and a bloody furrow carved all the way from the curve of her cheek bone to her hairline. He picked up the key from the carpet before touching her neck and feeling no pulse.

"Dodger?" the King whimpered as he fell to his knees beside the woman. "Dodger?" he called to her as if she were far away. He crinkled his nose and looked up at Doyle. "Goddamn, what's that smell."

"I think she shit herself," Doyle said.

The King poked her. "Goddamn," he said, sniffling, his voice catching as if it had been snagged on a hook. "I don't think she's...I don't think she's breathing. Ya...You...You killed Dodger." Then shouting, "You son-of-a-bitch, you killed my Dodger."

Doyle swung his open hand as hard as he could. The blow made a loud, hollow splat against the King's cheeks, sending his sunglasses flying and the big man tottering back and forth on his knees like a giant Elvis bobble-head doll.

"Shut up, you fat cow," Doyle snapped. "She's not your Dodger. This ain't Graceland. You're not Elvis. And... And, hell... I'm not either."

The King knelt there, his huge face engulfed in surprise before he broke into tears again. "What're we gonna do, little buddy?" he blubbered. "God, what're we gonna do?"

"Come on," Doyle said, grabbing the King by the stand-up collars of his shirt and coat and bringing him stumbling to his feet. "We're gonna get out of here."

"Out of here?" the King said, as if repeating a phrase from a foreign language he didn't understand. "Uh. Hey. Can't we wait till Mama comes back? She'll know what to do."

"Are you crazy?" Doyle said. "Didn't you just tell me they're going to kill you? And eventually they're going to kill me, too. And look at this," he said pointing down at the old woman on the floor. "They're going to blame you for this just as much as me. Our Mama is in this up to her sagging tits."

"Oh shit!" the King said.

"Exactly," Doyle said. "Let's go out to the barn and see if they've got a car that goes with this key."

"Le'me get my shades," the King said.

* * *

Back at the Office behind the Big House, Rhonda opened her purse and scrambled through its contents till she found her key ring. The key to the Mama car was missing all right. She figured Doyle must have searched her purse when she wasn't looking.

She stood there thinking of how many ways the world had ganged up on her since she whacked Elvis with that damned lion. Just when she thought she had escaped punishment for that little mishap, Elvis double crossed everybody by rejecting her at the Coming Out. She knew she was in trouble because the apostles felt they had license to talk dirty to her. Her drop in status even emboldened them to put their dirty hands on her. Those bastards would have been afraid to show her even a hint of disrespect back when she was in good standing with Mama. Now, on top of everything else, she was about to be accused of slipping Doyle a key to escape. Mama would think she had been betrayed.

She had seen people disappear for a lot less than that. And she could see no choice other than getting out. A flicker of hope had her rifling through her purse for the gate pass she'd used to pick Doyle up at the AMVETS. But that hope fizzled when she saw that the date had expired. For a moment she considered flirting her way through, maybe distracting Uncle Vester enough to make him overlook the date on her pass. But she was pretty sure he was still pissed at her for cracking Elvis's skull because when he'd stopped her the last time she went through the gate, he'd gone over her pass so carefully he looked as if he were searching for loopholes.

She sat at her desk frozen by worry before pushing herself up to walk, trembling, to the window. She wouldn't be surprised if Red and those goony Elvis apostles barged out of the house to come and get her at any minute.

A little squeak popped out of her throat when the back door at the carport sprang open. But instead of Red and the apostles, Doyle stepped out followed by the King. She watched in disbelief as they stumbled along in the sunshine toward the Cadillac barn like a couple of drunks, and all the while she thought, *They're going to try to leave.* After opening the cash drawer, she looked down on a thick stack of hundreds that she crammed into her purse. Those two clowns had less than a chance in hell to escape, but that was more of a chance than she had alone.

PART FIVE

ELVIS HAS LEFT

THE BUILDING

24

INTO THE WILDERNESS?

"God!" the King gasped as they stumbled along in the glaring sun and the damp heat. "It's too hot out here. I ain't gonna make it little buddy."

"It's just right over there," Doyle said, pointing at the barn. "Come on. Suck it up. You can make it." And as he fell in beside the King, alternating between pushing him along and holding him up when he stumbled, he looked behind them, then along the fence that snaked from the stone wall into the woods. He had a feeling that someone was watching them from somewhere. He just hoped they didn't know what they were seeing.

The King kept stumbling against him, and by the time they got halfway across the lot, the big man's sweaty arm wrapped around his neck felt as heavy as a sack full of rocks. "Gotta sit down little buddy," the King said.

"Can't sit down now," Doyle said, tugging on the King's belt hard enough to give him a wedgie. "Come on. You can make it."

When they got to the barn, Doyle tried the door and found it locked. "I'm going to try a window," he said. "You stay here."

While the King bent over, resting his hands on his knees, Doyle pushed on the closest of the three paned windows on the side of the barn. When it didn't budge, he picked up a sharp chunk of cinder block and smashed the glass. Then he reached in, found the latch and raised the window. He pushed himself up, swung his legs into the window and dropped into the dark hall.

The soles of his shoes smacked against concrete. With his fingers, he followed a line of exposed conduit to a row of light switches by the door. After turning on the lights, he pressed buttons on the wall till the door rattled and hummed and rolled up on the overhead tracks.

While squeezing the key in his hand, he surveyed the four vintage Cadillacs parked around the workshop. He didn't know which one the key fit, but he guessed it was the pink Mama car, the one that brought him into this place. After sliding under the steering wheel, he poked the key into the ignition, gave it a twist, and the engine roared to life.

He eased the big car through the door where the King now lay sprawled in the grass with Rhonda crouched over him. "What are you doing here?" Doyle said as he got out of the car.

"I'm going with you," she said.

"Don't take this bitch," the King gasped. "She'll rat us out the first chance she gets."

"I'm signed out for that key. If fatso here rejecting me last night didn't cook my goose, you coming up with it and driving out of here will finish me off for sure," she said.

"Can't trust the bitch," the King said. "I'm telling you."

"We don't have time to argue," Doyle said. "We'll get you out of here, but we're going to dump you at the first opportunity."

"Fair enough," she said. "Hadn't we better get going?"

The King turned himself around on his hands and knees and struggled to rise, his legs quivering with the effort. Finally, he slumped back in the grass. "Can you give me some help, little buddy?" he sighed.

Doyle thought for a moment about leaving both of them, but shrugged and said to the woman, "Help me get him into the car."

As they slid the King into the back seat, doors slammed over at the big house followed by shouting, and a cluster of men rushed past the Office and across the grass toward them. "Oh shit! Oh shit!" the King moaned.

"We'd better get going," Rhonda said. Doyle nodded, slid under the steering wheel and fumbled with the key. The car roared when he twisted the key and stomped the accelerator.

Doyle aimed the car at the men who were now charging toward them in the driveway. Red, with his eyes narrowed into two evil slits stood with Cholly at his side, his face twisted into a determined snarl while he pointed at Doyle with his cattle prod as if it were a magic wand that he thought would stop two tons of fast rolling steel.

The men scattered to safety. But Cholly, like a squirrel frozen by fear, stood in the path of the speeding car, his round face registering the oncoming horror before the car slammed into him with a sickening crunch. His face slammed against the hood, and he disappeared to become the dragging, scraping sound under the chassis, then the heavy bump under the left rear tire. "Oh shit!" yelled the King.

"We won't be able to get out the gate," Rhonda said.

"We'll bust through," Doyle said.

"I don't think you can," she said.

"Any other way out?" he said.

She shook her head. "I thought you knew what you were doing."

"You better hold on, because I'm not slowing down," Doyle said.

The gate was open with a red Coupe de Ville partially blocking the way and old Vester leaning on the roof of the car, his head thrown back, haw-hawing at something the driver had said. Doyle doubted he had enough room, but he knew he couldn't drive through the stone wall, and he would probably get shot by one of the guards if he tried to crash through the chain-link fence farther up.

He stomped the accelerator and crashed into the driver's side headlight of the de Ville and scraped the corner of the wall. The de Ville rolled backward. And with glass crashing and metal squealing against the crumbling stone, Vester tried to escape by climbing the de Ville, but he was too slow. When the pink Cadillac cleared the gate it slammed into the side of the de Ville, broadcasting a shrill squealing and squawking of metal against metal, against

Vester, against metal. Vester's blood splattered against the back passenger window of the Mama car and his scream stayed in Doyle's head miles down the road.

"God! Oh God!" the King gasped, pushing the words out through his labored breathing.

With a whirl of dust in its wake, the speeding car leaned heavily into the curves of the narrow dirt road, sending the wheels dipping through the ditches and into the weeds, the brush and brambles slapping against the doors and the glass. "Ohhh," the King moaned as he tossed about like a plastic bag in the wind.

Rhonda slammed into the dash and her head banged against Doyle and the passenger-side window a couple of times. They finally hit a flat stretch of asphalt where they ran a Toyota Camry off the road and blasted through a stop sign to the serenade of screeching brakes and an angry car horn. The heavy woods broke into pastures with little frame houses dotting the side of the road. A white steepled church zipped by the window; and men pumping gas at a convenience store jerked their heads around at the roaring pink blur.

Doyle didn't see anyone following him, but he didn't want to take any chances, so he let up on the accelerator only when he needed to keep control. He drove up on the interstate, weaving in and out of the traffic as the King's moans got louder and so mournful he ached inside. "Can you hold it down?" Doyle said. "I'm trying to concentrate up here."

He thought of the death he'd left behind him. And he cringed at the vision of poor Cholly's dumb face slamming into the hood of the car. But the sight of the Meditation Garden clouded out all other thoughts. The bastards had plans to plant him in one of those rectangles. It would be as if he had never been on the earth. His name had never done him much good, but he figured it would do to be etched into a tombstone one day after he died of old age.

"I think he's really sick," Rhonda said.

"I don't have time to think about him," Doyle said, now

thinking there was no way they could escape. The cops had to be after them by now.

"My neck's killing me," the King whined. "And my arm feels like it's 'bout to fall off." He gagged, bent his head over and puked, the rancid contents of his stomach splattering onto the floor.

"Oh, god!" Rhonda said. She tried to roll her window down, but finally gave up. "Roll your window down," she said. "Mine's stuck."

Doyle rolled his window down and spit a mouthful of his own bile into the wind. He turned on the radio, cranking up the volume of a country song to drown out the King's retching and moaning. He was feeling grateful for the hard rush of air through the window when the wailing of a siren blasted in his ears and a rack of revolving blue lights ignited across the roof of the black and white Dodge Charger racing along behind him.

"Damn," Doyle said, slowing down, maneuvering the van over to the right lane. "They've called the cops on us."

He pulled onto the shoulder, then stopped and turned off the radio. The smell of the vomit smothered him, but when he tried to open the door to get away from it, a voice from a loudspeaker behind him blared, "Sir! Stay in the vehicle, and keep both hands on the wheel."

Doyle had never been very fond of cops, but he always believed it was a pretty good idea to listen to anyone who got paid to carry a gun and a club. So he gripped the top of the steering wheel and looked in the rear-view mirror at the cop back in the Charger talking on his radio with the mic to the side of his mouth like he was having the most casual conversation in the world.

Doyle figured the cop was calling for back-up. He didn't blame him. After all, it was murder. No, triple murder. Next he'd be facing the gallows, the electric chair, gas chamber or whatever they did to mass murderers and thieves of vintage Cadillacs in Alabama these days. To fight back the tears, he slapped the steering wheel rhythmically and mindlessly hummed "Teddy Bear" while traffic whooshed by, heads turning to see the banged up pink Cadillac with the cop's whirling blue lights behind. Finally, the cop tossed the mic in the seat beside him, opened the door of the Charger and stood, hitching up his pants. Then he walked toward the Cadillac with a slow bandy-legged strut.

He was a hatless and buzz-cut young man with a cherubic face. The beginnings of a paunch gave his physique a premature middle-age bell-shape that protruded over his black plaited belt. On one hip, the thick belt held a pair of stainless handcuffs that gleamed in the sun as he walked along; and on the other, a holstered revolver whose snap he nervously thumbed as if he were getting ready to make a fast draw. "Where the hell you going in such a hurry?" he said in a quivering, high-breaking voice that sounded as if it belonged to a pubescent teenage boy. "I was doing seventy back there, and you blew by me in this thing like I was standing still."

Speeding? Doyle thought. *He spent all that time on the radio and all he can come up with is speeding?*

"Our friend back there's kind of sick," Rhonda said. "We were trying to get him to a doctor. That's why we were going so fast."

"Where'd all that blood come from?"

"Deer," Rhonda said. "He jumped out in front of us a ways back."

The cop walked around the car, shaking his head. When he got back to the driver's side, he said, "Must've been a monster to give up all this blood and do all that damage."

"We slammed into a tree after we hit him," Rhonda said.

The cop bent over and looked in the back seat where the King was stretched out. "Are you guys some kind of two man Elvis act?"

"That's right," Rhonda said. "Thin Elvis and fat Elvis."

"Hell, I'd like to see that," the cop said. "I've always been a big Elvis fan." He opened the back door of the Cadillac, and after wincing at the smell, he held one hand over his face and reached in to feel the King's neck. "You all right, buddy?"

The King moaned and the cop pulled his hand away and wiped it on his shirt. "Goddamn! He's still with us, but he's awful cold and clammy," he said. "Why didn't y'all call an ambulance?"

"They don't get to you so fast out in the country," Rhonda said.

"I can't tell how bad off he is, but you're right about him needing to get to a hospital. Tell you what, I'm going to pull around you, and I want you to fall in behind and follow me. You understand?"

"Yes, sir," Doyle said.

Doyle started the Cadillac as the cop jogged back to the Charger. "Pretty fast thinking," he said.

"Aren't you glad you brought me along?" Rhonda said.

"We'll see," he said.

During a break in the traffic, the cop whipped the cruiser out on the pavement. Doyle followed, tight on his bumper. They cruised into the left lane, the wailing siren as shrill as a pack of coyotes.

With his eyes riveted to the whirring blue lights, Doyle didn't even remember turning. But he glanced to his side and realized they were off the interstate and into the city, slowing at traffic lights before blazing on through the intersections. After wheeling into the emergency room entrance of the Hospital, the cop leaped from his car and made a mad dash through the automatic sliding door. He came out of the hospital running, followed by two men and a woman shoving a gurney along.

They loaded the King onto the gurney and hustled him through the glass doors. The cop stood, shaking his head, gasping for a moment. An ambulance pulled in behind the Cadillac, and the cop jogged around to the driver's side and said, "Get this thing out of the emergency entrance, then come back in. These folks'll want some information, and, to tell you the damn truth, I could use a little myself."

Doyle drove around the building, and not finding a parking space, he pulled into a loading zone. He was glad to finally get out of the stinking car whose headlights had been crushed, and the rear bumper dangling almost to the asphalt.

"We need to get out of here," Rhonda said as she slid across the seat and got out on the driver's side.

"What about Elvis?" Doyle said.

"Nothing we can do about him," she said. "But one thing's for sure, that car stands out like a sore thumb. The longer we hang around it, the more likely we are to get caught."

25

THE HIDEOUT

*I*t was her idea to throw the cops off their trail by walking a random zig-zag through an old community, shuffling over cracked sidewalks and through narrow streets made even narrower by the cars parked on both sides. Doyle kept thinking he heard footsteps behind him, but every time he turned around, the only things he saw were a canopy of gnarly oaks and a once-prosperous neighborhood slipping into disrepair.

"You hear the way I handled that cop back there?" Rhonda said as they walked along.

"You did all right," Doyle said. He wouldn't admit it out loud, but he was glad she'd been along because the memory of all that blood back at the compound had left him speechless in the presence of the cop.

He was exhausted. His feet felt so heavy they clomped under him like a couple of cinder blocks. She was now leading the way, marching ahead with her purse tucked under her arm. Her long hair swayed and her hips moved under those jeans in a way that would have made him regret all those lost opportunities back at the big house if he weren't so damned tired. As he trudged along he called out to her, "You even know where you're going?"

"No idea," she called back. "This street looks like it goes somewhere."

When the street intersected a busy avenue flanked by a string of payday loan joints and thrift stores, he had fallen way behind. His shirt, soaked with sweat, clung to his skin like a bandage. People staring from the passing cars made him wonder if he looked like a disheveled Elvis or just a homeless pervert stalking a beautiful woman. She waited for him on a bus stop bench. When he plopped down beside her, she said, "You didn't think this through very well, did you?"

"Didn't think it through at all," he said. "I saw a slim chance to get out, and I took it. You got any money? They took all mine."

"I've got some money," she said. "I bet that makes you even more glad you brought me along."

"How much you got?"

"Some."

"We need to catch the first thing smoking out of this town. You got enough for a couple of bus tickets?"

"I don't think we should do that," she said. "Lover, you just killed two people..."

"Three," he said.

"Three?" she snapped, looking at him as if she'd seen him for the first time.

"Yeah. Granny, right before we ran into you."

"Granny? No shit?" She said, a smile flickering through her gaze. "Couldn't have happened to a nicer person. Well, you'll have to tell me about it sometime. Right now, I think we need to stay out of the bus station. They'll be waiting for us there. We need to find somewhere to put up for a while."

He thought she was right—the cops had probably tossed up some kind of dragnet for them. Laying low for a couple of days might be the thing to do. Some comfortable and cool place to stretch out was sounding better and better all the time.

At a convenience store she bought three bags full of supplies and got the clerk to point them to the nearest motel, a horseshoe-shaped affair with a flickering vacancy sign and an empty swimming pool with blistered blue paint surrounding a nasty blanket of brown leaves on the bottom.

The dinging bell on the door as they entered the cramped little motel office didn't distract the clerk for a second from his session with "Grand Theft Auto" exploding from the monitor. They stood at the desk till he finally cursed before raising up to acknowledge their presence. He looked to be a teenager of Indian descent, copping a world-weary expression on a face the same color and expression as a sweet potato. He raised a half-interested eyebrow at their plastic bag luggage. When Rhonda told him they needed a room, Doyle expected to hear the stereotypical cab driver/7-11 accent, but his answer was more northeast Alabama than Mumbai. "Y'all gone hafta pay cash," he drawled.

The room had two beds and a flat-screen TV perched on a scuffed-up chest of drawers. Beside the chest stood a refrigerator so small Rhonda had to get down on her knees to access it. On top of the fridge sat a scarred micro-wave with a loose handle. A fading print of a plump rose with a thorny stem hung on one of the beige walls. But the thick scent of disinfectant hanging in the room didn't smell very rose-like.

"I don't know about you," she said. "But I'm going to take a shower."

"I'll be right behind you," he groaned as he dropped down on the bed.

"Hey," he said as she moved across the room in front of him. "Do I call you Rhonda or what?"

"Might as well," she said from the bathroom. "I don't think I'm going to be assuming any other identities anytime soon. Wow! I didn't know they even made towels this thin."

The sound of the water gushing into the tub made him want to pee, but not badly enough to get up. When he heard the water pelting the plastic shower curtain, he closed his eyes and imagined her naked, lathering her body with soap, her eyes closed as she felt the ecstasy of the steamy water beading on her sweaty skin. It was a pretty vivid image, and he figured he must really be tired because Little Elvis didn't even twitch once.

He raised up and clicked on the TV to see if he could find some local news, but after a few minutes of flipping through game shows, soap operas, and advertising lawyers he turned the thing off.

"What a day," he said, sprawling back across the bed.

Rhonda came out of the bathroom, bare except for a soaked towel wrapped across her shoulders. She dug the comb and styling brush she'd bought at the store out of one of the bags and after bending over and combing her long hair forward, she attacked it with a towel. She worked the brush through it a few times before rubbing it down with the towel again. "We would have picked the one dump without a hairdryer," she said. "When my hair dries out, I'm going to look like a windblown witch."

He'd turned away from her and curled into a fetal position when she popped his butt with the towel.

"Whaaa?" he said, and when he turned over, she startled him by hopping up on the bed and straddling him.

"We haven't got anything else to do," she said, looking down on him behind a seductive smile. "We could finish what we started. Well, we've never really started anything, have we?" She took a couple of sniffs and continued—"But you're going to have to take a shower. You smell like you've gone sour or something."

"Look," he said. "I just don't..."

"You don't what?" she said as she dismounted him and stood impatiently by the bed. "You don't want to? Again?"

"Well," he groaned. "I kinda want to."

"Kinda want to? You're not gay or anything, are you? I mean, it would be all right if you were gay. In fact it would be better because it would explain why you don't seem interested in all this." She made an elegant sweep over her body with her hands as if she were a model on a game show, pointing out a new washer and dryer.

"Hell no, I'm not gay," he said as he raised up. Then he collapsed back on the bed. "I'm just not feeling so good. Maybe after I rest a little. Is it cold in here?"

"Cold?" she said. "It's a sweat box. I was just thinking about cranking down the thermostat. Always something with you," she said, shaking her head as he pulled back the covers and crawled under them, shoes and all.

She shrugged, clicked on the TV, and while she worked on her hair she watched a bald, chunky moderator demean his guests for leading their dysfunctional lives.

He tossed and turned without sleeping. The ache, from deep inside him, seemed to be inching to the surface. After a while, he opened his eyes to see that the room had turned darker.

"Bad hair day or not, I'm getting pretty hungry," she said. "We passed a McDonalds, a meat-and-three joint and a pizza place when we came in. You interested in any of that?"

"No," he groaned. "I really couldn't eat a thing."

"Well, I'm going," she said. "Damn, I hate to put on these sweaty clothes over my nice, clean bod, but you gotta do what you gotta do."

He turned away from her, closed his eyes tight and listened to her scuffling around. After a few minutes the door opened and she said, "Sure I can't bring you something back?"

"No," he said. "Nothing for me."

26

COME TO MAMA

The last thing she wanted was to draw attention to herself. So she sat by the window, alternating between dabbing her lips with her napkin and sipping her Coke through the straw as daintily as she knew how, hoping no one noticed that she had just scarfed down her burger and fries like a starving hound. Outside, the blue, green and yellow plastic playground looked lonely and abandoned in the hard glow of the street light. And beyond the playground, the caravan of stragglers from the after-work rush hour slogged along the four-lane street. She'd given up the only real home she'd ever known, so she couldn't help but envy the drivers in those cars as they mindlessly traveled their well-worn paths back to their homes, confident that those homes would be the same as they were when they left that morning.

She knew it didn't solve any problems by regretting the decision she'd hastily made that afternoon. And her thoughts quickly turned to what she would do next. She'd been right saying that public transportation was a terrible idea, but staying put was not a long-term solution either. If trains, buses and planes were out, that left automobiles.

She remembered seeing one of those local auto sales magazines on a table in the little motel office when she paid for the room. If it was still there when she stopped by, she would grab it and do a little research. After laying low for a couple of days she would see about buying them a car that would at least get them into another state where they could change their identities.

Out of habit, she offered up a prayer to Elvis, but stopped half-way through when she began to doubt the King's spirit would be on her side at this point in the game. She imagined Him listening and quickly reporting her location back to Mama like some kind of celestial cop tracing a cell phone signal. It seemed unlikely, even silly, but there it was, embedded deep in her belief system like all those people who know that stepping on sidewalk cracks or walking under ladders can't possibly result in any real consequences but who avoid all those activities just in case.

Elvis. She had come this far without Him, so why not give up on Him? What had He done for her lately anyway? Doyle definitely needed to give up on Him. The Elvis image would be the first thing the cops would be looking for. And even if he didn't get them caught, going around doing an Elvis tribute act limits the hell out of his professional possibilities. The thing would attract only a small niche audience. He would wind up with a sad, mediocre career at best.

He had some talent though. There was no denying that. What he needed to do was create a different image. He could stop dying his hair black and let it grow onto his shoulder, cultivate a scruffy beard, and develop a totally different style. He could sing some of the edgy country songs with lyrics about drugs, sex, and turning your back on dysfunctional religions that she'd heard when she made recruiting trips among The Others. She could see him fronting a really tight band playing a revved-up rock-a-billy style with a jam groove, throwing in a few traditional tear-jerkers for a change of pace. She didn't know anything about entertainment management, but she felt confident that she could put the whole package together if she really tried.

He'd told her he didn't want anything to eat, but in case he changed his mind, she bought him a burger and some fries before leaving the restaurant. With her purse tucked under one arm and the take-out swinging at her side, she made her way across the street.

As she crossed the intersection in front of a cop waiting at the light she felt like a frightened kid whistling through a graveyard. But from the look on his face when she glanced back, she was fairly convinced that he'd been more interested in her ass than her identity.

With her eye on the little motel office, she walked beside the white van, not noticing it was there till the back door blocked her path and Red pulled her into the backseat with his hand clamped over her mouth. "Look who we got here," he said.

As she struggled, squirmed, and kicked, Red's grip on her tightened till she gave in to the inevitable and kept still in his arms.

"We going to pick up the boy?" Joe said from behind the wheel.

"Nah," Red said. "We'll send somebody back to watch him. But for now, we'll just let him stir in his juices a while. Mama's really anxious to have a little talk with this one."

"Hey," Sonny said from the front passenger seat. "That a Big Mac and fries I smell?"

They circled the Big House. After stopping the van in the carport, they led her into the Office where Mama sat behind the desk crying. "Oh, baby," she said when Red pushed Rhonda through the door. "How could you do this to me?"

The old woman came from behind the desk, wrapped her arms around Rhonda and wept with her face buried between Rhonda's breasts. "Why?" Mama said.

"Mama, you were going to have me disappeared."

"Oh, no, baby," Mama said, now sniffling. "Not you. Never you. You've always been my little girl. You were with me from the very beginning."

"Y'all were still mad at me for whacking Elvis with that lion in the Jungle Room. Then Elvis rejected me. And after everything else, it was my fault your key showed up in the boy's room. I just thought..."

"You should have come and talked to me. Honey, I would have done everything I could to protect you." Mama shook her head. "Lord, I still remember you as a dirty-faced little girl in that trailer park. Now what can I do? You've stole from the church and led Elvis and the boy away from the Land of Grace. Three of our people are dead. One of them an apostle. Everybody knows about it now. The Children are all in a twitter about how you tried to seduce their King away from them."

"Don't forget she wrecked your car," Sonny said.

"Yeah," Mama snapped, her brow furrowing, her mouth drawing up into a tight, little circle as if she were trying to slam the door on the salvo of profanities trying to escape. "There's that, too."

"I always heard there was no use crying over spilt milk," Red said. "My opinion? This one here's nothing but spilt milk."

"It breaks my heart," Mama said, shaking her head. "But I guess this is goodbye, baby."

Red and Sonny grabbed Rhonda's arms and pulled her back to the door.

"Wait! Wait!" Rhonda cried. "Mama, please!"

Mama nodded and the men stopped and released her arms.

"You got something else to say?" Mama said.

"Mama, all that we've meant to each other all these years. You've been the only mama I've ever had. You know that."

"I know, baby. And that's what hurts me so bad. You don't leave me any other choice. What's everybody going to say when I let you get away with all this? There's got to be some consequences."

"You mean there's no mercy in our religion?"

"Not any for you," Red said, and he and Sonny grabbed her arms again and pulled her toward the door. "Where you want to keep her?"

"Let's keep her in the bodyguard room for now," Mama said.

She said nothing as they shoved her into the Big House past the Jungle Room and down the stairs. Red unlocked the door across from the Pool Room, and pulled her into a bedroom she didn't know was there. After shoving her onto a couch, Red said, "Not much to look at, but it's more than you deserve."

"Does all of this make any sense to you, Red?" she asked, as she fought to keep the tears from taking her voice.

"Does it what?" Red said. "Make any sense?" He thought for a second and shook his head. "Honey, it's what we believe, ain't it? Hell, it don't have to make sense."

27

ARE YOU LONESOME AGAIN?

Doyle had no watch and the clock on the radio had been stuck on four o'clock since they checked in. But his increasing boredom and the changing shadows on the wall told him Rhonda had been gone a hell of a lot longer than necessary to eat dinner. If she had been arrested, the cops would have knocked the door down by now, so he figured she had just run out on him. He didn't really blame her. He had no money, and though he'd had more than ample opportunity, he hadn't exactly proven himself to be the most passionate lover in the world.

Whatever her reasons for splitting, he was too tired to care. At first, he thought the fatigue came from all the violence, the frantic escape and the long hike from the hospital to the motel in all that heat, but the ache he felt deep in his bones now reminded him of the early symptoms of the flu he'd caught back in Tonto Basin, Arizona, a couple of years ago. Back then he had stocked up on soup, crackers, aspirin and Pepsi and rode out a burning fever for over a week in the Tonto Basin Inn.

As the fatigue rose up in his muscles, he found it too painful to lie still. Yet he was too tired to stand. He spent the night and most of the next day alternating between squirming around on the bed and plodding around the room like an arthritic old man. Rhonda had bought him a six pack of Pepsi at the convenience store, but he threw up every swallow he tried to put down.

As sick as he felt, his curiosity over his fugitive status worried him. On the third morning in the motel, he wandered out to the curb on shaky legs, broke into a newspaper rack and stole a morning paper. Back in the room, his heart kicked into a fast gallop as he read the headline on the third column of the front page—

Elvis Lookalike Disappears from Hospital.

On the eve of the Anniversary of the death of Elvis Presley, an Elvis lookalike appeared only to disappear from University Hospital. Last night at 9:45 pm, University officials reported the disappearance of a critically ill patient from their cardiac intensive care unit. Because of patient privacy, the hospital officials would not comment on the man's condition, only saying that he was much too ill to have walked out of the hospital on his own.

The missing patient was admitted to the hospital late Tuesday afternoon by Springville Police officer Wendell Benefield who found the man slumped in the back seat of a pink antique Cadillac he had pulled over on I-59 for speeding. "For a second, I actually thought I was looking at two Elvises," Benefield told this reporter last night on the phone. "Then I said to myself, no, silly, it couldn't be. But one of the fellows was in pretty bad shape. His skin was cold and he looked kind of pasty like he'd been drained of blood or something. I made sure he was still breathing and just told the driver to fall in behind me, and we took him to the hospital where I checked him into the emergency room."

The identity of the missing patient is unknown at this time. Authorities describe him as a white male in his forties, around six feet tall and approximately 250 pounds. He has black hair styled in the manner of the late singer, Elvis Presley.

The car the patient was riding in was found abandoned in a loading zone behind the hospital. The car was impounded by police.

Another mystery swirls around the driver of the car and a woman passenger who are both now missing. Their identities are also unknown at this time. The woman was described by authorities as being in her mid-to-late twenties with long black hair, wear-

ing jeans and a blue and white top. The man was described as a white male around six feet tall who also looked like the deceased singer. He's in his mid-to-late twenties or early thirties, medium build, with dark black hair, styled in an Elvis look. He was last seen wearing jeans and a red and blue colored tee shirt. Anyone seeing either of these people should contact the Police Department ...

He read through the article a couple more times. Then he scoured the rest of the paper. But there was no mention of a triple murder anywhere. The whole thing had him thinking maybe they weren't hurt as bad as he thought. But then he slumped down on the bed, shaking his head. He thought Vester could have possibly lived through it, but he'd have to be messed up pretty bad. But Granny wasn't breathing. And Cholly? Poor Cholly. How could anybody live through being hit straight on by that monstrous car, then have the damn thing roll over the top of him?

When he saw *August 16, 2012* centered just below the masthead of the newspaper, he thought the King had known exactly what he was talking about. He envisioned them depositing the King's bloated corpse on the floor of the upstairs bathroom. Now they were going to dump him in the Meditation Garden under another one of those marble slabs with the others.

That night, the television news reported the story as a humorous break from all the shootings, drug overdoses and political prosecutions. "Has anybody seen Elvis lately?" the buxom anchor woman asked, introducing the story with a perky smirk.

28

ELVIS WEEK

The room had a green fabric couch, a coffee table, a twin bed and a bathroom. There was no TV, no music, no magazines or books. Since it was in the basement, Rhonda didn't expect windows, but the absence of even a picture on the pale blue wall told her they didn't want to divert her attention from waiting and worrying for a second. So she waited and worried.

The thing she worried about most was, what would happen to her? Since Mama had created her own special little heaven in The Land of Grace, Rhonda thought she was perfectly capable of designing some unique kind of hell. She couldn't imagine what it would be. But she knew for certain that waiting to find out was hell in itself.

She could tell someone had replaced Granny in the Kitchen because the food was amazing. From the omelets and pancakes in the morning to the pot roast and apple pie for dinner, they had her sniffing the air and listening for the door around meal time.

Three times a day the latch clicked and the door sprang open with one of the Kitchen help bringing in her meals under a silver domed tray and an apostle standing guard. She always tried to talk to them, but they were obviously under strict orders from Mama to avoid any communication with her. The woman bringing in the tray always shook her head as if she were deaf as a post, and the apostle stood at her side, ignoring her with a disinterested stare of an employee at the DMV.

She had nothing to do but eat and feel her time melting away. One day she was awakened by a loud commotion in the hallway, men rumbling and women crying as if they were all in some kind of pain. When they opened the door to bring her breakfast it seemed as if someone had turned the volume up to eleven on all that wailing as the sound of the grief flooded into the room. In the brief time the door was open, Rhonda saw people gathered across the way in the TV Room and the Pool Room. The woman carrying the tray sobbed and shook her head after Rhonda asked, "What's going on?" The apostle Jerry stood by the door, his stony eyes welling with tears.

After eating, she spent most of the morning with her ear to the door, listening to the rumbling voices and trying to imagine what could be happening. When the door opened for her lunch, Mama followed apostle Lamar into the room. She wore a black robe Rhonda had only seen her wear on two other occasions—the deaths of the King.

"Give us the room," Mama said after the woman from the Kitchen set the tray down on the coffee table.

"You sure?" Apostle Lamar said.

"Oh, I'll be all right," Mama said.

Once they were alone, Mama gathered Rhonda in her arms, squeezing her in a bear hug while trembling from grief. "He's gone," she sobbed. "My baby's gone."

"Gone?" Rhonda said. "Who's gone?"

"Why, my baby," Mama said, looking at her with surprise, her face a round mask of tears. "Elvis."

"But Elvis left," Rhonda said. "He's in the city."

"Oh, he came back," Mama said. "I knew he'd come back. My baby couldn't stay away from me for very long. Especially when he was sick. And he was sick. I mean, real sick. Honey, he was so sick there was nothing me and Dr. Nick could do. And we tried."

"Who are you trying to bullshit?" Rhonda said, her voice trembling with a mixture of fear of Mama and anger. She freed herself from Mama's grasp and pushed herself away.

"Baby, what're you...? How could you say something like that?"

"You don't have to waste this bereaved mother act on me," Rhonda said. "It's August the sixteenth. You made him sick, and you know it. You and Doctor Nick killed him like you killed the others."

"It's in the book," Mama said. "Of course I knew it was coming as well as I knew the sun was going to rise. But that don't mean it don't break my heart to lose him just the same."

Mama sniffled and wiped her nose with a tissue. Her eyes were too red and her lips too quivery for this to be just an act. Rhonda thought, *The bitch really is grieving*.

"That means Elvis Week's begun," Rhonda said.

"That's right," Mama said. "I don't think I've ever seen the Children so heart broke. How they love their grief. Sometimes I believe to my soul they love Elvis dying for them more than they love the resurrection."

"What are they going to do when Elvis doesn't rise up on the fifth day?"

Mama sniffed a couple of times and said, "Well, that's where you come in."

"I'm not going to talk the boy into coming back. You can forget that."

"Oh, honey. I don't want you to talk him into coming back. I want you to try to talk him into going away with you."

"You're not going to let me leave," Rhonda said. "Not after all I've done."

"You're wrong about that, baby. You know as well as I do that I could get Red and Sonny to go in that cheap motel room where you left him and fetch him back in a second. But that won't do. Won't do at all. See, he's got to want to come back. He's got to want to come back more than he wants your life. More than he wants his own life. If he don't want to come back more than he wants anything else, that means the spirit didn't quicken in him during rebirth."

"If you don't have an Elvis reborn, the Children are going to buckle on you," Rhonda said. "They won't believe anything in that book of yours or anything you say from now on."

"I know," Mama said. "But I'd rather have this whole

lash-up fall in than to have an Elvis who don't want to be Elvis. You know you're due for some serious reckoning, don't you, baby?"

Rhonda nodded.

"What you got coming." Mama shook her head. "Honey, what you got coming involves a visit from Doctor Nick."

"Oh, God," Rhonda whined like a wounded animal.

"I know. I know," Mama said. "It gives me the heebie-jeebies just to think of it. If you can talk the boy into staying away out there in the Wilderness with you and The Others, then we won't interfere. But if the boy wants to come back and claim his legacy? You'll have to come back too. And if you come back, Doctor Nick'll be waiting."

"But if I...if I talk him into leaving, you'll...you'll let us go?"

"If that's what the boy wants. You'll be free as a couple of birds. That's my word. And, Honey, you know my word is good."

29

THE TRIAL

The next day, instead of stumbling out to the curb to steal a paper, Doyle spent the morning vomiting until he thought his stomach would turn inside out. The nausea segued into dreams that ended with the image of a pink Cadillac crashing through the walls of the room and running him over. He was startled awake but wondered if he had actually been run over by a car when the cramps attacked his legs.

The cramps lasted so long that when they finally subsided he collapsed on the bed, exhausted, with his brain traveling through a flashing chain of fragmented images. He thought he heard Rhonda a couple of times, but when he raised up he was still alone. "That bitch is not coming back," he moaned. "The King was right. You can't trust her for a second. She probably made a deal for herself and ratted me out. I'd better get out of here before this stinking room fills up with cops." He struggled to his feet and stood on wobbly legs for a moment only to crumble back on the bed.

Through fevered images, he traveled back to San Angelo. He lost his breath when he found himself tied to his grandfather's wheelchair. The old man's voice crackled from the shadows, saying, "Now you can ride that chair for the rest of your life like I did. You little bastard."

He thought the old man's voice had jarred him awake, but he doubted his consciousness when the door to the room opened and Red and a man who looked like a cop crept in.

"What do you think, Uncle Buck?" Red said.

"I think I've seen better color on road-kill possums," the cop said.

"How you feeling, big man?" Red said.

Doyle lay staring up at the two. He felt as if he needed to get his eyes in focus, but after a while the two images looked as if they had more substance than the other apparitions he'd seen. But it still seemed like a dream because two more people slipped in the door and stood behind them like shadows moving along the wall.

The cop said, "Cat musta got his tongue."

The other dreams had clicked by like a slide show. But after this nightmare at the foot of his bed wouldn't change into something else, Doyle decided to speak to it. He raised up on his elbow and said in a quivering voice, "How...? How did you...?"

"How did we find you?" the cop said through a chuckle. "You gotta be shitting me. I have to say, I'm a pretty good skip-tracer. But it didn't take Sherlock Holmes to find your ass. I mean, a white male in jeans and a red and blue tee shirt who looks like Elvis, wandering around on foot with a beautiful brunette? Hell, we knew where you were a couple of hours after you left the hospital."

Red said, "When Uncle Buck slipped the pimple-faced desk clerk out there a twenty and asked if he had any big stars staying in this dump, the boy just shrugged and said kinda matter-of-fact, 'Got Elvis in 213.'"

Listening to the husky laughter filling the room made Doyle think this was too close to being real and struggled to rise. Red moved around the bed, clutched his arms and pulled him up. He thought this may be just another apparition, but if it was it had the firmest grip and the sourest breath of any dream character he'd ever encountered. "I guess he's here to arrest me?"

"Why would he want to arrest you? " Red said.

"Yeah, I'd like to arrest you, but I hadn't figured out what to charge you with." Buck said. "Driving Elvis to the hospital might sound crazy as hell, but last time I checked, it ain't against the damn law. And you think I'd come looking for somebody who illegally parked a wrecked Cadillac that hadn't been reported stolen?"

"But the...the murders," Doyle said.

"Murders?" Buck said. "Son, I'm the sheriff of Reece County and I ain't heard of any murders. You heard about any murders I need to be looking into, Red?"

"Not lately, Uncle Buck," Red said. "Closest thing to a murder was when we had some folks leave The Land of Grace without giving notice. I want to tell you, it pissed me off enough to kill somebody. That damned Vester for one. But I already got his sorry ass replaced. Wasn't any problem at all. Hell, I could teach a gorilla how to watch the gate.

"Then, of course, there was Cholly," Red continued. "Just up and quit for no reason at all. And I thought he was happy as a pig in shit. Oh, well." Red shrugged. "The Colonel's auditioning candidates for his spot as we speak. I understand ever' damned one of 'em is a better guitar player than the Cholly who left. But that's about all the changes we had."

"Granny," Doyle groaned. "She's all right then?"

"Oh, hell," Red chuckled. "How could I forget her? You gotta see this new Granny we got. I'll swear, she's older'n white dog shit, but she's sweeter than the banana puddin' she makes. The last one? Talk about murder, now. Hell, everybody wanted to murder that bitch. E liking her and calling her his Dodger was the only thing that saved her ugly ass. I don't know anybody that's not glad she's gone.

"Hey," Red said. "Got somebody wants to see you. Bring her on up here, Sonny. I promised Mama I'd give her a fair chance to make her little pitch."

Sonny shoved Rhonda to the other bed. After Sonny dropped down beside her, Doyle said, "Where did you go?"

"Now, let's get this straight right off the bat," Red said. "In all fairness, you can't blame her for leaving. She was even coming back with you a Big Mac and fries when I grabbed her out in the parking lot. She's been locked up in the basement of the Big House ever' since. Now, Sonny ate your Big Mac. And I have to admit, I had half your fries."

"Okay! Okay!" Buck said. "Let's get on with it. Mama told me to mediate this thing, and that's what I'm going to do. Now, let me tell you what this is all about, son. First of all, a while back, Miss Rhonda here assaulted Elvis. Now, according to the Book of Gladys, that alone is enough to make her disappear. But you know Mama. She's got big old soft spot in her heart, so she let her slide on that one. But then the girl stole money from the church, and encouraged you and Elvis to leave. In the process, she aided and abetted in the departure of certain of Mama's, shall we say, key employees, including an apostle. And then, if all that wasn't bad enough, Mama's car got all messed up.

"Now, you are supposed to be the chosen one. So, by the laws of the Land of Grace, you're exempt from any kind of punishment. But somebody's going to have to pay for all the shit that happened, and I'm afraid little Rhonda is it. That is, unless you decide to stay out here with her. In that case, both of you are free to go."

"I don't understand," Doyle groaned. With the throbbing ache in his body alternating with the stabbing pain between his eyes, he collapsed back on his pillow wishing they would all just go away and let him die. "Can you just come back later?"

"The way you look, there might not be a damn later," Red said.

"Listen, Boy," Rhonda said. "We can..."

"Boy?" he said, raising up on his elbow. The flash of anger almost strong enough to make him stand. "You don't even..." he said before catching his breath. "You don't even know my name, do you?" He fell back on the pillow, thinking he barely remembered it himself.

"We don't have time to argue about names," Buck said. "It's as simple as this—If you agree to go away with Miss Rhonda here, that's it. You can go with Mama's blessing. No hard feelings. Mama promised. I've known that woman all her life, and I can tell you, her word is as good as gold.

Go ahead Miss Rhonda."

"Boy, I've got plans for us," Rhonda said. "You've got a great voice. And you have an amazing stage presence. You really do. The most commanding I've ever seen. Except for Elvis of course. The problem is, you sound too much like Elvis. Shoot, you sound exactly like him. But we can fix that, maybe raise your voice a little, put a little more nasal whang into it. You can sing country. But a different kind of country. You know, develop your own style like I read about a guy named Waylon Jennings doing. You can be, uh, what *is* your name?"

"Doyle," he said, pulling the name out of the fog of his mind, thinking he could be wrong because it didn't sound right. "Doyle Brisendine."

Rhonda bit her lip and thought for a second. "Well," she said, shaking her head. "Maybe not that. But something other than Elvis. You might just make it big being yourself. I can see it all now. I really can."

"Red," Buck said. "You want to retort?"

"Think about all the other entertainers you've heard of," Red said. "I mean, the top entertainers. They've got their fans and all. People hoot and clap, buy their records, their t-shirts, get their autographs, and shit. But their fans don't adore them. They don't scream and wail and want to touch them. They don't worship them and line up by the thousands to visit their graves, their homes and their birthplaces after they die. The first Elvis has been dead for damn near forty years, and people pack into Memphis' Graceland every day from all over the world. The best entertainer out there now is only a shadow of what Elvis is even while he's dead. But odds are, you probably won't even make it to mediocre. What'll probably happen is, after being a miserable failure, you'll limp on back to Hop Toad, Texas..."

"San Angelo," Doyle said.

"Yeah. And you can spend the rest of your life in that shit hole bagging groceries and looking at the pity in everybody's eyes."

"That all, Red?" Buck said.

Red nodded.

Buck pointed to Rhonda and said, "Any rebuttal, Miss Rhonda?"

"Don't listen to him," Rhonda said. "You know why you're feeling so bad now? It's all their fault. Those vitamins Mama's been giving you? They're some kind of heavy shit that creep Doctor Nick brings in from Mexico. He calls them lightning in a bottle. You're feeling bad because your body's withdrawing from them. The first thing I'll do is get you to a hospital. They'll treat your withdrawal and bring you down from those things. Then we'll take a shot at you being a star on your own."

After a moment of silence, Buck said, "Those are some serious accusations, Red. You got anything to say about that?"

"Hell, I say we'll go about this another way," Red said. "We won't take those pills away from you for a second. In fact, first thing we'll do is get Doctor Nick to give you a couple more, maybe three or four more till he gets your blood all regulated again. Man, you'll feel gooood," he said, stretching out the word while twisting his head. "You know, like you did back in the Land of Grace. Then you can play all day and party all night. And late at night, Mama'll give you some of that good hot chocolate to slow your motor down to a gentle purr so you can get some sleep and have some of them sweet dreams you used to have. Once you get well? Which will be no more than a couple days, tops, you'll be rocking your ass off."

"Come with me, baby," Rhonda pleaded. "You know these creeps will use you up in five years. Five years! Then they'll dump what's left of you in a box and bury you out in that Meditation Garden with the others. Ask him if that's not true."

"Well, she's right about that, Hoss," Red said. "I'm not going to lie to you. It won't last forever. We decided at the beginning of this thing that the Children have to have somebody to die for them. If they don't have that, they might go ape shit on us. This whole thing is held together by the King's sacrifice.

"But just think about it for a second. Instead of being a mediocre singer, or sacking groceries and winding up an old man in a wheelchair, you'll have a whole pile of young women to love you and a few thousand people who'll not just love you, they'll worship your ass. You won't be just an Elvis imitator. Man, you'll *be* Elvis."

"Okay," Buck said. "That's enough. Miss Rhonda?"

"Remember, you'll have me," Rhonda said. "I know we got off to a bad start. But when you get all well, we can start all over, take our time and make it good. You know you want me, baby."

Red said, "You think a bitch that looks this good is going to stay with some Elvis-imitating, grocery-bagging motherfucker? Child, please! You come back with us and you'll have your pick of women. Every day you can pick a new one, or two or three of them for that matter."

"I need to be getting on back to Willow Ruth," Buck said. "Let's wrap this thing up. Miss Rhonda?"

Rhonda's lips trembled and her eyes welled with tears. "They're...they're going to kill me," she said.

"What?" Doyle said. "No. They're not going to..."

"Oh yes they are," she said. "If you go back, I have to go back. If I go back, they'll turn me over to Doctor Nick. Just ask Red."

"Red," Doyle said. "Is that true?"

Red shrugged. "What can I say?" He said. "She's got some serious shit to answer for. Getting you to leave is her last chance. Hey, I almost forgot the best thing of all— Mama. You know deep down in your heart that she's your mama now, don't you? Well, that little woman'll be with you all the way, hoss. She'll make sure you get your vitamins, tuck you in at night, and she'll always be just standing by being a proud mama as her boy reigns over The Land of Grace. And though you walked out on her, she forgives you. And you can bet your ass she'll never walk out on you."

PART SIX

ELVIS: THAT'S THE

WAY IT IS

30
MAMA'S LOVING HANDS

Rhonda lay strapped to a gurney, having to close her eyes and turn her head against the harsh glow of the huge lamp shining down from the white ceiling. The light was so bright that after she squeezed her eyelids together, red shapeless figures swam across her vision like jelly fish moving in the dark.

For the past two hours or so, she'd been alone, her cries muffled by a thick strip of tape covering her mouth. With tears tickling her cheeks, she worried about the hard rattling underneath her. It sounded like some fierce monster trying to escape from the bowels of the building, and she wondered what horror could be rising up to take her. But after she managed to be still for a moment, she realized it was just the tremors erupting from somewhere inside her, shaking the gurney and vibrating its wheels against the tile floor.

A door opened and someone entered the room. After closing the door behind him, he stood still for a moment and she could hear him breathing before he moved toward her. She had seen Doctor Nick in the Big House so many times she was sure it was him from the slow clicking of his footsteps against the tile. After squinting her eyes and turning her head toward the sound, she could see the outline of his thick hair on the shadow the bright light cast across the wall. While he walked around her, he sang a fragmented version of "Love Me Tender" in a scratchy tenor.

After butchering the song's first verse, he dropped a soft hand on her knee. His moist touch took her breath and ratcheted up her tremors. "I luh to hear Elwis sing that song, don't you?" he asked.

"What am I saying? Of course you luh it. All the girls

luh it. Sometimes I sit in the serwice and watch the girls and listen to them scream. I luh to hear them scream and think about them getting so wet for Elwis."

His breath quickened as his hand slid higher on the inside of her thigh. She would never have believed that Mama could invent a hell this horrible. While she bucked against the straps around her body, she thought that what was about to happen to her would be like getting raped by the angel of death.

"You screaming now, aren't you?" Doctor Nick said with a little delight in his voice. "Yes, I can tell you screaming. But you not screaming for Elwis, are you? No, you're screaming for me."

His hand inched up her thigh. "I'm now going to gib you what we call, informed consent. In my practice, I always gib patients informed consent. Well, I don't gib it to Elwis when I put him away. But that is not exactly *consent*, is it?" He fired off a sudden round of cackles that ended as suddenly as they began as his hand inched further up her leg.

"Let me tell you how special you are. The woman who was before you? I think her name was Sheila. Yes, Sheila. You remember her? I think she wrote a letter to someone out in the Wilderness. Sentenced to disappear for corrupting an apostle. Well, she got what most y-olators get." He reached up and tapped her temple. "Two raps to the head with a small hammer. I hope she died from the hammer blows because she would be in such pain down in that dark mineshaft with the rats and worms eating her flesh while she waits for death to take her.

"But that won't happen to you. I can see why Mama thinks you special." His hand slid up and down on the inside of her thigh. "Anybody ever tell you how soft your skin is? Oh, ob course they hab. Many times, huh? I bet Elwis used to tell you that all the time."

His breathing accelerated while hers already sounded like a runner at the end of a marathon.

"Well, Mama says you so special, you get treated like

a queen. In fact, you get the same, exact treatment I gib Elwis. Is a wonderful mixture of drugs. One to stop you lungs, one to stop you liwer and another to stop you heart. Of course, I hab not had this treatment myself, but I suspect it is quite uncomfortable." His hand slid to her crotch and he whispered, "If you're nice to me, I gib you Elwis' nice cocktail of walium and Demerol. I'm afraid the mine shaft will be the same though. Wary deep and wary dark."

He emitted a partial cackle before the door opened, and he sucked in a lungful of air. "What do you think you're doing?" Mama snapped.

"I was jus...jus... I was straightening her skirt. It had become all tangled in the straps."

"Bullshit!" Mama said as she moved close to the table. "You're not supposed to even be here for another twenty minutes."

"I finish at the clinic and thought I'd get set up."

"Yeah," Mama said. "I'll bet you did. It's a good thing for you that I got here a little early. I don't care if you are our only doctor. If you'd raped this child, believe me, I'd have Red and Sonny strap you to this table, and I would stand right here and make sure they went over your creepy ass real good with those ball-peen hammers of theirs."

"I was not..." Doctor Nick said, now moving away from the table. "I assure you, Mama, I was not..."

"Are you all right, baby?" Mama said in a soothing voice as she caressed Rhonda's cheek.

But Rhonda was not soothed, and she shook her head back and forth so hard her neck ached.

"My little girl," Mama cooed. "You didn't think I had forgotten you, did you? You should know I would come back and be with you in your final hour. Hey, you'll be glad to know that the boy's doing fine, and Elvis' spirit is moving strong inside him like we all thought it would. He's rehearsing real hard right now. He sends you his best and wants to thank you for bringing him to The Land of Grace.

"Baby, tonight we'll have the River of Lights. You remember how beautiful that is, don't you?"

Rhonda moaned, thinking how she didn't really give a shit.

"I know you do." Mama said, patting Rhonda's arm. "I'll anoint him right before the service tomorrow. He's real sorry you'll miss it, but he understands you've got obligations. So don't worry. You're not hurting his feelings for a second."

Mama gripped Rhonda's arm tightly. "Okay, Nick," Mama said. "You just make sure you treat this child gently."

"Yes ma'am," Doctor Nick said. He gripped Rhonda's other arm and said, "I'm sorry, Miss Rhonda, but this I-wee will stick a little."

Rhonda's throat made a sound like a whimpering puppy as the point of the needle jabbed into her vein.

"Our beloved Elvis," Mama said. "Who is always with us whether in times of trial or triumph. We pray that you accept this child. She's done some bad things, but we ask that you not overlook her contributions—how she helped us get started; how she recruited the Children; and how she brought your newest vessel into The Land of Grace. She..."

A chill seeped into Rhonda's arm, and she knew the exact moment the Valium and Demerol flooded in because she felt herself float away until Mama's voice sounded like someone had turned the volume way down on a radio dial. She opened her eyes wide when her lungs shut down, but she didn't panic and she wasn't blinded by the overhead lamp because more and more its light looked as if it glowed from a distant star.

31

RIVER OF LIGHTS

Claire believed that she would always remember this, her first River of Lights, as the most beautiful night of her life. She stood on the towering podium, clutching her father's hand while the long column of the Children held their lighted candles on their mile-long trek from the Village.

At the beginning she could only see the flickering lights on the dark road in the distance and hear a droning sound that, when they got closer, she could tell was all the Children singing, "American Trilogy" like a dirge.

First, they sang, "Battle Hymn of the Republic," then "Dixie" followed by "All My Trials." And they kept repeating the songs over and over till they finally reached the field beside the Big House. There, with their candles aloft, they coiled like a flaming ribbon around a mound of wooden pallets as wide as a basketball court and half as tall as the Cadillac Barn. On top of the pallets lay thousands of white poster boards on which they had earlier that day scrolled their prayers for Elvis' return.

Claire's father squeezed her hand and whispered with a tear in his voice, "I sure wish your mother could see this."

"Don't say that, Dad," she said, looking around to make sure that none of the apostles heard him. According to the book, *life was to proceed as if she'd never been.* And they might be reprimanded for even mentioning her name.

"Oh, I'm just saying, if she'd seen what we're seeing, she would never have done what she did."

Claire nodded.

With the glowing circles completed, the Children hushed while the voice of Elvis took up "American Trilogy" from a speaker placed somewhere in the trees beyond the field. The King's voice sounded as if it were echoing through a lonesome canyon. And Claire got all choked up when he got to the part in "All My Trials" where he sang about daddies bound to die.

Moans and cries swept across the crowd. Mama let them weep for a moment before stepping up to the microphone, and she stood until the cries and moans had withered before saying, "I am. I was. And I will be again."

The Children answered in a cacophony of "Amen!" "Blessed be!" "Hallelujah!" and "Praise Elvis!"

Mama waited till their praise ended.

"Beloved," she said. "Once again we have adored Him in life. We have mourned Him in death. And we have buried His body in our grief. Now we offer up our prayers for His return.

"A lot of things in this life are uncertain. But one thing we know for certain is that we cannot live without Him. Though He is gone, He promised He would return to us. This is our way of telling Him we love him and still need for Him to keep that promise. Now it is time to sacrifice the candles which represent the little insignificant lights of our own lives for the beautiful, flaming star that will be His again, knowing that while we do this we send our prayers up to him in heaven."

From the podium it looked to Claire as if circles of light were uncoiling below her as the Children passed the mound of wooden pallets and tossed their candles upon the stack on their way back to the Village. The pallets glowed and flickered at first. Then after more and more candles landed on the fuel, the flames popped and snapped as they licked fiercely at the dry wood. Before half of the people unwound from the circles and added their candles to the flame, the mound was a raging mountain of fire.

While the whole sight made her feel as if she could fly, she couldn't help being confused. Like her father, she regretted that her mother had written a letter to Claire's former Aunt Adele. And no doubt it was unforgivable for her to have tempted an apostle to mail that letter for her. But at the same time she thought that if her mother hadn't committed those serious sins she, Claire, wouldn't be viewing this beautiful ceremony from a privileged vantage point on this clear, starlit night. And she certainly wouldn't be Mama's favorite girl, soon-to-be Elvis' girlfriend and the possible if not probable future Priscilla. Like Mama always says, "He has a plan for all of us."

Apostle Red nudged her shoulder. "What do you think about your first River of Lights?" he said.

"It's just...just breathtaking," she said.

"I've seen it every time," Red said. "I don't think I'll ever get tired of it. But if you think this is something, wait till you see The Anointing tomorrow. Mama said you'll be in the dressing room with us. Not many get to witness that."

"I can't wait," Claire said.

"The whole thing kinda makes you glad you gave your heart to Elvis, don't it, little sister?"

"It does," Claire said. "It really does."

32

THE ANOINTED

The ceiling and each wall of the room was a solid gilded mirror. A gold-colored carpet covered the floor, and in the center of the room two black L-shaped couches faced each other across a highly polished coffee table that looked as if it had been crafted from a long piece of driftwood. On the center wall was a dressing table and a barber chair. A wet bar padded in gold-colored fabric stretched out against one wall and on the other, a long table covered with a gold-colored cloth bulged with food. From where he stood he could see: prime rib, a circle of shrimp around a crystal bowl of ice as big as a truck tire, as well as fruit, cheeses and plates of fancy little sandwiches he'd only seen people eat on TV. As he eased into the room, his reflections in the surrounding mirrors looked as nervous as he felt.

When he asked Red, "Whose dressing room is this?" Red burst out laughing.

"What'd he say?" Sonny said.

"He asked who this dressing room belongs to," Red said and he and he and Sonny cackled with laughter.

"What's so funny?" he asked.

"What's so funny?" Red, said still chuckling. "Hell, hoss, in twenty minutes this whole damned thing will be yours."

Mama, in her red robe, stood smiling behind the barber chair with her arms outstretched. "Are you ready to fully receive Him, baby?" she said in a voice so tender and at the same time so husky and strong that it made him think of one of her big hugs that comforted him with its warmth while squeezing the air out him at the same time. "Are you really ready?"

"Yes, ma'am," he said. "I'm ready."

"Then have a seat," she said, pointing to the barber

chair. She wrapped a black barber's cape around his neck and clapped her hands. The door swung open and a blonde teenage girl in a blue choir robe led the rest of the apostles into the room. The girl stood beside Mama as the apostles formed a circle around them.

He'd spent most of the morning combing his pompadour in place with Royal Crown Hair Dressing. Now Mama teased the front of his pomp with a comb. She looked at her handiwork and nodded before holding out her hand.

The girl handed her a bottle of Vaseline Hair Tonic from the dressing table. "Bow your heads," Mama said.

"Lord," she said. "This vessel has been reborn in your name. He has been tried and tempted in the Wilderness among The Others and he has come back to The Land of Grace, strong and true. He now sits here in the midst of this holy circle of your faithful to receive you into his heart. It is with this holy Vaseline that I anoint him in your spirit."

While Mama peppered his head with the slick oil, he felt as if something were rushing into his bloodstream to fill up a place inside him that had been hollow since the day he was born. She smiled as he wiped the tears from his eyes with the backs of his hands. Then she tilted his head up and ran a comb through his hair, teasing the front some more and sweeping the sides into a smooth ducktail in the back.

She gave the front of his pompadour a playful thump, sending a strand of slick, black hair tumbling onto his forehead. After combing it back in place, she looked deep in his eyes, smiled and said, "He is in our presence. Let us have the room."

After the apostles stepped out, Mama picked up a glass of water from the dressing table and held a vitamin between her thumb and forefinger. "Here, baby," she said. "I think you need another one of these."

He swallowed the pill as a deep hum rose from outside the door. After he set the glass on the dressing table, the water inside it trembled. "What's that sound, Mama?" he said.

"The Children," she said. "They know you've risen, and they can't wait to see you again. I need to go out and keep them company till you get there."

"I guess I'll see you there," he said.

She smiled. "I guess you will," she said, and she patted his cheek. "I swear, you are the sweetest thing."

After Mama left, he smiled at the girl as if seeing her for the first time. He liked her fresh-scrubbed face, and she looked as if she had something interesting going on under that robe. "What's your name honey?" he said.

"Claire. No, I mean, Linda,"

"Well, Claire-I-mean-Linda, looks like we're going to have a little party after the show. You want to come back with me and be my date?"

"Yes," she said with a little chirp in her voice, looking as if she were going to hop with joy.

"After we've had a drink and said hello to everybody," he said, "we can go back to the Big House, maybe go upstairs and have a little private party of our own. You know. Just you and me."

"I..." she said, taking a deep breath. "I'd like that."

I bet you would, he thought as he lifted the comb from the dressing table and swept it through the sides of his hair. She unpinned the cape and swirled it around to uncover his torso as if she were unveiling a sculpture. He patted his hair and rose slowly while checking out his look in all the mirrors. He had on black and white loafers with pink socks. His gray pants were baggy in the legs and had a thin pink stripe down each out seam. They were cinched to his waist with a pencil-thin white belt, and he wore a black shirt with a thin white tie knotted under the collar.

From a rack by the wall, Linda pulled a charcoal tweed sport coat spattered in little pink flecks and held it out for him. When the rumble grew a little louder, the door opened and Red poked his head in. "Children getting restless out there, E. We better get going."

"Hold your horses," he said. "I'll be right with you." He swept the girl into his arms and kissed her. When he released her, she stood wobbly, gasping for breath. "For luck," he said. Then he slipped into the coat and followed Red out the door where the apostles lined both sides of the hallway. "Look at him, boys," Joe said. "If that ain't one cool cat, I never seen one."

"Man, you gonna kill 'em out there today, E," Lamar said, patting him on the shoulder. "Way you look, you won't even have to sing."

"My boy, my boy," Billy chanted.

"Purtiest thing I ever seen."

"You're the man, E."

"Nineteen-fifty-six all over again baby."

"The King has risen for damn sure."

While absorbing their praise, a smile curled his lip. Then he said, "Let's go." He turned toward the rumbling sound and began the long trek down the hallway to the stage. The tramping of their shoes blended with the rumble of the rest-less Children that grew louder as they moved down the hall. Little butterflies danced in his belly, but the hand-trembling jitters he'd had before he stepped into the dressing room had left him. Leading the apostles down the hall, he felt as if he were a big daddy goose, flying point in a southbound V.

Ahead, Cholly stood in the light of the stage entrance, holding an acoustic guitar with a leather-covered sound board. Elvis took the instrument and slung the strap over his head as if he were shouldering a weapon. Cholly said some-thing he couldn't hear because when the curtain rose and the Children saw Scotty, Bill and D.J. waiting center stage they emitted a roar that sounded loud enough to threaten the bolts holding the building together.

In a moment there would be nothing behind him. No Nashville. No San Angelo. No grimy little towns with their AMVETS and American Legion halls. No old man in a wheelchair. No sad-eyed girl smiling wistfully from a crumpled photo. Not even a speck would be left of some-one named Doyle Brisendine because everything would be blown away by the fierce storm that would strike the second he hit the stage. The Children would be the thunder. And He would be the lightning.

— *END* —

Mike Burrell was raised in DeKalb County, Alabama. He now lives in Birmingham, Alabama, with his wife, Debra. He has earned his living as: a farm laborer, a grocery clerk, a military intelligence analyst, a revenue agent, and a lawyer. He received an MFA in creative writing from Queens University of Charlotte. His short fiction has appeared in: *Southern Humanities Review; The McGuffin; Kennesaw Review;* and the Livingston Press anthology, *Climbing Mt. Cheaha: Emerging Alabama Writers. The Land of Grace* is his first novel.